DOWN AMONG THE DEAD MEN

Also by Kerry Wilkinson

The Jessica Daniel series

LOCKED IN

VIGILANTE

THE WOMAN IN BLACK

THINK OF THE CHILDREN

PLAYING WITH FIRE

THICKER THAN WATER

BEHIND CLOSED DOORS

CROSSING THE LINE

SCARRED FOR LIFE

The Andrew Hunter series

SOMETHING WICKED

The Silver Blackthorn Trilogy

RECKONING

RENEGADE

KERRY WILKINSON

DOWN AMONG THE DEAD MEN

MACMILLAN

First published 2015 by Macmillan
an imprint of Pan Macmillan
20 New Wharf Road, London N1 9RR
Associated companies throughout the world
www.panmacmillan.com

ISBN 978-1-5098-0461-0

1 3 5 7 9 8 6 4 2

A CIP catalogue record for this book is available from the British Library.

Typeset by Ellipsis Digital Limited, Glasgow
Printed and bound by CPI Group (UK) Ltd, Croydon, CR0 4YY

Visit **www.panmacmillan.com** to read more about all our books
and to buy them. You will also find features, author interviews and
news of any author events, and you can sign up for e-newsletters
so that you're always first to hear about our new releases.

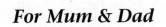

For Mum & Dad

1

As Jason Green scuffed his trainers along the pavement, he could hear his mother's voice in his head telling him how much they cost. They had been a combined Christmas and thirteenth birthday present: a rare instance of him getting what he asked for. Being born on Boxing Day meant he'd never had a proper birthday party. Everything was always a joint Christmas and birthday celebration where he had to watch his younger brother get presents too. It was a bit of a con, really.

At least he'd got his trainers at the end of last year. Big air cushions in the heel, the spring underneath and the big red swoosh along the side. When Jason had taken them out of the box on Christmas morning – technically an early birthday present – he couldn't believe how light they were. His mum had told him not to wear them to school but if he couldn't show them off, there was no point in having them.

Jason was busy staring at his feet, trying not to scuff them, when he heard the voices in front of him. The alleyway was an easy cut-through from the main road to his estate, taking five minutes off his journey compared to going the long way around. It meant he got to pass the sweet shop too, not that he had any money on him. He peered up to see the five teenagers leaning against the wall, baseball caps at an angle, two of them with cigarettes, one on a BMX, all wearing big puffed-out jackets as if they'd been bubbled-wrapped. Their conversation dropped to silence in the time it took Jason to glimpse up and there was a moment of clarity as they all realised what was going to happen next.

The boy on the bike peered down at Jason's trainers, then up to his face. 'What size shoe are you?'

Jason took a step backwards, glancing over his shoulder towards the main road. On either side were tall red-brick walls from the surrounding blocks of flats – only one way out.

'Small.'

Another step back. The boy on the BMX shunted himself forward, putting one foot on the pedal, using the other to hold himself up. One of his friends spat his cigarette to the ground with a saliva-filled puff of his lips.

Jason took another step backwards and the other boys moved forward in unison. He might not be big, strong or even particularly brave – but he was quick and had top-of-the-range trainers. Spinning on the spot, Jason was rushing towards the main road before the boys had realised what was happening. Knowing he couldn't outrun a bike, he dashed left as he reached the end of the alley, feeling the breeze through his short brown hair as he headed past the chippy, kebab shop, bookies and off-licence, rushing towards the car park of the Fox and Hounds pub on the corner.

Voices called angrily after him, the teenagers' footsteps clattering on the tarmac. Jason didn't look backwards, breathing the cold air deeply and kicking his knees high, thundering across the hard ground.

With a squeal of an all-too-close BMX tyre, Jason leapt onto the bonnet of a parked Vauxhall Astra, stumbling and using the windscreen to steady himself. Risking a glance over his shoulder, he could see four of the boys twenty or so metres behind – but the one with the bike was picking himself up from the tarmac, snarling and spluttering in fury. Jason hopped onto the roof of the car, the soles of his shoes sliding on the shiny paintwork, almost slipping off as he jumped over the wooden fence that ran around the car park. The kids might outnumber him but he knew the back streets of Hulme as well as anyone.

Overgrown trees hung low over the crumbling path, blocking what little light there was as Jason ploughed forward, head down, following the trail that looped back around the car park to where he'd been in the first place. Somewhere in the distance, there were still voices howling after him but the paths at the rear of the pub weaved their labyrinth-like way through the nearby estates. Unless one of his pursuers had seen in which direction he'd headed, they could be anywhere.

Jason allowed himself to slow slightly as the tree branches began to thin, allowing the January sun to spill through. Now he was close to houses again, tall wooden fences were on either side of him, rattling slightly in the breeze and dousing the patches of frost in shadow.

Emerging onto the main road close to the chippy, Jason

came to a halt, peering both ways along the street before wriggling through the ice-cold metal gate and stepping back onto the spot he'd dashed past minutes before. Back at walking speed, he could feel the cold air in his lungs as his breath spiralled in front of him. Flicking his hood up again and wishing his trainers weren't quite so clean and bright, Jason moved quickly back in the direction he'd originally been heading in. He made a quick check over his shoulder before re-entering the cut-through but there was no sign of the gang either in front or behind him. Hopefully they were lost somewhere in the maze of paths, being preyed upon by the needle-users and paedos who hung around in the dark corners. Well, those were the names the kids on the estate called the blokes in dirty coats anyway.

At the end of the alley, Jason glanced both ways and then turned right, following the two-storey row of grimy flats that had muddy patches of garden at the front.

It dawned on him that this was probably the reason his mum had told him not to wear the trainers to school in the first place. He'd wanted to show off to his mates but she knew there were plenty of people who lived around Manchester's underbelly that didn't like having expensive things waved in their faces. He wondered how she'd found the money to buy them. Had one of the men who hung around his house – one of his 'uncles' – got them from the back of a lorry? That was where a lot of things in his life seemed to come from. Jason had long since learned not to ask too many questions.

The path opened into a courtyard, with flats surrounding all four sides and narrow archways in the corners allowing residents to get from one end to the other without having to go the long way around. A dog was barking somewhere nearby, coupled with the sound of a man's voice bellowing at it to shut up. In a moment of self-awareness, Jason stopped halfway across the concreted space, turning a full circle. He couldn't see anyone but it felt like he was being watched. He peered towards the four corners but there was no one there, with the windows above offering only the glare of the winter sun.

Yap, yap, yap.

The man shouted something about tanning the dog's 'sodding arse' but Jason couldn't even see them. His flat was only a short distance away: through the archway in the corner, across the road, around the park and up the stairs. Suddenly it felt like it was the entire way across the city.

Jason felt the chill skim through his jacket and then they were in front of him, the kid on the BMX wheeling himself through the archway. Somewhere along the way he'd lost his baseball cap, exposing a thin spiky mass of dark hair, hollow cheeks and big ears. Behind him were the other four, out of breath but smiling menacingly.

Jason took off again, bounding towards the corner through which he'd entered. Slowing to a walk had been a mistake – if he'd continued running, he would have been home by now but the strength in his legs had gone and they felt heavy as he tried to sprint. He reached the arch-way just as something crashed into his lower back. Falling forward, Jason felt the weight of someone rolling with him, an errant elbow catching him under the ribs and taking what little breath he had left. His head collided with concrete and something that felt like his nose went splat. By the time he'd stopped sliding, Jason was a little outside the darkness of the passages which led into the courtyard, on his backside, on the freezing pavement.

The winter sun seemed brighter as he stared into it, vision scarred by bright stars and shapes from where he'd hit his head. Jason tried to push himself to his feet but whoever had rugby-tackled him was clinging onto his legs as the other boys' blurry outlines emerged from the shadows.

Jason expected taunting, swearing, vague threats; instead nobody spoke. The BMX clattered to the pavement and then the shape of its rider was over him. The teenager didn't even bother going for the trainers, instead reeling back and crunching his fist underneath Jason's ribs in the exact spot where the other boy's elbow had caught him.

If there was one thing learned from growing up on the estate where Jason lived, it was how to take a beating. He curled his knees up and covered his head as a second blow rattled into his lower back. Jason could taste blood but tucked his tongue into the top of his mouth so that he wouldn't accidentally bite through it. There was little point in fighting back against five of them: he'd have to take the battering and hope he was in enough of one piece to haul himself home afterwards. The last time he'd felt someone's fists pounding him, it had been one of those 'uncles' who'd had too much to drink and fallen over in the hallway. Jason had made the mistake of laughing, which wasn't one he'd repeated. His mother had seen his black eyes the next day and said nothing, an unspoken reminder of what she valued in her life. Another reason why the trainers had been such a surprise.

Jason screwed his eyes shut as the first kick came. When his 'uncle' had kicked him into the wall at home, he'd been wearing heavy steel toe-capped work shoes that had left Jason with black, blue, purple and yellow marks around his torso for weeks. For the first day he hadn't been able to eat or drink because every movement of his stomach left him in agony.

Luckily the teenager's trainers had been made out of the lightest materials by some Chinese kid for two pence a day. If nothing else, it ensured a near pain-free kicking experience. Jason barely felt the first two blows: it was only when the other boys joined in that his head started to go fuzzy again. One of them was stamping on his legs, two more working on his back, another trying to wedge his feet into his ribs and the final one attempting to kick through the hands covering his head.

Jason almost felt like he was out of his body, watching himself, hearing the blows but not feeling them. He kept his mouth firmly closed, his knees curled, fists clenched.

Doof, doof, doof.

Suddenly, everything stopped.

Jason screwed his eyes further closed, wondering if it was a moment's respite before the violence began again, but there was a voice – a man's, he thought, although there was blood in his ear and it was as if he was trying to eavesdrop on something while at the bottom of the swimming pool. He rolled onto his back, turning towards the road where there was a black shape. A car, a man. Perhaps a second man? It was just colour: the fading blue of the sky and black.

Jason was trying to ignore the pain under his ribs and around his back as he slowly shuffled into a sitting position, using his arms as his legs weren't responding. The teenagers were still around him, forming a semicircle. One of them said something to the black shape that was steadily swimming into view.

The scene was almost clear now: a smooth, shiny black car with tinted windows was parked on the side of the road, its back door open. Standing in front was a man in a suit and long dark coat. His hair was bristling in the gentle breeze, a mix of black and silvery grey.

'What's your name, son?'

Jason blinked and realised the man was talking to him. He opened his mouth but one of the kicks must have caught him in the jaw because pain shot through him, making his spine tingle and body shiver.

The man peered up from Jason towards the five teenagers, scanning across them. When he spoke, he exuded a cool authority: the kind of tone that couldn't be taught, each word deliberate. 'What do you think you're doing?'

The teenager who had been on the bike stepped forward, fists balled. 'What's it to you, old man?'

The man didn't seem to be that old, perhaps forty, maybe fifty. Jason wasn't good at judging adults' ages at the best of times, let alone when his vision was so hazy. He could see the smile spread across the man's face though, slightly lop-sided, a twinkle in his eye.

'I suppose you think you're big men, don't you – five of you picking on one.'

'What if the five of us pick on you?'

The man grinned more widely, not even glancing towards the car behind him. His arms were loose at his sides, palms out, almost welcoming.

'I don't think that's a good idea.'

The teenager turned towards his friends, his sneer not as pronounced as earlier, an inkling of doubt etched across the lines in his forehead. 'Well, *we* think it's a good idea, don't we, lads?'

His friends didn't move.

The man was tapping his shiny black shoes on the concrete. 'I'm going to do you a favour: I'm going to tell you my name and then I'm going to give you thirty seconds to turn and run. If any of you are still here after those thirty seconds, then we're going to have a problem.' His lips twitched slightly, the grin slipping as he peered across at the five boys, steel in his dark eyes. 'You might not have seen me around much – not here anyway, but I wonder if the name Irwell means anything to you. Harry Irwell.'

'Shite.'

The word came from one of the teenagers surrounding Jason. With a scrape of trainers and another swear word, he was scrambling away, legs flailing as he scarpered along the street back towards the shops without a glance over his shoulder. In an instant, two of his friends were joining him, leaving the lad with the bike and one other.

The BMX rider had taken two steps backwards and jumped as his friend placed a hand on his shoulder.

'Come on, let's go.' The teenager nodded towards Harry. 'You know who that is, don't you? Don't be a dick.'

In the second of hesitation, he had turned and run too, leaving just the bike rider. Without taking his eyes from the man, he picked up his BMX, sat astride it, glanced quickly at Jason – and then pedalled as quickly as his legs would let him in the direction his friends had taken.

Jason watched him cycle away, his vision still slightly woozy. As he turned back towards the car, he jumped at the dark figure hunching over him, hand outstretched. Jason hadn't heard Mr Irwell approach but took his hand, feeling the strength in the man's grip as he allowed himself to be hauled upwards. Jason's knees felt a little wobbly but Mr Irwell had a hand on his shoulder, steadying him.

'What's your name?' the man asked.

'Jason.'

'How old are you?'

'Thirteen.'

'Why were those boys after you, Jason?'

Jason peered down to see the red smears of blood on the white of his shoes. 'They wanted my trainers.'

'Do you know who I am, Jason?'

'Mr Irwell.'

The man smiled again in the fatherly way none of Jason's uncles ever did. His fingers twitched on Jason's shoulder, holding him firmly but reassuringly.

'Call me Harry, but that's not what I'm asking you. Do you know *who* I am?'

'I think so.'

The hand slid down to Jason's back. 'Would you like a lift home?'

2

Jason sat in the van staring through the night towards the off-licence's fire exit. The alley along the back of the shop was littered with fluttering newspapers and crisp packets spilling from the metal bin at the far end that had its hinged lid hanging open. The van was parked across the road, giving Jason a perfect view of the alley from the driver's seat. It was cloudy, as ever, meaning the gentle orange of the surrounding street lights was the only illumination – at least until it was interrupted by the white light coming from behind him.

'Will you turn that sodding phone off?' Jason hissed.

'I just got a text from Carly,' came the reply. 'She wants to know if I'm going over tonight.'

Jason stifled a sigh. 'Just turn it off. All of you.'

There was a shuffling from the back of the van, more white light, a succession of tinny-sounding ringtones and then a moment of silence before they started gabbling again.

Jason tried to blank out what they were talking about. They weren't exactly friends, more acquaintances. He didn't even really know them. The four of them were all in their early twenties with no particular ties but the difference was that they were amateurs – idiots – while he knew what he was doing. The shop had closed four minutes earlier, meaning the owner would currently be sweeping up and tidying the inside. At some point in the next ten minutes, he would open the fire exit, go to the bin, empty the day's rubbish, and then return inside, before locking up and driving home.

'. . . so, Carly, she does this thing with her tongue, right, where she rubs it against her bottom lip and then . . .'

Jason checked his cheap plastic watch: five past ten. It wasn't particularly late but he was a little tired, his warm bed seeming particularly appealing.

'. . . then she licks upwards. It's like she's got two tongues or something. Honestly, one of these days I'll get you round and you can have a go. She's always saying—'

'For Christ's sake, will you shut up back there?'

Jason half-turned, taking in the figures dressed in black. Four sets of eyes stared back at him, not exactly defiantly – they knew who the orders came from, more wondering why he was so bothered.

Turning back to the fire exit, Jason enjoyed the moment of silence before the voices began again. 'So, I'm thinking about getting a new car. That Corsa's been shite since the day I got it. I took it down the garages last week but the bastard wanted fifteen hundred to fix it. Bloody thing's not even worth that. I can probably afford something new anyway. You know that dealership at the end of the M602? They've had this new Audi out front for the past month and—'

Jason interrupted without turning. 'You're not buying a new Audi.'

'Who says?'

'*I* say.'

'You can't tell me how to spend my money.'

Jason didn't reply for a moment, focusing on the fire door and willing it to open so that he didn't have to have this conversation.

Again.

'If you want,' Jason said, 'I can ask the person who pays us to tell you. Would you rather hear it from me or him?'

Silence.

Jason's eyes flickered down to his watch again. It had cost him under a tenner but that was the golden rule, well, *his* golden rule: don't stand out. The moment someone started flashing the money around was the moment it all came crumbling down.

Seven minutes past ten.

Ahead, there was a crinkling of light as the fire exit opened a fraction and an Asian man's head peeped out. With a shove and a kick, he wrestled with the door and then turned inside to pick up the bin.

'Now,' Jason said.

Pulling his balaclava down, Jason opened the driver's door and began striding across the road. He heard the van's side doors sliding open and footsteps behind him on the echoing tarmac. The shopkeeper had already emptied the bin and turned back to the shop when he noticed the five men approaching. Jason saw the whites of the man's eyes blazing with fear as he ran towards the fire exit, wanting to wrench it closed.

It was already too late.

The biggest of Jason's balaclava-clad associates – Kev – kicked the door away from the shopkeeper's grasp, simultaneously shoving him inside. Jason didn't break stride, marching through the fire exit behind the others and pulling it closed.

Three of the black figures had rushed into the main area of the shop, cackling as the rampage began. Jason nodded at Kev, who had one hand across the shopkeeper's mouth, his other arm clamping the man's arms painfully behind him.

Jason crouched in front of him: 'What's the safe code, Namdev?'

From somewhere in the main area of the shop, there was a crash as one of the displays was sent tumbling. Jason asked the struggling shopkeeper to give him a second and then he moved through to the front. The shutters were already down, blocking anyone outside from seeing what was going on. He stood silently, waiting for the men in black to notice him. When they finally did, there was a moment of silence, of understanding, before Jason spun on his heels and returned to the back room. The noise from the front was now more restrained – a targeted and tactical pattern of destruction, not the wild hyenas from before.

Namdev gasped as Kev removed the hand from his mouth. His eyes were wide, white, but he didn't call out.

'Five-five-five-eight-two-one.'

'Thank you, Namdev.'

Jason nodded to Kev and he headed towards the main area of the shop, leaving the two of them alone.

Namdev shuffled backwards slightly until he was resting against a wall of cardboard boxes packed with crisps.

'You've been a very silly man, Namdev,' Jason said.

'Who are you?'

Jason shook his head, feeling the itch of the balaclava wool on his forehead. 'You don't want to be asking questions like that. You know why we're here, though, don't you?'

Namdev's eyes shot towards the fire exit but he would've known there was no way he'd get there before Jason slammed him into the floor. 'No . . .'

'This isn't a good place from which to sell drugs, Namdev.'

'I'm not—'

'We both know that's a lie.' Jason reached into his pocket and took out the blue plastic bag containing half-a-dozen pills. He tossed them at the shopkeeper, who picked them up from his lap. 'You can't just open a shop and start selling extra merchandise under the counter. Anyone could come in – you're lucky we're not the police.'

Namdev's voice trembled: 'Who are you?'

'You already asked that. Let me ask *you* a question – why did you choose to open your shop here?'

Namdev peered up, wondering if it was a serious query. When Jason nodded, he stumbled a reply. 'I suppose I thought there'd be a lot of through traffic.'

'Exactly. You saw a gap in the market because there were

no other shops selling milk, papers and sandwiches on this stretch of road. How's business?'

'Um . . .'

'It's a simple question.'

'It's okay.'

'Right – but what would happen if someone moved in next door selling the exact same goods as you?'

'Um . . .'

'It's an easy question, Namdev, basic business. It would halve your income. You'd have to compete on price – so then you'd have to lower the cost, meaning that even if you got the customers back you'd be making less money. That's true, isn't it?'

Namdev nodded. There was a gash just above his eye, a small trickle of blood seeping into his black brow. His brown eyes flickered towards the fire exit again.

'It's supply and demand. Too much supply overwhelms the demand, meaning there's less money to go around.' Jason pointed at the blue packet in Namdev's hand. 'When you started selling your produce, that meant there was too much supply, which affected the profits of anybody else trying to sell similar goods in this area. Understand?'

Another nod.

'What were you using the money for?'

'Um . . .'

'Don't mess me around, Namdev.'

'It was expensive to fit this place. It was run-down when I bought it.'

Jason turned towards the door that led into the main area of the shop. A row of shelves had been tipped sideways, the contents emptied onto the floor. He waited until Namdev was looking too. 'What good is that to you now?'

Namdev gulped. There was a small trickle of blood from the corner of his mouth. 'I don't know,' he said.

'Exactly – perhaps you should have thought of that. Now, where is your camera footage stored?'

Jason already knew but Namdev's nerves gave him away as he glanced towards the camera over the fire exit that had recorded them breaking in. 'That's the one,' Jason added.

'I don't . . . I . . .'

Jason launched himself forward, pressing his left forearm across Namdev's throat and pushing him into the boxes. With his free hand, he rested his right thumb on the man's eye, not forcefully – not yet – but enough to feel Namdev's eyelashes fluttering against the underside of his thumb.

'You don't want me to push, do you?'

Namdev tried to shake his head but Jason was holding him too tightly. Jason glared unblinkingly into the untouched eye and then swiftly released him again, brushing down the man's top.

'So where's the footage?' Jason demanded.

'Upstairs.'

Jason whistled sharply, waiting until Pete appeared in the doorway.

'*Where* upstairs?' Jason growled.

'There's a computer in the room at the top of the stairs. Everything is stored on that.'

Without a word, Pete headed around the stack of confectionery and crisp boxes and thumped up the stairs two at a time.

The two men sat silently, watching each other. Every few moments, Namdev's gaze would slip to the fire exit and back again. Soon after, the footsteps clumped back down the stairs and a laptop was tossed onto the floor next to Jason, followed by a silver metal box.

'Is this computer and hard drive everything that stores the CCTV recordings, Namdev?' Jason asked.

The man nodded.

Jason leant forward, not even raising his arm as Namdev flinched away from him. 'Are you sure? No hidden back-ups?'

'Yes.'

CRUNCH.

Pete stepped forward and slammed his boot into the laptop, stamping on it another half-dozen times just to make sure. Then he repeated the act with the hard drive, grunting with each thrust of his foot. Soon, there was only a scattering of metal, plastic and silicon.

The noise from the main part of the shop had stopped, with the other men in black waiting close to the fire exit. Jason pushed himself up to his feet, keen to get the balaclava off. It was always so itchy and he could never breathe properly underneath it.

'Have you got the message, Namdev?' Jason asked.

The shopkeeper nodded.

'Paki scum.'

Jason turned to Kev. He was wiping his mouth, as if having to cleanse the words from his lips. With a stride,

Jason was in front of him, hand flashing through the air, back-handing the man as brutally as he could manage. Kev's head snapped sideways and back again, his blue eyes blazing through the holes in his balaclava. Jason used his forearm to force him back against the fire exit, going eyeball-to-eyeball with him, silently daring Kev to raise a hand back.

'Apologise,' Jason ordered.

There was a moment of defiance but Kev knew it wasn't just Jason he was eyeballing: there was the person who paid them. Jason shoved the larger man one final time and then stepped away. Kev straightened his clothes, not turning from Jason.

'I'm sorry, like.'

Jason waved his hand dismissively. 'Apologise to Namdev. Not me.'

Kev turned slowly, turning to the downed shopkeeper, before repeating himself.

'Did you get the money?' Jason asked.

'Yes.'

'Good – sod off then.'

Kev and the other men hurried through the fire exit as Jason turned back to Namdev, who was squirming on the floor. 'I'm sorry we had to do this, Namdev, but you brought this on yourself. No more selling drugs, okay? Not to adults, kids, men, women, anyone. Got it?'

The shopkeeper nodded.

'Next time, it won't just be your shop – we'll burn your house down with you, Padma, Hamid, Ishrat and little Jalaja inside. Got it?'

Namdev's eyes were bulging, mouth hanging open at the mention of his family.

'Got it?' Jason repeated, more firmly this time.

Namdev nodded again, mouth still open.

'Good – now what happened here tonight?'

'Nothing.'

'Exactly – nothing. Now don't make me come back.'

3

Jason drove steadily through the streets, avoiding the main roads but not going down the needless route of weaving in and out of the tiny suburban lanes. The chances of being pulled over were minimal but he was more likely to stand out if he tried to manoeuvre through rows of parked cars and then had to reverse to let someone through. Jason had always known the shadier areas of Manchester as well as anyone. For some, it was all about the lights of the centre: the colour of Piccadilly Gardens; the rows of brightly lit shops; the theatres, the huge advertising posters and the market stalls. With Jason, it was about the ginnels and snickets that sliced through one estate to the next; the dark paths around the various parks; the bridges and shadows that lay underneath.

The chatter from the back of the van was down to the odd comment as the four of them tried to count the money. Without taking their respective shoes off, Jason knew they could get up to forty quid and then it was all guesswork.

'There's about two and a half here,' Pete said.

'You've not done anything stupid, have you?' Jason replied.

'Like what?'

'You know "like what". Everything's in the bag, isn't it?'

For a moment there was no reply and then: 'Of course, what do you take us for?'

Jason knew *exactly* what he took them for – which is why they were the amateurs and he was the professional. The fact he was smaller physically than any of them was irrelevant. They all knew who had the real power and it was none of them.

'Let's have it then,' Jason said.

There was a soft thud as a plastic bag landed on the empty passenger seat, tied at the top. Jason glanced away from the road and then back again. There was muttering from behind – probably Kev telling the others what he'd do to Jason if they were alone and he could act without the wrath of God coming down upon him. Well, the closest thing they knew to God anyway.

Jason cut across the main road that separated Hulme from Trafford and eased the van past a row of shops. He headed into an adjacent alley, slowing close to a row of garages. With almost rehearsed precision, the side doors slid open before he had stopped and Pete strode to the row of metal doors, opening the one in the centre with a creaking moan of rusting metal. The others hopped out and Jason reversed the van inside, wondering if the top was going to hit the metal door, even though he'd parked the vehicle inside many times before.

As the headlights blinked off, the disintegrating patch of tarmac outside the garages was thrust into darkness. Jason's eyes took a few moments to adjust to the shapes of the men undressing in front of him. He pulled a black bin bag from the roll just inside the garage door and started taking his own clothes off, packing his jeans, top, gloves and bala-clava inside, then scooping up the others' and squeezing them inside too.

New sets of work clothes always appeared inside the garage when required.

Jason slunk across to his car that was parked in the shadow of a tree. Autumn was in full swing, piles of leaves gathering on his windscreen and around the wheels. He opened the boot, dropped the bin bag and money inside, and then began changing into his own clothes: more jeans, a shirt and his denim jacket. Nothing too fancy, nothing too slummy, just like his car: a mid-range five-year-old Ford with dirty silver paint, tax that was up to date and an MOT which was always renewed in plenty of time.

Nobody bothered saying goodbye, not that Jason expected or wanted them to. The first car slipped through the alley, lights off, before the engine roared into the distance. Jason watched the others leave. Were their cars too fancy? Had Pete put on a suit that was too tightly cut? Were Kev's shoes too shiny? Jason knew he shouldn't be too concerned – even if one of them were picked up, they knew that talking would bring consequences that stretched far beyond just them. Everyone had family members some-where.

The fourth car revved away, leaving Jason alone in the car park with his thoughts. Was he paranoid – or had he got by for this long because he noticed those details? Was thinking that he *might* be paranoid the thing that *actually* made him paranoid, or did that prove he wasn't? Jason stared into the gloom and took a breath. He hated being out this late, even though it was part of the job.

If it could be called a job.

Already knowing the route, Jason drove almost on auto-pilot away from Trafford towards the ring road, heading underneath and keeping going along the darkened country lanes until he reached the layby with which he was so familiar. He pulled in, turned the lights and engine off, took the bin bag from the boot and headed along the muddy path that separated two fields. Falling leaves had blown from the woods at the far end of the path, gathering and mulching into the ground from the rain and array of dog-walkers.

Jason couldn't stop himself sticking to the area where the leaves were thickest, not that anyone would be looking for footprints. When he reached the end, the curving hedge around the rim of the field dipped down into a natural bowl-shaped hollow. He dropped the bag in, squirted a generous helping of lighter fluid onto it, and then tossed a match on top. Flames leapt into the air, though the height of the hedge shielded him from the main road. For a moment, Jason stood, watching the orange and black lick into the night air. He held his hands out, enjoying the warmth as the material of the clothes caught fire and began to disintegrate in front of his eyes. Because of the shape of the earth and the way the rain drained from the fields, nothing ever burned for long in this spot – just long enough.

Back in the car, Jason did a U-turn and began driving back to the centre. He should probably go home but, despite his dislike of late nights, knew he wouldn't be able to sleep yet. Traffic was non-existent, with a succession of green lights lining up for him as he followed the main road to Oxford Road and the student area. On a Monday night, there were only a few places that opened past eleven, almost all of them on this small stretch of road that led away from the city centre, past the university buildings.

After parking in the gated NCP close to the Aquatics Centre – as secure as it got in the city – Jason headed along the road towards the pub he often visited after he'd been on a job. At his age, he could just about get away with not standing out in a student joint without being the creepy older man in the corner.

Pop music pounded from the speaker above the door as Jason walked in, his shoes instantly sticking to the booze- and who-knew-what-soaked floor. On the dance floor to his right, lads and lasses swayed to the music, limbs entangled, chests pressed against each other. To his left, a group of young men were crowded around a pool table, cackling and egging each other on. Jason walked straight ahead to the bar, eyeing the array of bottles in the brightly lit cabinets and the brand names on the pumps at the front. Some-times it was a scramble to be served but he must have picked his moment perfectly because, despite the fact the place was almost full, the bar was almost empty. He sat on a stool, listening to the thump of the music as the young blonde girl on the other side of the bar nodded at him without moving.

'Whatcha after?' she asked.

The beers were the usual selection – swill from Australia

that wasn't actually Australian; some shite from the Netherlands which no Dutch man or woman in their right mind would go near; something Italian-sounding that was brewed in Essex. Jason tapped the pump with the logo of an ale he'd never heard of – at least that way it might taste of something – and then squinted to read the '5.6%' printed underneath. He knew his limits. He would never drive home after drinking – there was no stupider way to get caught, especially when there was two-and-a-half grand in cash in the boot – plus it wasn't worth it. He'd do what he always did: get the late bus back to Hulme, or a taxi if it was too late. Pay in cash, leave a small tip, don't talk too much. Pick up the car the next day.

With the ale he'd chosen, Jason knew it meant he couldn't have any more than two pints – that would get him tipsy but not too drunk. He never let himself get to that point where his lips started flapping and too many truths might slip out. Two pints – that was all.

The first arrived with condensation running down the outside of the glass and a perfect frothy head. Jason paid with a five-pound note, pocketed the change, and then turned to face the room.

He sipped and watched. Girls dancing, lads dancing. Thump-thump-thump. The rattle of a pool ball into a pocket; a drunken stumble sideways; 'oops, sorry mate', 'don't worry about it'. Thump-thump-thump. Crotches grinding; a couple kissing in the corner; three girls heading into the toilets together hand in hand; different songs but the same thump-thump-thump.

Another sip.

Was this the life he could have had? People his age having fun: dancing, singing, snogging, laughing. How did people even talk to each other? Did one person say 'hello' and the other say 'hello' back? Could this still be his life?

Thump-thump-thump.

'Hello.'

Jason turned in surprise. There was someone sitting on the stool next to him. Not just someone: a girl . . . a woman. She was cupping a large purple purse in her lap that matched the colour of her tight short dress. Her long legs were crossed, the tan apparent even in the strobe of red, green, yellow and blue lights that were eating into dim pub lighting. Jason's eyes darted across the V-cut at the top of her dress that exposed a hint of what lay underneath. With a blink he was looking into the woman's face, know-ing that's where he should have started. She had long dark hair that had a gentle wave to it, brown eyes and a round nose. Jason couldn't think of a better word for it: she was pretty – and she was talking to him.

His uninspiring reply was a mix of a cough and a word: 'Hello.'

Half a grin crept across her face as she leant forward. It took Jason a second to realise it was so she could talk into his ear. 'What's your name?'

He tilted his face to reply into hers. 'Jason.'

She offered him her hand, long thin fingers gripping his and shaking as she replied: 'Natalie.'

Jason was desperately trying to think of what to say next. Should he offer to buy her a drink? No, she already had one. Ask her to dance? Did he even know how to dance? Didn't people just flail a bit and hope for the best? That's what it looked like the other lads on the dance floor were doing.

She pressed in again: 'How old are you?'

Was that a normal question? He didn't have time to think of a sensible lie or even figure out if he needed one. 'Twenty-four,' Jason replied. The truth.

She angled back and took a sip from her glass of wine, smiling slightly. She was definitely older than him, though it was hard to know for sure. There was something about her that made him think she had seen a lot: a sort of wisdom around her eyes. But then there was her smooth skin, straight teeth and hint of playfulness. Perhaps she was younger than him after all? Maybe they were the same age? Should he ask? Wasn't there something about it being rude to ask a woman her age?

In the absence of knowing what to do, Jason drank from his pint, leaving only a tot of froth and dark-coloured liquid at the bottom.

Natalie didn't lean forward to speak but Jason could read her lips anyway: 'Do you want a drink?'

This would be his second and final pint. Loose lips were a dangerous thing. But if she bought him a drink, did that mean he had to buy her a drink? And, if so, could he buy a non-alcoholic drink next time around? This was so much more complicated than when it was just him sitting by himself, watching.

Jason pointed to the pump. 'Same again.'

A clunk of glasses, hiss of the pipes, clang of the till. A

sip mainly of froth, a stifled cough, Natalie's knowing giggle.

She pressed closer again, breath flittering across his ear. 'Are you a student?'

'No. You?'

'No. What do you do for a living?'

Jason offered the answer he always gave. 'This and that.'

Natalie smiled and took another sip from her drink. 'Is that supposed to impress a girl?'

He tried to reply with a grin of his own but instead hid his mouth behind the pint and took two quick swallows. He didn't have a better answer – it wasn't as if he could tell her the truth. He held the glass in his lap and leant in. 'What about you?'

Natalie's top lip twitched as she took a gulp, holding the wine in her mouth before swallowing. 'This and that.'

This time, Jason actually laughed. He hadn't even planned to, it simply slipped out in a way that he would never usually allow it. Was it the alcohol? He had to be smart, straight, and in control. She was only a woman, for God's sake.

Natalie's eyes narrowed as she waved him forward, mouth slightly open, tongue resting on her top row of teeth. 'What's it like working for Harry Irwell?' she asked.

4

Natalie pressed back on the stool and took another sip of her drink, eyes never leaving Jason's. He couldn't break her gaze, feeling her searching into his soul. He wanted to reply 'who?' – but it was clear she already knew the truth. Fumbling for the bar, Jason put the glass down and slid off his chair. The music thumped around him, lights strobing. He pushed himself up until he was standing. His legs felt slightly wobbly, head clouding, confusion and panic rippling through him.

He turned abruptly, bumping into a lad carrying a bottle of something red and sickly looking. The other man apologised even though it wasn't his fault but Jason didn't stop either to apologise himself or reply, rushing towards the exit, clattering through the door and skidding down the steps. At the bottom was a girl with a bird's nest of blonde hair smoking with one hand and holding her phone to her mouth with the other.

'. . . Honestly, Jem, it's the smallest thing I've ever seen. It's like the end of one of those pepperami things with a pair of peanuts underneath. I couldn't stop myself from laughing . . .'

Jason knew he had to get a bus or a taxi – something not to stand out – but then he'd *already* stood out because

Natalie, if that was her real name, knew who he worked for. That meant she might know other things too.

Thrusting his hands into his pockets, Jason dashed across the road away from the girl with the phone, checking over his shoulder to make sure he wasn't being followed. The pub door remained closed.

The night was colder than earlier and his denim jacket wasn't offering much protection against the chill. Why had he even bothered to come out? The job had been completed, the clothes dealt with and everyone sent packing with the minimum of fuss. He could have been at home, in bed or in front of the television. Instead, he'd come out to the same pub he often did. Doing the same thing too often, developing a pattern, was clumsy and stupid. What was he thinking?

Who was Natalie? Police seemed the obvious answer but did officers really look like that: all long hair, short dresses and legs?

Jason looked both ways along the street – no parked taxi and no bus lights, even in the distance. He checked the pub door again but it was still closed.

Making a decision he hoped he wouldn't regret, Jason slipped his collar up, dropped his head down and walked as quickly as he could along the road, turning by the Aquatics Centre and heading back to his car. By the time he had paid and reached his vehicle, Jason hadn't seen a single person. He'd not heard the echo of anyone's footsteps but his own. He fumbled with the keys, using the remote to open the door and then dived inside before locking it.

Sinking down into the driver's seat, Jason peeped over the steering wheel, looking for a hint of movement.

Nothing. There were other vehicles in the car park but no people.

Count to ten. Deep breath. Count to twenty. Another.

Still nothing.

Jason eased the key into the ignition, knowing it was reckless and that he shouldn't. This was the exact type of thing he didn't do. Needless risks would get him caught. He could still find a taxi somewhere and come back for the car and money tomorrow.

The engine chuntered to life with a gasp and Jason flicked the headlights on instinctively without realising he'd done it.

The journey home was as uneventful as any he'd made, except that it was punctuated by moments of panic the situation didn't warrant. Passing cars were viewed suspiciously in case they were unmarked police vehicles; amber traffic lights were treated with the utmost respect as he didn't dare go through them; the speed limit was something he adhered to rigidly.

Jason spent almost as much time peering in his mirrors as he did watching through the windscreen. At one point a lorry slotted in behind him before taking the turn for Salford, then there was a powerful BMW which overtook him in a thirty zone and sped into the distance, exhaust sputtering in protest.

The roads around the Hulme housing estate where Jason lived were quiet aside from a handful of late-night dog-walkers and the usual dodgy sorts who strutted around, hoods up, hands in pockets, thinking they were hard. Jason parked in one of the bays on the road, took the carrier bag of money from the boot, and headed through the wide, brightly lit passage between two flanks of ground-floor flats until he emerged on his own row.

The area had been built some time shortly after the Second World War but a good bomb would have left as positive an impression on the area as the choice of housing. Long rows of two-storey flats stretched into the distance surrounding three sides of a green that had more mud, carrier bags and used condoms than it did grass. Across the bottom, grubby windows overlooked white-washed walls and washing lines that residents only hung clothes on if they never wanted to see them again. That was pleasant compared to the stairwells that led to the first floor. As well as the grey concrete straight out of an Eastern Bloc colour chart, imaginative graffiti listing people who 'liked cock' and the ever-present smell of piss, there were the scattered needles, blood spatters and general sense that at least ten per cent of the people who lived in the complex had lost their virginity somewhere between the ground and first floors.

Jason made his way up the stairs, trying to ignore the toxic mix of cannabis, urine and tobacco, before emerging onto the balcony that ran the entire way around the three-sided block.

The first floor was marginally worse than the ground, largely because everyone chose to leave their rubbish bags outside their flats. The squeal of rats was as common as the satellite dishes welded to the side of every front door.

It was gone midnight but someone was revving a motor-cycle somewhere on the far side of the complex, hidden by the shadows. Elsewhere, there was music blazing from one of the flats on the adjacent row. In any gathering of people, there was always that guy everyone knew was The Prick. A place such as this attracted more than its fair share.

Jason reached his front door and turned, resting on the balcony rail, peering into the shade beyond to see if Natalie – or anyone – was watching. A stray dog plodded out from of one of the flats, a woman bellowing abuse before slamming the door behind it. Padding wistfully across the green, the animal sniffed at something in the mud, took one look at the flat from which it had just been ejected, and then trudged away into the gloom.

After one final scan, Jason spun back and unlocked the front door, shoving it with his shoulder and stepping inside. He closed it quietly, waiting for any hint of movement to indicate someone was actually in but, aside from the faint murmur of the living-room television, there was nothing.

Despite the lack of sound, Jason found himself creeping through the hallway anyway, the dent his younger self's head had made in the wall to his left an endless reminder about keeping quiet.

In the darkened living room, the television was casting an eerie blue-grey glow as the motionless figure slept in front of it. Apart from the sofa, holed carpet, television stand and smattering of empty disc cases, there was little else to look at. Even the photos of Jason as a child had disappeared at some point over the past few years. Once they had hung on the walls and rested on the television stand, now they were probably in a landfill somewhere.

Jason rounded the sofa and stared down at his mother, watching her eyelids flutter in the light. An arm was cradling a cushion, one knee curled into her belly, the other leg out flat. Her mouth was open as she breathed in and out deeply, her other arm hanging limply off the edge as if reaching for the empty vodka bottle on the floor. If she was dreaming, she probably was.

As Jason plucked the blanket from the back of the sofa and placed it over his mother, she groaned and rolled until she was facing the other way but her eyes didn't open. She murmured something that might have been 'Chris' but it was hard to tell as her acid breath made Jason wince and he had to turn away.

Jason finished tucking her in, turned the television off, left the remote control on the floor in front of the sofa so his mother couldn't miss it, and then took the empty bottle into the kitchen. After dropping it in the bin under the sink, he downed a glass of water and then thought he should probably check on his brother, given their mother might well have whispered his name.

Crossing the hallway, Jason knocked gently on Chris's door and then nudged it open a crack when there was no reply. Aside from the smell of deodorant and the vague shape of someone sleeping on his front, there was nothing to see. Jason closed the door again and went to his own bedroom, peering through the window onto the darkened, empty street below.

*

Jason woke with a jolt, as if there was an icy spider creeping along his naked skin. He rolled onto his back, gasping for breath, wondering where he was and scratching the area where he had felt the arachnid's feathery touch. There was nothing on his skin, or the bed – or the floor for that matter. Jason's eyes darted around the room, searching for what was wrong. The carrier bag of money was still tucked under his pillow, his clothes from the night before were still neatly folded on his nightstand, his door was shut, his phone was charging on the floor.

All exactly as it should be.

Except that the window was open a crack, the latch hooked over the metal cylinder poking up from the frame. Jason crossed the room, resting his hand against the freezing glass and feeling the chill blowing through the gap. The housing association had been promising to install double-glazing for years but it hadn't happened. It probably never would. They'd be better knocking the whole place down and starting again.

Jason hooked the window closed and then stared down to the road outside. Kids in school uniform were bouncing along in twos and threes as parents on the school run weaved dangerously in between them, tooting their horns and shaking their fists.

Had the window really been open all night? Wouldn't he have noticed the cold? Jason had stared into the still darkness the night before, looking for Natalie, but there was no one there.

Putting the thought to the back of his mind, Jason grabbed a hooded top from the floor, tugged his pyjama bottoms out of his arse crack, and headed into the living room.

His mother was rocking back and forward on the sofa, cackling to herself and having a conversation with someone who wasn't there. 'Did you hear that?' she said. 'Cheese? He's having a laugh.'

When he was younger, Jason remembered his mum as having a delicate high-pitched giggle; now it was throaty and rough. She turned as Jason entered, reaching out to tug him towards the sofa. 'You should watch this – they're showing clips of some quiz show where they get all the answers wrong.'

Jason glanced at the screen where a breakfast television presenter was looking far too awake for this time of the morning. He was gurning smugly at a guest and asking inane questions he probably knew the answer to already.

'Isn't that every quiz show?' Jason said.

His mother didn't turn from the set. Her straggly once-brown hair was a knot of wiry grey strands knitted into each other, her skin like the bottom of a well-worn shoe, her hands wrinkled and frail. She was forty-four but no one would have guessed within ten years, regardless of how much money was riding on it.

'Go and get your mother a cup of tea, will you?'

'Mum.'

'What?'

'Did you open my window?'

'What?'

'I think my window was shut last night but it was open this morning.'

'What are you talking about? Where's my tea?'

Jason noticed the almost-full vodka bottle at her feet, wondering where she'd got it from before figuring that if she wanted to drink something else, then he may as well help her.

The view from the kitchen window was almost identical to the one Jason had from his bedroom. The number of schoolchildren had started to tail off but there were still motorists driving too quickly, weaving in and out of the parked vehicles and blazing away in a cloud of exhaust fumes.

As the kettle fizzed and hissed, Jason peered through the glass for a few moments, searching for a hint of anything out of the ordinary.

Lamppost, bench, parked cars, corner of grass, graffiti, dirt, mad old woman with a shopping trolley.

Seeing someone pushing a trolley along the road wasn't exactly normal but it was hardly extraordinary either. Either way, she didn't glance towards Jason's flat, instead jabbing a finger towards an errant cat and shouting something he couldn't hear.

The click of the kettle snapped Jason back into the room. He hunted through the cupboards for the box of teabags, sniffed the milk and then heaped four teaspoons of sugar into his mother's cup before mixing everything together.

Two teas later and he was on the sofa next to his mum as she continued laughing at the television. The presenters weren't even telling jokes but she had the giggles, like a child at the funeral of somebody they didn't know.

'Mum.'

'What?'

'Have you seen Chris this morning?'

'He went out.'

'Where did he go?'

'Out.'

Jason had endured similar one-word conversations every day for too many years to count. He wondered why he'd bothered to make himself a tea when he had no intention of drinking it. His mother sipped at hers.

'This is too hot,' she said.

'It's tea, Mum, it's supposed to be hot.'

'Don't take that tone with me. I'm still your mother.'

In name only.

'Sorry, I was just wondering if you knew where Chris was.'

'He's *your* brother.'

And your son.

Jason stood, returning to the kitchen and tipping his tea away. He dressed properly, before double-checking all the money was still in the carrier bag and tucking it under his jacket.

He had one hand on the front door when his mother's gravelly voice echoed from the living room: 'Jason.'

Taking a breath, Jason closed his eyes, knowing he should leave. There was nothing she could say that would make his day any better. Against his better judgement, Jason returned to the living room. Despite the fact his mother's eyes didn't shift from the television, she somehow knew he was in the doorway.

'Have you got any money?' she asked.

'What do you want money for?'

'There's nothing in the house – the cupboards are empty and the milk's going off.'

'What happened to your disability money?'

'I need that.'

Jason didn't need to ask what for.

'I'll go to the supermarket later.'

'Just leave the money here.'

Another sigh. Another conversation they'd had over and over. 'I'll pick some food up later, Mum.'

For what was likely the first time that morning, her eyes left the television – but it was only to spin and call Jason a word few mothers ever used on their sons, not that it was the worst thing she'd ever called him. Her follow-up was familiar too: 'You never do anything around here – you're always out. What is it you do? Whoring? Are you some rent boy offering yourself for a tenner a time? I don't want your money anyway. Go on, get out of my house – run away to your sugar daddies. See if I care.'

Jason turned to leave but his eyes were drawn to the screen where the news had come on. There was a fire engine and police tape in the background, a presenter standing at the front. '. . . as I said, firefighters have been working through the night here in Rusholme where neighbours and local residents are in shock. Bodies have been removed under cover and, though the police are yet to release a formal statement, local reports indicate there was an entire family inside the burning house. I'll remind you that this is currently unconfirmed but sources have named the homeowners as Namdev and Padma Gupta . . .'

5

Jason sat on his bed next to Chris, watching television. Their backs were pressed against the wall, legs outstretched across the covers.

'What's on ITV?' Chris asked.

Jason slid across the bed and stood, crossing the room. The remote was somewhere around, not that it mattered considering it hadn't had batteries in months. He changed the channel to number three but there was something about animals on so he flicked it back to the BBC and returned to the bed.

On the other side of the closed door, their mother's voice continued to rage: 'Don't you take that tone with me. This is my house and—'

Thwack.

The crunch echoed from the living room along the hall-way, into the bedroom. Neither of the boys said anything.

'You're the one who's always pissing money up the wall,' a man's voice shouted. 'What happened to that tenner?'

'We needed milk.'

Thwack.

'You must think I'm a mug. Milk doesn't cost a tenner. What did you do with it?'

Jason slipped off the bed again and crossed the room to the television, turning the volume up. He'd gone to the living room in the past but it never ended well.

He returned to the bed, taking the pillow and handing it to Chris, who hugged it into himself. Jason tried to concentrate on the screen but wasn't taking it in. There was a woman in bright clothes grinning and having a conversation with a talking flower. At fourteen, he was definitely too old for it but it was probably too juvenile for Chris, who was half his age. Whatever it was didn't really matter, as long as the noise was drowning out what was happening in the other room.

The two boys sat in silence, Chris with the pillow, Jason gripping the covers, pretending he hadn't heard the thud through the wall.

As the programme finished, the credits began with an upbeat, poppy theme that was louder than the programme had been. Jason knew there was a line between drowning out the argument and . . .

The door thundered open, bouncing off the side of the bed with a clunk as Uncle Graham stormed into the room, boots clumping on the hard floor. He glanced towards the two boys and then stepped across to the television, picking it up and throwing it at the wall. As it sailed through the air, the tangle of leads caught on the corner of the dresser and the TV swung downwards, clattering into the floor. For good measure, Graham swung a boot like a rugby player taking a conversion and clattered it into the wall. With a fizz and a pop, the room was silent.

Then he turned around.

Uncle Graham had been living with them for a few months and Jason didn't think he'd shaved in all that time. His dark beard had grown and was now matted with spilled alcohol and bits of food, a complete contrast to his bald head.

His dark eyes glared towards the bed. 'Which one of you little shites turned that up?'

Jason stood. 'Me.'

Before he could say anything else, Graham pounced across, slapping him hard across the face. The crack echoed around the room as Jason stumbled sideways into the dresser, his face burning. Graham stopped Jason from falling by grabbing his collar and hurling him towards the shattered television as if he was a flimsy doll. He was about to pick him up again when Chris's voice sounded: 'Leave him alone.'

Jason was on the floor, head spinning from the blow, but he saw Graham's feet turn until he was facing the other direction. 'Whatcha gonna do about it, little man?' He took a step towards the bed but Jason heaved himself to his feet and hurled himself at the man.

Some fourteen-year-olds were the same size as adults but Jason hadn't really grown any bigger than when he was ten. He wasn't skinny but there was no strength to any of his limbs either. Graham was a bull of a man, with a thick neck that had bulging blue veins on top of powerful shoulders and upper arms. His thighs were like the giant joint of ham they'd had a couple of Christmases ago. Jason's shoulder bounced off Graham, barely making him stumble.

As Jason tried to pick himself up from the floor, he felt Graham's vice-grip squeezing his shoulder, hauling him to his feet. Jason tried to kick his legs but the man clasped him even tighter, making him squeal with pain. He wasn't sure if he'd been picked up or if Graham had bent low but Jason found himself staring directly into the man's icy gaze.

'Do you want to go to war with me, boy?'

'No.'

'No what?'

'No, Sir.'

Graham flicked his head forward, butting Jason just above the nose. As he fell backwards, the man kept hold of his shoulder and threw him against the dresser again.

'The pair of you need to learn some respect.'

Not for the first time, there were stars clouding the grey haze around Jason's vision. He tried to stare up at Graham but the man was simply a hulking dark shape standing in the doorway. With a slam, he was gone.

There was a scrambling of bedcovers and legs and then Chris was at Jason's side, his fair hair bright against the haze of grey. 'Are you all right?'

'I think so.'

'There's blood over your eye.'

Chris brushed a spot above Jason's eyebrow and held his thumb up to show the red liquid.

Jason rubbed it and then reached across for the box of tissues which had fallen onto the floor and began mopping himself up. Everything above his nose ached.

Chris's voice sounded so hollow it made Jason shiver: 'What are we going to do?'

Jason was trying to think but it was hard to blink the pain away. 'I don't know.'

'He could kill us.'

'He won't.'

'Or Mum.'

'He won't.'

'How do you know?'

Jason didn't reply but used the corner of the dresser to pull his body up and looked at himself in the mirror. A crescent moon-shaped cut had opened above his right eyebrow and there was already dark shading forming around both eyes. A dribble of bright blood trickled from his nose.

Jason caught his brother's eyes in the mirror.

'You look like a boxer,' Chris said.

'A shite one.'

'Are you going to tell someone?'

Jason turned, kneeling so he could look at his brother properly. 'I'm going to go out. I want you to go back to your room, close the door and push your dressing table up against it. Do it as quietly as you can and then don't say anything.'

'Where are you going?'

'Out. When I get back, I'll knock three times on your door to let you know it's me. You can sleep in here tonight if you want.'

'How long are you going to be?'

'I don't know – but if Graham comes for you, if he breaks into your room, then run for the front door and scream as loudly as you can.'

'Okay.'

*

Jason clicked the front door open and closed it as quietly as he could. Graham and his mother had already gone off to their bedroom and wouldn't be leaving any time soon. He weaved his way in and out of the clutter that littered the balcony around their flat and descended the hard concrete steps to ground level before dashing across the green.

At the back of their complex was a housing estate with paths and alleyways woven throughout. Jason resisted the urge to join in with the football game going on against the wall with the 'No ball games' sign and crossed to the row of shops.

Jason scanned the surroundings: a woman was waiting for the bus with two bulging bags of shopping at her feet and a toddler in a pushchair; a delivery driver was running from his van into the pizza place, having left his keys in the ignition – always a dangerous idea around this area; a couple were wedged into the cubby hole between the take-away and the paper shop eating each other's faces.

None of them was who he was looking for.

Heading towards the cut-through that linked his estate with the park, Jason clenched his fists and put them in his pockets, trying to keep them warm. He ducked his head and put his hood up, not wanting anyone to see the marks on his skin – not yet anyway. Upping his pace, Jason skirted through the alley and crossed the next road, finally spot-ting the person he wanted a few metres inside the park gates sitting on a bench in the shadows.

Dropping his hood again and standing up slightly straighter, Jason began walking as normally as he could manage – not too quickly, not slouching. He wanted to be noticed without making it look like he'd gone out of his way to be seen. As he passed the bench, he heard the man say his name.

'Jason?'

He turned. 'Mr Carter?'

'Just Carter. I'm only a few years older than you, kid.'

Jason didn't know how old Carter was but 'a few years' was probably pushing it. It was more like ten to fifteen years older. Carter was built like Graham but he was all muscle, no fat. He had short blond hair and a weathered clean-shaven face. The type of person that could be stared at for five minutes and then instantly forgotten. There was nothing memorable about him aside from his size – and even then, he wore his bulk well with crisply cut clothes that didn't make him stand out.

Across the path, a teenager with shoulder-length dark hair glanced nervously in their direction. Carter looked both ways and then called out. 'Give us ten minutes, eh, kid?'

The hoody nodded and hurried away without a word.

'Have I just cost you a sale?' Jason asked.

Carter licked his lips as he peered at Jason. 'He'll be back. He's one of the regulars.'

'What does he buy?'

Carter patted the bench and Jason sat next to him. 'Kid like you shouldn't be worrying about things like that. Now, where did those marks on your face come from?'

Jason glimpsed away self-consciously. 'Nowhere.'

'So you woke up this morning and someone had done a number on you?'

'Not exactly.'

'Some kids at school giving you grief?'

'No.'

'Who is it then?'

'I shouldn't say.'

Carter blew into his hands and put them in his coat pockets. He was wearing a semi-shiny black jacket over the top of something else dark. No jewellery, no tattoos. Jason glanced down at his own hands knowing this was the example he should follow: be anonymous – a man in a plain coat on a park bench that nobody looks at twice.

Carter clucked his tongue. 'Don't be silly, Jase. We're all pals here, aren't we? You remember what Mr Irwell told you – you do right by us, we'll do right by you.'

'I don't want to get into trouble.'

'Who's going to put you in trouble?'

'*He* is.'

Carter laughed humourlessly. 'How about you tell me who "he" is and we'll see who ends up in trouble.'

Jason took a deep breath, playing the game. The hoody was sitting on a bench fifty or sixty metres away watching them, while a woman with a pushchair had already passed them twice, anxiously glancing both times towards Carter and then scratching the inside of her arms before continuing on.

'His name's Graham,' Jason whispered.

'And do you know where this Graham lives?'

'At our house.'

'Does he go out much?'

'He goes to the paper shop around the corner to get some fags every morning at nine.'

Carter took his hands out of his pockets and cracked his knuckles. 'Does he indeed?'

'Yes.'

'Every morning?'

'Yes.'

'Right – how about you leave things with me?'

6

NOW

Jason hurried along Quay Street, hands in pockets, head down: jeans, dark top, denim jacket, not being noticed. He offered a quick nod to the security officers standing at the front of the casino and walked inside, making sure he glanced at the camera above the doors before bounding onto the main floor.

Even though it was early, the establishment was beginning to fill up with the ding-ding-ding of the slot machines and the caller in the bingo area blathering number after number as rows of women breezed through their pensions one stabbing permanent marker dot at a time. Jason stopped to watch for a moment, transfixed by the rhythm of the calls and subsequent arm movements. He had never visited Las Vegas but assumed the servers there weren't bustling through the aisles with teapots and bone china.

Only in England . . .

Remembering why he was there, Jason turned and weaved his way through the machines, around the table games, until he reached the door at the back next to the bar. A suited man was standing, arms crossed, gazing directly ahead. His eyes flickered to Jason and then away again. Turning swiftly, he pressed four numbers into the keypad next to him and then spun back to face the floor. 'Make sure you knock.'

Jason pushed open the first door and headed along the familiar dark corridor until he reached the door at the end. As instructed, he knocked but the 'come in' came almost instantly.

The casino's office was decorated with crimson walls and a cherry-wood border with matching chairs and an enormous table in the centre. Harry and Carter were sitting on the far side of the desk, hunched over a large sheet of paper.

Harry didn't have the same physical presence he'd had when Jason had first met him; however, even though his hair might be greyer and he might wince slightly each time he stood, he could still command the attention of a room with the raise of a bushy white eyebrow.

Carter was much the same as he had always been. He'd lost a little weight but kept the same cropped hair, athletic build and non-descript appearance. The only difference was that cold park benches and dealing to hoodies and single mothers was a thing of the past. During business hours, he went everywhere Harry did.

With a dismissive wave of his arm, Carter made it clear what he thought about Jason's arrival. 'Can you come back later, kid? We're busy here.'

Jason waited for Harry but the older man was tutting. 'Now, now. We're all one family here. Come here, m'boy.'

On the other side of the table, Harry nodded towards the paper. 'This is the casino's floor plan. Legally, we're allowed another dozen machines but it's finding room for them.' He pointed at a spot on the page. 'We were thinking that if we shrunk the kitchen and moved this wall, it'd let us shift the craps tables over and then we'd have the space. We'd have to contract some of the food in but the extra income from the machines would be more than enough to cover it.' Harry peered up, holding Jason's eye. 'What do you think?'

'It sounds like a nice idea.'

Harry nodded. 'That's what my other boy here was saying but I'm not so sure.' He rubbed his chin and sat, poking the leather-backed chair next to him and waiting for Jason to sit before turning to Carter. 'Will you give us ten minutes?'

'You sure?'

'Absolutely – and get someone to sort some teas out, will you?'

Carter glanced at Jason and then stood, walking to the door and leaving without turning. When it was just them, Harry pushed himself to his feet and deliberately crossed to the bar, where a record player was perched. He opened a dark-wood cabinet and took out a record sleeve, sliding out the vinyl disc and placing it on the turntable. In an instant, classical music filled the room: a beautiful medley of instruments.

Harry crossed back to the table and sat next to Jason, leaning in. 'You can have your CDs, downloads, or whatever else you kids have these days – but there's something quite magnificent about an old-fashioned seventy-eight.'

The chorus boomed through the speakers so loudly that Jason had to shuffle his chair closer to hear. 'Is that a record?'

Harry laughed. 'Oh, my boy. I'll make you a promise now – when I'm gone, I'm going to leave you all of my *records*.'

'Thank you.'

'How's your mother?'

'Same as ever.'

'And the brother?'

'The same.'

The older man nodded approvingly. 'So why are you here? It's been a little while since we've seen you around these parts.'

'Last night . . . the shopkeeper.'

Jason wanted to say Namdev's name but couldn't bring himself to do it. Instead, he stared at his feet. There was no reply but Jason could feel Harry's eyes searching for his and when he finally peered up again, the older man replied in a whisper, barely audible over the music.

'What do you think happened to him?' Harry asked.

'You asked me to deliver the message.'

'And you did that, didn't you?'

'Yes.'

'So what's the problem?'

'I saw on the news . . . there was a fire.'

'Perhaps I wanted more than one message delivering?'

Jason took a second to absorb the information. 'Why?'

Harry began sucking on his teeth and then stood abruptly, crossing to the bar and waving a hand towards Jason, who followed.

'How long does it take to make a cup of tea around here?'

He stared at Jason, raising his eyebrows, expecting an answer.

'I, er . . .'

Harry twisted the dial on the record player and, as if on cue, there was a rap on the door. Harry called 'come in' and a slim, tanned woman wearing a sparkly short skirt, huge heels, a matching glittering bra-top and a smile entered with a tray. She bowed her head and then crossed to the table, putting it down before asking if Harry required anything else. He scanned the contents of the tray and shook his head. After she had closed the door, he turned the music back up and then returned to the table, tipping the contents of the teapot into two cups, followed by a splash of milk from a small porcelain jug and a single sugar cube. Jason sat back next to him as Harry stirred his cup and put it back down.

He picked up a ginger nut from the tray. 'What's your favourite biscuit?' Harry asked.

'I, er . . . I've never really thought about it.'

'Think now.'

'I don't really have a sweet tooth.'

Harry took another small bite of the biscuit. 'You can have all these extravagant things – triple chocolate-this, mocha cream-that. It's a whole industry nowadays: deluxe boxes of six cookies costing a fortune, those imported American things. Back in the day, we had ginger nuts, custard creams, digestives, rich teas and Bourbons. No sodding about.' He took another bite, chewing thoughtfully, staring at Jason. 'There's only one king of biscuits – the ginger nut. No fancy shite, no showing off. From the name, you know it's got ginger in it and you know it's rock hard.' Another bite, his gaze still not moving. 'You're a good boy, Jason. You're my ginger nut – no elaborate arsing about. You keep your head down, you don't go throwing money around, you don't blow it on girls or merchandise. You're what every father wishes for.'

Jason didn't know if he expected a reply. What was there to say? Harry finished the biscuit and had a sip of his tea, motioning for Jason to do the same. Jason took the dainty cup and gulped a mouthful, even though he never usually had sugar.

Harry swallowed, waiting for Jason to do the same before continuing. 'Sometimes, a message needs to be sent and you need someone else to send it. I'm sure you did a grand job but this needed something bigger. It's about respect – it's not just about that Paki.'

For a moment, Jason thought Harry was going to name the person he was really sending a message to. It definitely wasn't Namdev Gupta. Anyone who was remotely close to Harry was aware of who he was constantly trying to ward off. The rivalry had been going on for years and the Guptas had the misfortune of being in the middle.

Before he got to the name that was really on his mind, Harry took another drink of his tea. 'How much did you get?'

Jason started to unzip his coat to take the bag out but Harry wagged a finger. 'Two thousand, six hundred and twenty,' Jason said. 'Do you want it?'

Harry shook his head. 'Consider it a bonus.'

'Thank you.'

'Is there anything else bothering you?'

Jason thought of Natalie but it was almost as if he had dreamed her. Had she really mentioned Harry's name in that pub last night? Perhaps he'd misheard her and she'd said something else entirely? The music was loud and they'd had to whisper in each other's ears. He hadn't stopped to ask her to repeat herself – he had panicked and run for it.

'No.'

Harry nodded and then crossed to the bar, lowering the volume of the music until it was a background hum. Back at the table, he pointed to the blueprints as he had earlier.

'Aside from making the kitchen smaller, the other option is to try to buy the land next door. It's owned by the council, so it would take years to get through.'

Jason stood, zipping his coat all the way up again. 'I'm sure you'll make the right decision.'

'Feel free to stay for a drink if you wish.' Harry turned towards the bar. 'It's fully stocked if you prefer something a little stronger.'

'No thank you.'

Harry clapped Jason on the back. 'Well then. I'll be in touch soon, m'boy. Thank you for your hard work. I'm sure you'll be very pleased with the reward.'

Jason mumbled another 'thank you' and headed towards the door. He passed Carter in the corridor and offered a half-hearted 'see you', before returning to the main casino floor.

In the short period he had been in the back room, it had filled up even further. A woman with a supermarket canvas bag for life at her feet was sitting at a slot machine, gazing hypnotically as she fed plastic coins in and pulled the lever. Behind her, two men in suits were sitting on opposite sides of a blackjack table, chests out, posturing like two wild animals about to fight over a mate. Jason skimmed around the edges, staying away from the dings and rattles as he found himself back at the bingo room. All the seats were taken but there were still half-a-dozen women at the back resting on the pint-glass-width ledges stuck to the walls, dabbing away at their cards as the caller went through the routine.

Outside and the air was cool. Jason had his hands in his pockets and could feel the bag of money under his clothes. The only reason they'd stolen from the off-licence was in case Namdev did call the police. He'd never be able to mention the drugs, so they'd label it as a robbery, rather than the intimidation it actually was. Who knew what the police would make of it now?

Jason returned to his car and threw the bag in the boot before climbing into the driver's seat. The radio sprang to life as he turned the key, just as the news was beginning. The top story was the obvious one: Namdev Gupta, his wife Padma, his brother Hamid and their children Ishrat and Jalaja were all officially dead – burned alive in a suspected arson attack on their home. In the second before Jason reached across to turn it off, the police spokesman had time to call it 'an extermination'.

And then there was only the hum of the engine.

7

Jason drove away from the city centre back towards Hulme, parking just off the main road and crossing into the library. He swiped his card, nodded a non-committal 'hello' at the man behind the desk, and then headed towards the bank of computers in the far corner.

There was something about the peace of the place that Jason always enjoyed. Libraries should, of course, be quiet – but even the noises people made were somehow satisfying. Any coughs were muffled, sneezes suppressed; any necessary conversations were whispered as if muttering a swear word around a baby. That left only the gentle tapping of computer keys and the fluttering of book pages – something that Jason found inherently peaceful.

The row of computers was seemingly always occupied by at least one pensioner but Jason logged onto the one at the far end, facing the rest of the library where the only chance of anyone watching him was if they were browsing the Medieval History section – which no one ever did.

Jason opened two tabs on the Internet browser and navigated to the same pair of pages he always did: one showing the weather in Crete, the other his bank's website.

Well, one of his banks.

His main account was just like anyone else's: a High Street branch, with a small, stable stream of wages dropping in each month and a slightly less steady string of direct debits emptying it again. He was paid as a courier by one of Harry's various companies. In many ways, it wasn't an inaccurate description of what he did: he delivered messages and, occasionally, he picked packages up. Everything from that stream of income was whiter than white, with tax and National Insurance paid, annual statements produced and nothing that had even a whiff of not being quite right. Jason's mother might complain that he never did anything around the flat, but the money to pay for the TV licence, electricity and gas bills, council tax and every other thing society managed to bleed from a person came from that account. His wages didn't add up to a large amount of money but it was calculated carefully to make sure he had just enough after all of the deductions to be certain he didn't have to ask for anything extra.

Jason never checked that account because there was no need. Like clockwork, money went in, money went out. The one he logged into was the one Harry had set up for him. It was registered somewhere in the Caribbean where no one bothered to ask questions and he knew he could have everything transferred wherever he wanted with a click of a mouse or a phone call.

The screen flashed cream, then grey before the page with his bank account's details came into view. Harry had said he'd be 'very pleased' with the reward, which was true. Jason had expected a couple of thousand but he'd been paid five, plus the two and a bit in cash in his car. Over seven thousand for a simple message delivery: something he'd done many times before and been paid a lot less for.

None of those had ended with him hearing about house fires on the news, though.

Jason scrolled down to the bottom of the page and stared at the total, doing a quick piece of mental arithmetic. He knew the exchange rate from the foreign currency into British pounds perfectly.

£325,420.

If someone had told him five years ago that he'd have that sort of money, Jason would have laughed at them. He certainly wouldn't have thought he'd be sitting in a library staring at the figure thinking that it wasn't enough.

The reason the amateurs wanted to blow their money was only partly because they were stupid – it was also because they couldn't plan. Harry was right about Jason: he didn't waste his money on girls, drugs, booze, cars or anything else. That didn't mean he wouldn't one day – but it definitely wouldn't be in England, let alone Manchester. He'd wait, bide his time and let that money grow.

Jason logged out of the site and hit the home button, which made a news website load.

'FAMILY PERISH IN HOUSE BLAZE'

With a blink, he clicked the cross on the tab to close the site, leaving only the weather website open. It was warm in Crete – twenty-two degrees with a gentle five-mile-an-hour breeze. Jason closed his eyes and he was almost there: soft white sand, rippling blue waters, the bustle of tourists, the heat on his skin—

'Looking at Crete again?'

Jason's eyes shot open and he realised there was someone at his shoulder. He spun to see the semi-familiar face smiling down at him. He focused on her name tag – LUCY – and found himself having to stifle a yawn.

'Sorry,' she said.

Lucy was carrying half-a-dozen hardbacks but put them down next to the computer and sat in the seat next to Jason. He couldn't remember the first time he'd spoken to her but it felt as if they'd always had a strange relationship of saying 'hello' and nodding to each other across the library. They'd gradually started to have short conversations about the weather and other things going on in their lives. The only time anyone had ever caught him out was when Lucy had been adding a book to the Medieval History section and he'd been looking at the weather in Crete.

She had long butter-blonde hair weaved tightly into a bun and watery blue eyes that never seemed to leave the person she was talking to. Jason didn't know how old she was but it was somewhere around his age, perhaps a little younger. He couldn't fail to notice how tight her pencil skirt was, not to mention her well-fitting white blouse. The girls in the casino showed pretty much everything off but there was something to be said for leaving it to the imagination.

Jason suddenly felt nervous, forgetting what Lucy had said to him. It was only when she nodded towards the screen that he remembered.

'I went to Crete when I was a kid,' Jason replied in a raised whisper. 'It was warm and seems to be nice the whole year round.'

'Are you thinking of going back?'

'Maybe. Not yet.'

'Next summer?'

'Something like that.'

Lucy rested a hand on the books, a hint of a smile on her face. 'So, how are you?'

'All right. I didn't realise you were working today.'

'Oh aye, you're not a stalker, are you?'

'No, I—'

Lucy nudged his shoulder with the palm of her hand. 'I'm joking.'

'Right.'

She glanced towards the rest of the library, making sure there was nobody near, and then turned back. 'Can I ask you something?' Lucy said.

'Okay.'

'Why haven't you got the Internet at home? Or why don't you use your phone? It's only usually schools or older people who come here to use the computers but you're in once or twice a week. I always want to ask you.'

Jason shrugged. He couldn't tell her the real reason, that he was paranoid about Chris or his mother being able to trace what he was looking at, let alone anyone else getting hold of his hard drive.

'It's really distracting to have the Internet all the time,' Jason replied. 'If you want to get some work done, it's always there putting you off.'

Lucy grinned more widely, making the darker freckles across the tops of her cheeks stretch. 'You're probably right – every time I start a project I usually get about half an hour in and then I'm drifting off to use my phone for something.'

'How is your course going?'

Lucy dug her fingers into her hair, forgetting it was tied up, and then pulled them out again, biting her bottom lip. 'Did you go to university?'

'No.'

'Do you really want to know?'

'Yes.'

She reached forward and took Jason's hand, standing and pulling him around the bank of computers before letting him go. The books she had been carrying were abandoned as she hurried in between bookcases, slaloming knowledgeably through the children's section, past Sci-Fi and Fantasy, around Crime and up a flight of stairs, not even turning to see if Jason was still behind her.

Lucy eventually stopped in front of a section with books so large that the shelves were spaced further apart.

She spun, throwing her arms wide. 'Ta-da!'

'Aren't you supposed to be quiet in a library?'

She grinned mischievously, her high cheekbones rising even further. She flung her arms open and whispered: 'Ta-da!'

'The history of art section?'

'It's interesting.'

'What do they teach you? Someone once picked up a paintbrush and a thousand years later, people are still doing it?'

The top half of her face was frowning but her lips were smiling. 'I wouldn't have thought you a cynic.'

'I just don't know anything about it.'

Lucy spun and ran her hand along the uneven thick

spines of the books, humming quietly to herself. She reached the end of the row and then crouched, repeating herself until she found the book she was looking for. She heaved the wide hardback from the shelf and put it on the nearby table with a thump that boomed around the otherwise silent building.

'Oops,' she whispered, not sounding as if she meant it.

'Do people really borrow those things?' Jason asked. 'How would they get them home?'

'Fork-lift.'

'Really?'

Lucy turned to look at him, eyebrows dipped in the middle. 'Of course not really. Most people would read these books here. They're for research. Do you believe everything you're told?' She didn't wait for a reply before opening the book, scanning her hand along the chapter titles and then finding the right page. She jabbed it with a finger. 'What do you think of that?'

The picture was a close-up of a man's face, his mouth wide open, eyes wide with bony thin fingers on his cheeks and what looked like cornet-shaped horns coming out of his head. In the top corner was a woman wearing a long flowing dress, staring into the distance and shielding her eyes from a sun that wasn't visible.

Jason panicked slightly, not having a clue. If it had been a picture of a house, a sunset, or a real person, then he might have had an opinion but the horns were off-putting. Was it supposed to be a man? A demon? And who was the woman?

'It's, er, nice,' he mumbled.

Lucy whispered without turning away from the page. 'You can say if you don't like it.'

'No, I do. I just . . .'

'You don't know what to make of it.'

'Right.'

'It's called Expressionism. The artist takes a subject and distorts it, putting their own slant on what they see. I'm doing a year-long project about it as the final part of my art degree.'

'Okay.'

Jason hadn't known she was doing something arty, just that she was on some sort of course.

'Which is where you come in,' Lucy added.

'Do I?'

She turned to face him again. 'I was hoping you'd pose for me.'

'Me?'

'You're the one I'm looking at.'

'Why me?'

Lucy pursed her lips, genuinely thinking. She started tugging at the small strand of hair that had become disentangled from the rest. 'Because you come in here all the time, you spend a few minutes on the computer and then you're gone again. You never borrow a book, you never even *read* a book. You always say hello and then scuttle away. You're interesting.'

'Really?'

'I never know what you're thinking. Sometimes it gets boring around here and you end up watching the people that come in, wondering what their stories are. There's this woman who's sixty- or seventy-odd. She's always glammed up and heads to the film and television non-fiction section. She'll spend hours picking books off the shelves, skimming through them and putting them back. I always wondered if she's some actress from the old days. Then there's this man: scruffy, long hair, unshaven, always wearing T-shirts even when it's cold. He goes to the crime section and always borrows books from the same series, even though he's had them all out before. He'll go through the series and then go back to the start again but never borrows anything else. I wondered if maybe he's the author and he keeps taking his own books out because he gets money. With you . . . I don't know what to think. You're this curious Internet man.'

Jason couldn't hold her gaze for any longer. He didn't realise anyone had bothered to pay so much attention to him. It was a tiny bit worrying that someone else knew his routine but flattering too.

Before he could reply, she added: 'And you've never asked me out.'

'No.'

The word had blurted out before Jason had a chance to stop it. Had she said that because she wanted him to ask her out? Or was she genuinely happy about it because lads were chasing after her all of the time? Or did she already have a boyfriend – or girlfriend? – and she didn't want anyone else trying it on? Perhaps she was just stating a fact – he hadn't asked her out, after all.

Lucy didn't seem too bothered by his instant response. 'So, whaddya say?'

'About what?'

'About posing for my painting.'

'What do I need to do?'

'Just sort of sit around and not move very much.'

'Do I keep my clothes on?'

Lucy snorted and back-handed him gently on the shoulder. 'Why would you take your clothes off?'

'I don't know – you hear about people posing for things with their . . . bits . . . out.'

She shook her head. 'All you need to do is come to my flat, keep your clothes on, sit still, keep your clothes on, look into the distance, keep your clothes on, and keep me company.'

'When?'

'Whenever you're free. I'm off tomorrow morning if you are.'

'I am if nothing comes up.'

'Brilliant.' Lucy closed the book and held her hand out. 'Let's have your phone.'

Without thinking, or questioning, Jason took it out of his pocket, tapped the unlock code in and handed it over. She flashed through the screens quicker than Jason ever could and a moment later something in her pocket began to vibrate.

She handed his phone back: 'That's supposed to be off in here by the way . . .' She took her own out with a grin. '. . . not that anyone ever obeys that rule. I've sent myself a text from your phone so we've got each other's numbers. I'll send you my address. Come over for about eleven. Will you call if you can't make it?'

'Okay.'

Lucy stood and picked the book back up. 'And smile once in a while. How bad can it all be?'

8

Jason left the library feeling more than a little confused. Was that flirting? Had Lucy asked him out? Was sitting in her flat posing for a painting classified as a date? And what did she mean when she said he was 'interesting'? He'd been called many things in his life but never that. Perhaps she wouldn't think that if she knew how much money was in his Caribbean bank account.

He wondered if Lucy knew about the second part of his routine.

Jason left the library, crossed the road and headed into the newsagent. He waited in line as the man at the front counted out pennies to pay for a packet of cigarettes and then tried to haggle when he was ten pence short. In the end, the man behind him in the queue flipped a coin onto the counter and said he'd cover it. It was likely he'd done it so he could get on with paying for his top-shelf magazine, tabloid newspaper to cover it with, and packet of chewing gum.

When Jason reached the front, it was just him and the shopkeeper. He bought his usual ten scratch cards, paid in cash and then turned to lean on the ice-cream freezer.

As Jason scraped away the first patch of silver, the man behind the counter called across to him. 'You ever won anything on one of those?'

'Bits and pieces.'

'What's the most you've ever won?'

Jason scratched away the second silver square. The shape underneath didn't match the first. 'Hundred and twenty quid.'

'One of my cousins won seven grand, the lucky bastard.'

'What did he spend it on?'

'Christ knows. A holiday, I think.'

Jason tossed the card in the bin and started on the second.

'What's the jackpot on that one?' the man asked.

'Quarter of a million.'

The man whistled extravagantly. 'What would you do with that much?'

'I don't need it all.'

'How much do you need?'

The second card was flung in the same direction as the first. 'One hundred and seventy-four thousand, five hundred and eighty quid.'

There was a pause as the third card was scratched and binned.

'That's a very precise amount,' the shopkeeper said.

Jason didn't reply, scratching through the fourth and fifth cards with no result.

Clearly wanting someone to talk to, the man continued: 'I always think thirty grand would be a nice amount. Nothing too silly but just enough. If you stuck it in a savings account, you'd be able to have nice holidays every year but you'd still carry on your day-to-day work like normal. You hear all these stories about people who win millions and then they blow it all and end up hanging themselves or whatever. Who wants all that money and responsibility? The begging letters, people outside your door and so on?'

Cards six, seven and eight went into the bin.

'. . . Still, I wouldn't complain about your hundred and seventy grand either. I'd find something to spend it on. Well, the wife would. Christ, imagine sending her to the Trafford Centre with that – she'd blow through the bloody lot.'

Nine followed the first eight but Jason held up the tenth with triumph. 'Aha!'

'You won?'

'Two quid.'

'Wanna go again?'

Jason tossed the winning card across the counter. The man checked it over, grinned, and then took a fresh card from his roll, passing it to Jason.

'So, whatcha going to do if you win your hundred and seventy grand then?'

'Emigrate to Crete with my mum.'

The shopkeeper scratched his head. 'That in Spain?'

'Not quite. It's sunny all year round.'

'You'll be taking some gorgeous girl too, I'll bet. Sun, sea, sand, gorgeous girl – yeah, I could live with that. Sod the missus. Not sure about my mum, though. She can win her own lottery.'

Jason scratched off the first patch of silver: a red heart.

He tried to think of how long he'd have to work to earn the money he wanted to get himself up to half a million. He'd made his three-and-a-bit hundred thousand in around seven years, so it would be another three or so. Perhaps a little less if Harry continued to be generous.

The second patch: a red heart.

Jason had thought a lot about why he was so obsessed with the half-a-million figure but there was no logical reason. It simply seemed like a nice amount so that he'd not have to worry about money when he was abroad.

The third patch: a red heart.

He thought he could buy a small restaurant somewhere on the edge of one of the resorts and then a house up in the hills. The restaurant wouldn't turn over too much but he'd pay the manager well enough to keep him honest and then live off the returns. He didn't need the extravagant things some people did in their lives. Food would be cheap, he could ride a bike to get around, do his own cooking and cleaning. It wouldn't cost that much.

The fourth patch: a black spade.

Jason flipped the card over to check the result. Four hearts was the jackpot. Four reds would be a fiver but three hearts meant nothing. He turned and threw it into the bin after the others.

'Not your day, eh, pal?' the shopkeeper said. 'Never mind.'

Jason ignored him, heading outside to where the skies had clouded over into a regular north-west squall. The breeze was up, whipping the faint drizzle directly into Jason's face. As he blinked away the rain, he noticed the metallic-red estate car parked in front of the shop on a single yellow line. More importantly, he spotted who was leaning against the bonnet, dressed in a professional-looking smart dark suit.

'How's the head?' Natalie asked. She didn't look as glamorous as she had in the purple dress but she was still something of a head-turner.

Jason put his head down and set off along the road, looking both ways and hoping that no one he knew was watching him. He could hear her footsteps and then she was alongside him.

'You didn't drive home last night, did you?' she asked.

'What do you want?'

'The same as I wanted last night – a chat.'

'Are you following me?'

'Not really.'

'So how did you know where I was?'

'You remember when you had your tonsils out when you were five? We stuck a microchip in your arse.'

Jason stopped and turned to face her. Natalie's long dark hair was in a ponytail but billowing in the wind. She looked so different to how she had the previous evening in her short dress and yet somehow still the same. She had a smirk on her face.

'Really?' he said.

'Of course not really. Do you believe everything you're told?'

'Pardon?'

'That's very polite.'

'What did you say?'

The smile slipped from Natalie's face, unsure why he was asking. 'I asked if you believe everything you're told.'

Jason looked past her, towards the library. 'Why did you say that specifically?' he asked, turning back to Natalie.

'Because it's preposterous that anyone would put a microchip in your backside. I was joking.'

'But why did you phrase it like that?'

Natalie's eyes narrowed. 'I don't know. It just came out.'

Jason continued staring at her. Had he imagined that Lucy had said the exact same thing? Word for word? Perhaps it was a coincidence – he had responded to both ridiculous statements in the same fashion, after all.

'What do you want?' he asked.

'A chat.'

'I don't want to talk to you.'

'How do you know that until you've heard what I have to say?'

Jason glanced across the road and then peered both ways along the street. Aside from a battered silver Yaris being driven erratically, there was no one else around.

Natalie continued: 'I've got a nice car with tinted windows. It'll just be you and me. You can either come along for a ride or I'll follow you the entire day.'

He gazed along the road again where the Yaris was stopped at a set of traffic lights in the left-hand lane indicating right as the panicking driver checked over her shoulder to see if she would be able to weave across the traffic.

Without replying, Jason spun and strode past Natalie, breaking into a jog. The vehicle remotely unlocked as he got close and he grabbed the passenger's side door, throwing himself in and ducking his head down. He watched through the windscreen as Natalie took her time, not worrying about the drizzle, strutting along the pavement, hair wafting, one hand in her pocket, the other clutching the car keys.

When she finally got into the vehicle, she didn't acknowledge that Jason was there, switching the engine on, silencing the Radio Two DJ's monotonous drone with a thumb-jab into the central panel, and then easing onto the road. The locks on the doors clicked ominously.

'Where are you parked?' Natalie eventually asked.

'Just around the corner.'

'I'm going to do a loop of the area and then I'll bring you back. Don't worry – I'm not abducting you.'

The thought hadn't crossed Jason's mind.

'Who are you?' he asked.

'Who do you think I am?'

'Police.'

He turned sideways to see the thin smirk on her face. 'I'm your salvation, Jason Green.'

9

Jason walked into the flat to be met by the cacophony of cupboard doors being opened and slammed. He headed into the kitchen, where Chris was facing away from him and in the process of crashing the fridge door closed.

The kitchen was poky at the best of times: counters along three sides, a cooker that was more brown than white, a grime-covered green plastic toaster with matching kettle, a metal sink with a window above it, a draining board speckled with white scum spots and cheap brown lino that was peeling in all four corners with a deep red stain in the centre that had been there for as long as Jason could remember.

Chris's fair hair had become darker over the years but it was still a lot lighter than Jason's. He'd also shot up by a foot or so over the past couple of years and now stood a few inches taller than his older brother.

He spun around at the sound of Jason's footsteps and scowled. 'There's never any food in.'

'Why don't you buy some then?'

'Why do you think? Have you got any money?'

'I meant to go shopping earlier but got side-tracked. I'll go out later or tomorrow.'

'You could just give me the money and I'll go. It'll save you having to worry about it.'

Jason marvelled at how appalling his brother was at

masking even the most basic of ill intentions. He nervously chewed his lip and stared over Jason's shoulder rather than attempt to make eye contact.

'It's fine – I'll sort it,' Jason said.

Chris screwed his lips up and then blew out. 'Right – can I borrow some money then?'

'What for?'

'Nothing much – I'm just a bit short.'

Jason crossed to the sink and poured himself a glass of water. 'A bit short for what?'

With a sigh, Chris moved to the doorway, blocking the only way out with his arms. He was thinner than Jason and, with his height, looked like he'd been stretched on a rack because his limbs were a little too long for the rest of his body.

'It's Kat's birthday next week,' Chris said.

Jason didn't know if that was true but doubted that's what the money was for. 'You want *me* to buy a present for *your* girlfriend?'

'Well, I wouldn't put it like that.'

'How much do you want?'

'Two.'

'Two hundred?'

'Two grand.'

Jason had just taken a sip of the water but coughed on it, sending a thin spray into the centre of the room, before turning and choking the rest into the sink, only regaining the ability to speak a minute later.

'You're eighteen years old,' Jason spluttered. 'What are you buying her – a sodding yacht?'

'No.'

'Christ's sake – you're not asking if she wants to get married, are you?'

'No.'

'Is she pregnant?'

'No!'

'So what do you want two grand for?'

Chris shuffled nervously on the spot. 'Have you got it?'

Jason had that two-and-a-bit-thousand in the boot of his car, plus more in his current account that he could take out if he wanted.

'Tell me what you want it for and I'll tell you if I've got it.'

Chris did what he always did – lost it. He aimed a kick at the bin, missing, and then took a stride forward, jabbing a finger towards his brother. 'You're so selfish. It's always about you, isn't it? You love lording it over me and Mum, so we have to come to you with a begging bowl. It gets you off, doesn't it?'

Jason tried to brush past him to head to his room but Chris shoved him backwards. 'I can't wait for the day when you come to me asking for something. I'll ask you a load of questions and then turn around and tell you to get stuffed.'

'I wasn't telling you to get stuffed – but if I'm going to give you two thousand pounds, it'd be nice to know what it's going on.'

'"*Give*"? I asked to borrow it.'

Jason pushed his brother away, sighing. He'd heard it so many times before. 'When am I going to get it back then? You haven't got a job and didn't stay on at school. Do you

79

want to do it all properly – we'll sit down and work out some payment plan with compound interest? What do you want – twelve months? Twenty-four?'

'You're such a prick.'

'Whatever.'

Jason motioned to move past his brother again, but Chris held an arm out, blocking him.

'Are you going to let me past?' Jason said, trying to stay calm.

Chris's eyes were lighter than Jason's, as were his skin and hair. Neither of them knew who Chris's father was but it was a fair bet he was an Aryan dream, as opposed to Jason's, who'd been dark-haired, brown-skinned, and brown-eyed. The two brothers glared at each other before Jason felt the burst of fire in his stomach. He thrust his right forearm up, catching Chris under the chin and shoving him back against the wall. The younger brother might have the height advantage but neither of them was in any doubt about who the scrapper was.

Jason pressed hard into his brother's sternum, peering into his eyes and speaking steadily, calmly. 'I do everything for this house. It's me who pays the bills, me who buys the food. I'm the one who comes home each evening to make sure Mum hasn't choked on her own vomit. What do you do? Eat the food, sleep at home every now and again, and then flit off to Kat's house whenever she's after a shag.'

Chris tried to force Jason back but he pressed him harder into the wall, showing how much stronger he was. 'If you're so concerned, why don't you go out and get a job? Why not go to college? Or move out?'

Jason relaxed his grip slightly as Chris angled his head forward. 'What, a job like yours?'

The two brothers continued staring at each other as their mother breezed into the kitchen, smelling like a burned-down brewery. She glanced at them and then headed to the cupboard under the sink. 'What have I told you two about fighting?'

Jason shoved his brother away but continued staring.

'You've been like this since you were kids,' their mother continued, scrabbling to the back of the cupboard. 'I thought you'd grow out of it. How old are you now? Thirty?'

Jason answered: 'I'm twenty-four, Mum.'

'Still, you should know better.'

Jason knew there were so many ways he could reply. What about the beatings she'd given them over the years? Or the times he'd had to pull her hair back as she vomited in various corners around the flat – the toilet bowl if they were really lucky. Being told off by their mother was like being called a liar by a politician.

Chris didn't bother waiting for his rebuke, slamming the kitchen door and then following it up moments later by making the front door rattle on its hinges.

'What are you doing, Mum?' Jason asked.

'Looking for something.'

'What?'

She emerged with a triumphant 'aha!' and a slight wobble as she tried to stand, using the sink to steady herself. In her hand was a full bottle of vodka.

'Where did you get that from?'

'Under the sink.'

'But where did you get it from before that? I know you're out of money and I didn't buy it.'

Jason's mother was struggling to twist the plastic lid. 'Never you mind.' She offered him the bottle, leaning forward and sending her stinking breath into his face. 'Open that.'

Jason took it but only made a half-hearted attempt at getting the lid off.

His mother slurred her words slightly. 'You shouldn't be so hard on your brother.'

'I'm not being hard on him. He wanted to borrow a lot of money.'

'He's your brother, isn't he?'

'That's not the point.'

His mother stood with her hands on her hips. 'Are you going to open that?'

Jason thought about doing so and emptying the lot down the sink but he'd only have to listen to her wailing for the rest of the afternoon. She probably had another half-dozen bottles hidden around the flat anyway. He pulled his sleeve down to get a grip and then wrenched the lid around until it unclicked. His mother held her hand out and then snatched it away when Jason didn't offer it quickly enough.

She headed past him towards the living room. 'Remember what I told you.'

'About fighting?'

'About your brother – you've only got one, so play nice.

10

Jason poked his head around the pub door, looked both ways and then stepped back outside again, peering up at the 'No Under-18s EVER' sign. He'd already stuffed his school uniform into his bag and changed into jeans, a T-shirt and a jacket, plus put on the baseball cap he'd nicked from the school's lost property room. He didn't exactly look eighteen, but he probably didn't look fifteen either. Well, maybe he did – either way, he was supposed to be at school.

After counting to thirty, Jason poked his head inside again. This time, the landlord was on the far side of the bar, dealing with the customer who was slumped to one side, probably drunk, hopefully not dead. As the barman patted the man on the head, muttering, 'Can you hear me, Stanley?' Jason rushed inside, heading around the opposite side of the bar to the row of three arcade machines. He dropped his bag on the floor and glanced behind at the middle-aged man cradling his pint of Boddington's as he watched the television above the bar. He had apparently not noticed anyone passing him, with the barman's voice still drifting across from the other side of the pub as he tried to rouse Stanley.

The machines were in a crook next to a row of dirty soft-red sofas, only visible from the bar if the server stuck his head around the corner.

Jason dug into his pocket, took out a pound coin and fed it into the machine's slot. He had no idea how he was so good at general knowledge given that he never read and only watched whatever it was his mother had on the television. It would only be factual if she'd fallen asleep – yet somehow he could almost always win his money back on the games machines. Frequently, he'd win the lower prizes too, meaning he could spend hours answering questions and come away with at least as much as he walked in with. That was if the various landlords and arcade owners didn't notice him playing and throw him out, of course.

Question one was about the capital of Israel, which was easy. Harry was always complaining about 'dirty Jews' buying businesses around the city and Jason had gone away to find out exactly what a Jew was.

The next question was about football, one of Jason's weaker subjects. He didn't mind the odd kickaround when he was younger but didn't follow it. He went fifty-fifty and guessed the right answer.

Question three was about weights and measurements: another strong point – especially as Harry dealt in imperial measurements while they taught metric at school. Jason made the conversion instantly.

Up next was history: 'In which year was Oliver Cromwell executed?' A trick question. Cromwell had *died* in 1658 but had been dug back up three years later and *executed* for symbolic reasons. Jason knew because Harry often talked about the need for 'another civil war'. When Jason said he didn't know what that meant, Harry had given him a brief history lesson.

Jason grinned as the fifth question appeared. Geography: 'Which river connects Manchester to the River Mersey?' How could he not know that? He pressed the button for 'Irwell' and smiled as the man on the screen told him he'd done enough to get his pound back.

Six, anatomy: 'Where would you find a human spleen?' There was a picture of a human body – another easy one. Jason had once heard Harry tell Carter to 'rip that arsehole's spleen out – via his arsehole if you can'. Given he had no idea what a spleen was, Jason had made an effort to look it up at school the next day.

He reached forward to press the correct option when he heard the dreaded voice behind him: 'What have I told you about coming in here?'

Jason felt the landlord's hand on his shoulder, tugging him away from the machine. By the time he stretched out, the time was up and his pound was dropping into the slot.

'I knew the answer to that!'

The landlord was somewhere in his forties, unshaven, with tight dark curly hair sprouting from his head, ears, sideburns – everywhere, really. He pointed towards the front door. 'You know you're not allowed in here – take your money and sod off.'

He reached forward again but Jason brushed him away. 'Stop trying to feel me up, you paedo.'

The man stepped back, rolling his eyes. 'Just piss off,

will ya? I'm going to lose my licence if they catch you in here.'

'You cost me a fiver.'

'Bollocks did I. You should be at school. Take your quid and get lost.'

'I'm going to tell the police on you – trying to feel me up. You're disgusting.'

'Yeah, whatever – you tell the police. Now hop it before I call them myself.'

The landlord was stronger than he looked. He grabbed the collar on Jason's coat and dragged him to the door, despite the protests and swear words. With his free hand, he opened it – and then pushed Jason outside with just enough force to get him moving without making him fall over.

'I'm going to get my mates on you,' Jason yelled. 'We'll shite through your letterbox and tell everyone you touch kids up.'

The landlord offered him a cheery wave. 'You do that.'

SLAM!

Jason straightened his coat, slung his bag over his back again before setting off in the vague direction of home. There was at least one more pub he could try to get into on the way, two if he went to the other side of the park.

As he walked, a few adults gave him a second glance as if to ask why he wasn't at school but kids bunking off weren't entirely uncommon in the area. The last thing most people wanted to do was antagonise their neighbours by pointing out to various authorities that their children weren't where they were supposed to be. That was as sure a way as any to get your windows smashed or, if you told on the wrong person, your head caved in.

Jason had only reached the end of the road when the shiny black car with the blacked-out windows slid in alongside him. He stopped as the door clunked open and Carter's suited frame appeared.

'Get in.'

Jason did as he was told, sliding past Carter onto the luxury of the brown leather seats. He slipped across the side seat, resisting the urge to giggle, even though it was ridiculously satisfying. Harry was opposite him, heavy crystal glass partially filled with whisky in his hand.

'Want a drink?' Harry asked as Carter slammed the door and sat in the back area of the U-shaped seat.

'What have you got?'

'You're not drinking. There's water and I think we've got some Coke for mixing.'

'Coke's good.'

Harry's eyes flicked to the side and Carter did the honours, taking a thick tumbler from a rack next to his head and opening a fridge underneath his seat as the car moved away.

'Aren't you supposed to be at school?' Harry asked, the lines in his forehead folding into one another.

'I don't like it.'

'Nobody likes it – you still have to go.'

'I'll go tomorrow.'

'We all have to do things in our lives that we don't like.'

Carter passed Jason his drink and then reclined into the seat, watching in silence.

'Do you do things you don't like?' Jason asked with a grin.

Harry clucked his tongue and returned the smile. 'You're a cheeky one, m'boy. That's why I like you – but being cocky at fifteen is one thing. If you're still like that at eighteen, you're going to fall out with a lot of people. Now what were you doing in that pub?'

Jason stopped mid-drink. 'How do you know?'

'It doesn't matter how I know – that's one of my pubs if you don't already know. I can't have it losing its licence because some kid keeps going in without permission – get it?'

Jason knew when to mess around and when not to. 'Yes,' he replied solemnly.

'What were you doing in there? They're not serving you, are they?'

'No – I like the games machines.'

Carter and Harry exchanged a glance but Jason didn't get the significance.

'How are things going at home?' Harry asked.

'Okay.'

'No one's giving you stick any longer, are they?'

Jason finished his drink and put the empty glass on the table between them. 'No but Mum's been a lot quieter since Uncle Graham . . . disappeared.'

Harry didn't take the bait. 'Are there any other "uncles" in the picture?'

'No.'

The older man nodded crisply. 'We're going to take you

back to school and you're going to spend the afternoon doing whatever it is you're supposed to be doing.'

Jason sighed and stared at his feet. 'All right.'

'We've just got a little pit-stop to make first if you want to come along.'

'Okay.'

'You're good at keeping your mouth shut, aren't you, Jason?'

'Yes.'

'Good.'

Jason peered up to see the hint of a smirk on Harry's face but Carter definitely wasn't pleased. He was biting his lip, blinking quickly.

A few minutes later, the car eased to a stop and Harry pulled himself up. He was wearing a dark suit, not too expensive but a nice fit nonetheless. He winked at Jason, holding the door open for him. When they'd climbed out, Carter emerged from the vehicle, tightening his tie with one hand, clasping a metal baseball bat in the other.

Harry reached forward and put a hand on the car door and then turned to Jason. 'Are you sure you don't want to wait in the car?'

'No.'

Harry slammed it. 'Good.' He turned to Carter. 'After you.'

Carter walked straight ahead, through a set of double doors into a pub. Jason started to follow but Harry rested a hand on his shoulder. Twenty seconds later, three men emerged, none of them offering Harry or Jason a second glance as they rushed down the street. Harry tapped Jason on the shoulder and then led the way into the pub. When they were both inside, he turned and reached up, sliding the bolt into place, locking the door as Jason took in the room.

Off to the left was a pair of pool tables, the green felt stained by various pint glass-shaped rings. Around the walls were a host of Manchester United football shirts and scarves, alongside photographs of various title-winning teams. The carpets and soft seats had a vague musty smell as if they hadn't been washed at any point in the past twenty years or so, with the ceiling a grimy brown.

Behind the bar, a man with a shaggy greying-black beard and hair to match was glancing nervously towards Carter, who was resting on the bar.

Harry turned, taking a few moments to examine the room himself. 'You really need to get a deep cleaning company to take a look at this place, Michael. It stinks.'

The barman's accent was broad Mancunian. 'Sorry.'

'Oh, don't apologise to me. It's your pub – it's the brewery you should be apologising to. If you want, I can pass on the names of a few cleaning companies. Every now and then, I need people to come in and give one of my places a thorough scrub.'

'Right, Mr, er, Irwell.'

Harry strode to the bar, shifted a beer mat to the side and then started drumming his fingers on the wood. 'I'm not here to talk about cleaning companies, though, am I?'

'No, Mr, er—'

'Call me Harry. We're all friends here, aren't we?'

Michael glanced from Carter to Harry and stammered. 'Yes, Mr, er, Harry. Sorry.'

'The problem is, Michael, that friends usually pay their debts to each other – and I've heard that you've not made this month's payment.'

'It's been awkward . . .'

Harry slapped his palm down on the counter extravagantly. '"Awkward" is the correct word – but I don't like things being awkward when it comes to money – especially not when it's my money.'

'Sorry, er, Harry.'

'So where's my money, Michael?'

The man's gaze flickered towards Jason and then back to Harry again. 'The brewery put their rates up, plus there was that cold spell where people weren't going out. We tried to have a few themed nights to get people in but no one wants to go out when it's snowing.'

'My pubs have been doing all right through the winter.'

'Sorry—'

'Stop telling me you're sorry and tell me where my money is.'

'I don't have it. Takings are down – I've already laid Vanessa off and she's pregnant.'

'So she was going to be leaving anyway, where's the problem?'

'It's just that there's nothing spare. If things pick up again this month then I'll be able to pay everything I owe, plus a bit more.'

'But that will still leave you a month behind.'

Carter lifted the hatch and made his way around to the

other side of the bar. Michael winced away from him but Carter simply picked up a pint glass from underneath the bar and filled it up from the tap. He handed Harry the baseball bat and then drank deeply as everyone watched in silence.

'I'm sor—'

Harry slapped his hand on the bar again, louder this time. 'Don't you dare say you're sorry again.'

Michael flinched. 'I don't have anything to give you.'

'What would you do if this place got firebombed with you and Susan asleep upstairs? Even if you got yourselves out, there'd be no money then.'

'I know.'

Harry leant forward, lips tight. 'That's the *exact* kind of thing I'm protecting you from, Michael. If the brewery put their rates up, bollocks to them. Water the swill down – none of your punters are going to notice anyway. If your staff can't keep their legs closed then bollocks to them too. Get your missus down here pulling pints. That's two of you – how many more staff members do you need? You can't put a price on safety, can you?'

'No.'

Harry pointed to the row of spirit bottles hanging upside down in the optics behind the bar. 'Got anything good in?'

Michael took a side-step away from Carter. 'There's a twenty-five-year-old malt in the back. The brewery sent all of us one bottle each at Christmas.'

Harry sat on the stool and splayed his legs, leaning on the bar. 'Well, why didn't you say so?'

With a nod of the head, Michael scarpered into the back room as Harry waved Jason towards the bar and handed him the bat. 'Ever played baseball?' he asked.

'No – cricket at school a few times.'

'No matter – it's a stupid Yank game anyway. Glorified rounders, and that's a girl's game.'

Jason weighed the bat in his hand – it wasn't as heavy as it looked. The rubber handle was comfy and he took a couple of air swings, enjoying the swish it made.

Michael soon rushed back, arm outstretched with the bottle. Harry took it from him and turned the bottle around, smiling approvingly. 'Nice – perhaps your brewery aren't so bad, after all.' He unscrewed the lid and sniffed the liquid, then nodded towards the row of glasses behind the bar. Michael picked one up, cleaned it with a tea towel, and then placed it on the bar. Harry poured himself a small measure, took another sniff, and then downed it in one. He nodded approvingly: 'This is fabulous stuff. I'll have to see if I can get a case sent down from Scotland.'

Jason peered over the bar to see Carter cracking his knuckles. Michael glanced at him nervously and then back to Harry.

'Are we . . . ?' he stammered.

'What?' Harry replied.

'Are we done?'

Harry snorted. 'You give me a bottle of whisky worth a couple of hundred quid when you owe me over a grand and you think we're done?'

'No, I—'

Michael didn't get the chance to finish his sentence

because Carter stepped forward and elbowed him brutally in the windpipe. Michael half-coughed, half-choked as Carter used the side of his hand to clatter the man across the temples, following it up with one, two, three short, sharp slaps to his ears.

Carter wasn't even touching him but Michael had lost all sense of what was up and down, stumbling sideways and sending a row of glasses tumbling to the ground. As he tried to right himself, he reached out but only succeeded in bumping into Carter, who pinned him to the bar, wrenching Michael's arms up behind him and making the man squeal like a trapped piglet.

Harry pointed towards the open hatch, waving Jason around to the other side. 'Pick a bottle, son,' he said.

Jason scanned along the row of spirit bottles, picking one with a red stag on the front. He pointed at it, turning to check he had Harry's permission. When the older man nodded, Jason reared back and sliced the bat through the bottle, taking half-a-dozen glasses out with it for good measure.

Carter heaved Michael backwards until he was standing almost straight again, though the pressure on his arms was making him sob. Harry leant across the bar until he was only a few centimetres away from the landlord. 'When will I get my money, Michael?'

'Soon!'

Harry nodded to Jason and the teenager swung again, taking out a bottle of vodka and sending the liquid spraying across the back of the bar.

'When?'

'I don't know.'

Another nod, another crash of metal on glass – this time a bottle of white rum.

'I want a day, Michael.'

Carter screwed the man's arms back again, twisting him until it looked as if the man's shoulders were going to pop.

'Aaaaaaagggrh!'

Harry's voice remained utterly calm. 'A day, Michael.'

'Friday.'

Nod-crash. There goes the amaretto, whatever that is.

'*Thursday*,' Harry insisted.

'Owww. Pleeeeeease . . . okay, Thursday.'

Carter released Michael's arms and the man slumped forward, catching his chin on the edge of the bar and rocking backwards until he collapsed on the floor. Carter stepped over him, took the bat from Jason and then walked towards the front door without a word. Harry nodded again and Jason took the hint, crossing towards where Carter was waiting.

Carter unlocked the door and the three of them left together, Harry offering the final parting shot: 'Don't make me come back at the end of the week, Michael.'

With that, he slammed the door into place and the three of them piled back into the car.

They were barely in their seats when Harry asked which school Jason attended. Jason told him and Harry tapped the window that separated them from the driver's seat. The glass hummed down and he told the driver where they were going. Once the glass was back in place, he relaxed into his seat and the car gently pulled away.

'Did you see what Carter did in there?' Harry asked.

Jason nodded.

'You don't have to be a massive brute of a man to make people take you seriously. Carter can teach you a few tricks. It isn't about hitting hard, it's knowing where to hit. Our barman friend will barely have a mark on him tomorrow. You can't fight back if you can't see out of your eyes, you can't balance if your ears don't work.'

Harry flicked a hand towards Carter, who nodded towards Jason. 'We'll sort something out,' he said.

'You have to promise not to use anything you learn on the wrong people,' Harry said. 'It's not about being a bully or showing off – it's acting when you need to. Do you understand?'

'Yes.'

'Good boy. First, you need to go back to school and stay there. You've only got a little while left and then you're done for ever. Do you understand?'

'Not really.'

Harry sniggered. 'Tough luck – sometimes you've got to listen to your elders.'

11

Jason jumped awake, a breath catching in his chest. That icy spider was creeping along his naked torso again. He lay, staring up at the ceiling and gasping for breath, repeating over and over in his mind that he was at home, in his bed – the same place where he always woke up. As he felt another tingle along his side, Jason rubbed it, digging his fingernails in until he felt the tug of skin. There was no spider, no anything and the room was exactly as it should be: clothes folded on his nightstand, door shut, phone charging on the floor.

But the window was open a crack again. Jason crossed the room and pressed his hand to the freezing glass, feeling the breeze seeping through the gap. That sodding housing association and their empty double-glazing promises.

Jason closed the window and stared down to the road outside. More children in school uniform in twos and threes; more parents on the school run driving dangerously. Someone with shopping bags wobbling along, trying not to overbalance; a flat-capped old man trapping an errant football that rolled his way and then curling a pinpoint pass back to the kid who'd kicked it. He offered a thumbs-up to the lad and grinned as if he was playing in a cup final.

Not everything about the estate was shite.

After a glass of water from the kitchen, Jason checked Chris's room. His brother's duvet was half on the floor, the sheet twisted in the centre of the bed and both pillows covering the alarm clock. As messy as Chris was, no one had slept there the night before.

Jason moved into the living room where his mother was asleep on the sofa, the television blaring out as ever. He switched it off and was about to leave when he noticed a single white pill on the floor next to an almost-empty vodka bottle. For a few moments, Jason simply stared at it, unsure what to do. When he picked it up, he turned it over, wondering if it might possibly have the name or identifying letter on the side. His mother had always been a drinker but it had been years since she'd been into anything else.

Starting with the obvious places – the dark corners, the drawers, under the sofa, behind the television, behind the empty flower pots – Jason got nowhere in finding where it had come from. The one thing he knew was that if his mother was hiding a stash of pills somewhere, it would be in the living room. She only got up to use the toilet or get a new bottle, so it would be close.

Jason checked on top of the curtain rail, even though his mother would be too short to reach, and then he began going through the various scattered movie cases. Still nothing. He looked underneath the coffee table to make sure nothing had been taped there and then removed the smoke alarm and checked inside, only to see that the battery compartment was empty – as it had been for years.

Hmm.

His mother was many things but clever wasn't one of them when it came to something like this. Jason stared down at her unmoving, barely breathing figure underneath the blanket cradling a cushion. He was just about to move into the kitchen just in case she had another hiding place in there after all when he found his eyes drawn to the shape of the cushion. Instead of being soft and puffy, it was decidedly flat and un-squishy. Jason plucked a second cushion from the floor and delicately used it to replace the one his mum was holding. She stirred but only briefly, her eyelids fluttering as she rolled over.

Jason left the room, pulling the door closed behind him, and headed into his bedroom. When he unzipped the cushion cover, the contents left him staring open-mouthed: boxes and tubs of pills. He scanned along the names: oxycodone, hydrocodone, diazepam, temazepam, doxylamine and a few others he couldn't pronounce. He didn't know much about medicine but the large 'DO NOT TAKE WITH ALCOHOL' was a basic enough giveaway that his mother shouldn't have them anywhere near her. Quite how she'd got hold of them, he had no idea – though it wouldn't surprise him if Chris was involved somewhere along the line. The only relief was that she must have been taking them in small doses, else she wouldn't be breathing at all.

Jason was going to take them all down to the large wheelie bin at the back of the shops when he realised it would do no good. If he got rid of them, she'd simply find a new source – and a better hiding place. If he was going to do something, he'd have to be smart.

Jason walked into the off-licence / pharmacy / sandwich shop / paper shop / ice-cream shop / confectionery stall / general-bit-of-everything-place that was close to their estate. After hours it was like a military installation with thick metal shutters at the front and rear, and four CCTV cameras high on the roof surrounded by twists of barbed wire. Inside, there were another eight cameras, with everything costing more than four pounds safely behind the counter – meaning razor blades, cigarettes and all the spirits were locked in a cabinet next to the condoms and tampons. Presumably there was an epidemic of contraception and sanitary-related thefts around the estate.

He hovered around the rear of the shop scanning the headlines before deciding that 'BLAZE FAMILY'S SISTER TELLS OF HEARTACHE' wasn't something he wanted to read. He didn't even know who might have set the fire – arson wasn't the type of thing with which Carter got involved, while Harry's greatest strength was that he kept all areas of his business separate. He could have Jason and his crew delivering something in one area of the city, with a completely different group doing something else in another spot. Neither would know about the other. It was no wonder Harry had been untouchable for such a long time.

When the shop was finally empty, Jason picked up one of each of the basic-looking medicines – aspirin, a selection of vitamin pills, indigestion tablets – and took the packets to the counter.

The man serving was definitely younger than Jason: ginger with freckles and fading acne. He shook his head. 'You can't buy all of them.'

'Why not?'

'Some law. I can sell you two packets and that's it.'

'Can I buy two, go home, put them down, turn around and come back to buy two more?'

'Er . . . I guess.'

'So why can't I just buy them all now?'

The man nodded nervously upwards towards the camera above his head. 'I could lose my job.'

Jason took out a ten-pound note. 'How about you keep the change?'

'That's not much if I lose my job, is it?'

'I could go elsewhere.'

'Feel free.'

Jason sighed, dug back into his pocket and pulled out an additional fiver. 'Fifteen quid – I'm not paying any more than that.'

The young man picked up the first packet of aspirin. 'Done.'

Back at the flat, Jason emptied all of his mother's pills onto his bed, mixing them together. He was going to flush them but then remembered his own hiding place. High on the wall close to the window was an old grate. Someone had once screwed a plastic cover over the top but they hadn't used rawl-plugs and it had begun to work its way out of the wall years ago. When he was younger, Jason would remove it and wedge mucky magazines inside, then replace the cover. He'd not hidden anything in there for years, mainly because he was pretty sure nobody bothered coming into his room, but the fact his window had apparently twice opened itself was worrying. Either someone was coming into his room while he slept, or . . . he didn't know. Was he doing it himself? Or imagining things? Perhaps he'd not closed it in the first place.

Either way, Jason emptied the cocktail of pills into the largest of the tubs, pressed the lid on and then eased it into the hiding place behind the grate cover.

When he was done, he popped all of the painkillers and indigestion medicines out of their packets and dropped them into the now-empty containers marked with the various prescription names. His mother might notice that the shapes were different but Jason seriously doubted it. After dropping all of the tubs, packets and boxes back into the cushion, he rearranged what little stuffing was still inside and then returned to the living room.

At some point his mother had rolled over and switched the television back on but she was fast asleep again as Jason delicately swapped the cushions.

As he was turning to leave, the jingle came on for the news and the reader began speaking: '. . . and the headlines this morning. Police are appealing for witnesses to the attack that killed an entire family in Manchester. Arsonists targeted Namdev Gupta's house in Rusholme on Monday night and police have also revealed there was an attack on the Guptas' shop earlier in the evening. Police are treating it as murder. In other news . . .'

Jason picked the remote up once more and switched it off.

Even though it was half past ten on a Wednesday morning, the traffic along Oxford Road was still backed up into the centre of Manchester. If the city was defined by something other than grey clouds, it was traffic jams.

Jason risked turning the radio on, only to hear some woman telling everyone how a lorry had jack-knifed on the M602. The motorway had been shut, meaning that traffic was flooding into the city from all other available routes. It was always the lorry drivers – if they weren't busy killing cyclists, overtaking each other and blocking two-thirds of the motorway, or parking in the bus lanes for 'deliveries', then they were smashing into central barriers and bringing the entire city to a standstill.

Jason parked his car on a side street that ran parallel to the main road and weaved his way through the hordes of students heading from their houses to lectures. They were almost entirely decked out in huge coats, hats, hoods and scarves, firmly expecting the north-west weather to drench them at any given moment.

Lucy's flat was tucked in next to a laundrette, at the beginning of a row of identical red-brick terraced houses. Lines of cars were parked on either side of the street, with a van driver and someone in a Skoda standing in the centre arguing over who had right of way.

When she opened the door, Lucy peeped outside and shook her head at the scene going on in the middle of the road. 'That's the fourth time this week,' she said, holding the door open for Jason to enter. She turned and waved him along the hallway, leading the way through the flat. Her hair was down – the first time Jason had ever seen it not tied up – and she was wearing tight jeans, socks and a T-shirt that hung limply at the bottom while still clinging to her top half.

Lucy's living room was small but homely, with various prints around the walls, plants on the tables and window-sill and a scattering of throws and cushions. She had already arranged her easel and canvas in the corner, with a plain dining chair in the centre of the room and a sofa pushed to the side.

'Sorry about the heat,' Lucy said, sitting on a stool behind the easel. 'The heating's either on or off – there aren't any dials on the radiator and I don't know how to turn anything up or down. The landlord mentioned some-thing about a thermostat when I moved in but I've never found it.' As Jason sat, Lucy grinned at him, showing off her freckles again. 'Still, at least you'll be warm when you get your kit off.'

He returned her smile, trying to work out if she was being serious.

She bit her bottom lip, eyes narrowing mischievously. 'You really don't know when someone's joking, do you?'

'I didn't want to laugh in case you were being serious.'

Lucy bent down and picked up a hat from the floor, spinning it across the room to him. 'Will you put that on?'

Jason twisted it around in his hand – it was a plain black trilby, the type of thing he'd never worn in his life. 'Why?'

'Because I think it will look good in my painting.'

'Really?'

'Try it on.'

Jason flipped it onto his head and turned to look at himself in the mirror over the boarded-up fireplace. It looked okay in a strange thing-he'd-never-wear way. He turned back to Lucy, who was nodding thoughtfully. 'It suits you.'

'What do I need to do now?'

'Just sit still.'

Jason wriggled onto the chair. 'Should I be looking in a particular direction?'

'Just sit comfortably. I'm going to need you to be there for an hour, perhaps two. Then I'll need to rest my arm.'

Slumping slightly, Jason fidgeted into a position that wasn't too uncomfortable and began staring at a spot a little over the top of the easel. There was some sort of painting with a rainbow on the wall but, more importantly, it meant he could risk quick glances at Lucy when she wasn't looking at him.

'Am I allowed to talk?' he asked.

Lucy dabbed her brush into the palette of paints and began with a swish. 'What do you want to talk about?'

'I don't know.'

She reached forward and smeared paint onto the canvas. 'Do you like books?'

The question took Jason so much by surprise that he mumbled an 'erm' before he'd even thought about it. The true answer was no – but he didn't think that was what she wanted to hear.

'It's just you're in the library a lot,' Lucy added. 'I know you use the computers but I wondered if you actually liked books. It's okay if you don't.'

'I've never really read books.'

Lucy peered around the canvas. *Really?*'

'Not like a proper book. Sometimes I look things up but it's all on computers nowadays. My mum never read and I wasn't very good at school.'

Lucy turned back to the canvas and Jason chanced a glimpse down from the wall to look at her. She was completely different with her hair down. It curved around her cheeks, making her skin seem slightly browner, plus it was an interesting colour – definitely blonde but there were light and dark streaks. He wondered why she'd left it down even though it was surely going to get in her way at some point. Was it for him? Or did she prefer it that way?

Lost in the shape of her face, Jason only realised Lucy was staring back at him when she cracked into a smile.

'Sorry,' Jason said, peering back towards the wall.

Lucy giggled slightly. 'It's fine.' She leant in closer to the canvas, putting the brush down and using her fingers to dab paint. 'So if you don't read, what do you do?'

'This and that.'

'What does that mean?'

Jason wasn't used to being called on his evasion. 'I suppose I buy a few things and sell a few things.'

'But not during the day?'

'Sorry?'

'Well you go to the library during the day and you're here on a morning. So are you buying and selling at night?'

She continued rubbing her fingers on the canvas, not looking up. It sounded like a genuine question.

'It's complicated,' he said.

'Assuming you don't mind, we're going to be sitting around a lot over the next week or two.'

Jason paused, thinking about his answer. 'It's not time-specific. Sometimes I'll have lots on, other times not much. Plus I work as a courier: delivering parcels and so on. It's really intermittent.'

Lucy picked up her brush again for a couple of elaborate swipes. 'What about family?'

'I've got a younger brother, plus my mum's still around.'

'I come from Skipton in Yorkshire originally. My parents wanted me to go to Leeds Uni because it's just down the road – plus I think my Dad preferred it because it's in York-shire. I just know they would've been over every weekend if I'd gone there, though, so I came here. It's close enough to get home but far enough away that I've not had any surprise visits. Well, not yet, anyway.'

Jason didn't reply, not wanting to reveal that he still lived with his mum.

Lucy delved back into her paints, scooping a splodge of purple onto her thumb and reaching towards the canvas. Jason peered down at her again. If he looked really hard, the way her T-shirt was hanging left a gap in the armhole that meant he could see the dark colour of her bra straps. Or was it just a shadow? He squinted, trying to work it out, and then glanced back to his spot on the wall as she shuffled slightly.

'So,' Lucy said. 'Buying a few things, selling a few things, delivering packages – that can't be what you wanted to do with your life. How old are you now?'

'Twenty-four.'

'What would you like to be doing when you're thirty?'

Jason knew exactly what he wanted to be doing – sitting in Crete with his half a million. He could hardly say that, though.

'I don't know – I quite like the idea of running a business.'

Lucy peered around the canvas again. There was a smudge of white on her nose, which, if anything, made her even more attractive. 'At least you have some desire. My mum's always going on about how I have no ambition.' She picked up a dollop of brown and began dotting it onto the painting with her fingers. 'I think it's because I'm doing art. She wanted me to be a doctor or a lawyer, something like that. You know what parents are like – they always want you to *be* something . . .'

Jason had no idea what that felt like.

'. . . so when I told her I was doing art, she kept saying, "Well, what are you going to do *after* your course?" and "What are you going to do with a degree like that?" I'd say I didn't know, which only made her more annoyed. She's a teacher, so it's a big deal for her.'

'What *are* you going to do?'

'Now you sound just like her.'

'Sorry.'

Another peep around the canvas. 'I'm joking, Jase.'

'Oh.'

She called him 'Jase'. It sounded nice. He'd never heard

a female say it like that before. When his mother called him 'Jase', it was usually when she was asking for money. He'd never been sure if he liked the abbreviation but definitely didn't mind when Lucy said it.

Lucy grinned at him and then turned back to her work. 'I know my parents will go batshit but I'd like to go travelling. I had a gap year in South America and it was amazing. I want to go back – plus there are so many other things to see and places to visit.' She paused to wash her finger in a cup of water and then picked the brush back up. 'Have you been abroad much?'

'Only Crete.'

'When you were a kid, right?'

'Before my brother was born.'

'How old is he?'

'He turned eighteen last month.'

Lucy took a moment to do the maths. 'So you were really young, then?'

'I suppose.'

'And you've not been abroad since?'

'No, I . . .'

Jason realised he'd barely left Manchester in that time. In fact, if the surrounding district was discounted, he'd not been beyond a fifteen-mile radius of his house in . . . he didn't even know how long. That surely wasn't normal, was it?

'It's okay,' Lucy said, perhaps sensing what he was thinking, 'travelling isn't for everyone. I did this Amazon trip in South America and, even now, I'm not sure if I enjoyed it. I was in a tent but all you could hear through the night were the howls of the various animals. The guides kept telling you about all of the creatures that could kill you, plus there was nowhere to go to the toilet or anything like that. It was sort of good but I doubt I'd go again. Beaches aren't for everyone, either. I wouldn't want to spend all day lying in the sun – I like to go and get into trouble.'

She met his eye and winked. A thin smear of brown had joined the white, stretching across underneath her eye. Her hair was messy, her skin blemished, her fingers covered in paint – but in the instant that she winked at him, Jason felt something squeeze the inside of his stomach so hard that he had to gulp down a breath.

'What's Crete like?' she added.

Jason tried to breathe but his throat felt like it had tightened. His eventual reply grated: 'The sun was out all of the time.'

'Was it just you and your mum?'

'Yes, she was . . . happy.'

The word crept out because Jason couldn't remember a time when she had genuinely been content, other than when they were on holiday. For the past few years, he'd had the idea of saving his money to eventually return to the island but there hadn't been any serious thought as to why. Now, with a few simple questions, Lucy had brought the moment back to him.

It had been the best week of his life.

'I've never been,' Lucy replied. 'I went to Cyprus but it was all touristy and I try to avoid that. Morocco's nice, plus Turkey's okay when people aren't constantly trying to sell you things on the street. I had this bloke follow me, trying to sell me some wooden piece of tat.'

She sighed but was smiling too as she caught his eye. 'There's a whole world out there, Jason, more than just Manchester – and I'm going to see at least some of it.'

12

Jason eased his car into the empty space on the road outside the flats a little after half past one and closed the doors. There were a few kids hanging around on the corner smoking but none of them gave him a second look. He had a strange relationship with the people around him – no one bothered to harass him, no one would dare break into his car, let alone their flat, and yet Jason had never formally mentioned his job to anyone. Somehow, through word of mouth or assumption, people knew that he wasn't someone they should mess with. Despite that, he had almost anonymity too. Until Natalie had cornered him in the pub, he would have put a large chunk of his money on the fact that no one in Greater Manchester Police even knew who he was. Now . . . he wasn't sure. Was he being followed? Had someone talked? He eyed the youngsters but they didn't return his stare, instead passing around one of their mobile phones and laughing at whatever was on the screen.

He went to the boot of his car and took out the four shopping bags, then wedged the carrier bag of cash into a pocket next to the wheel rim that contained a bottle of oil and some rags.

Jason wobbled his way up the hard steps to the first floor and dropped the bags on the sodden mat outside his front door. As he delved into his pockets wondering where his keys were, he saw a flash of movement around the top of the stairs at the far end of the rank. He stepped across to the balcony, peering towards the far end of the row, but whatever the dark shape was had disappeared into the stairwell.

He unlocked the front door and carried the bags into the kitchen, putting them on the table. He thought about packing it all away, knowing his mother and Chris – if he was in – would be pawing through everything if he didn't take what he wanted for himself. Something about the shape outside was bothering him, though.

He leant over the sink, peering through the window to the street below: more kids smoking, a woman getting on a bus, rubbish blowing along the road . . . nothing out of the ordinary. Nobody stopping, nobody watching his window. Was that stranger than if there was someone acting suspiciously? If somebody was keeping an eye on him, they wouldn't be standing on the street, they'd be in the back of a van or jogging past in a loop. He squinted to try to get a closer view of the woman getting on the bus. Was she wearing an earpiece? Was she reporting back? Or was it just an earring?

With a blink, Jason stepped backwards, feeling an itch just above his right eye. He rubbed it hard until flakes of skin tumbled in front of his eyes. This was madness: he'd just had an amazing few hours with a girl he couldn't believe would give him the time of day. He really thought Lucy had been flirting with him. She smiled, she flicked her hair, she winked, she called him 'Jase'. That was flirting, wasn't it?

Jason grabbed a glass from the draining board and filled it with tap water, downing it in one and then re-filling it. This time, he sipped the liquid, enjoying how cool it was. This was silly: no one was following him – Natalie had promised him that in the car.

He ran the water into his hands and scrubbed his face with his palms. In the window, he could just about see his reflection. He looked slightly pale but that was most likely the glare. Lucy had been right – the trilby did suit him. Still, he couldn't start wearing one now – it would give people a reason to look at him. Plus Chris would probably take the piss, not to mention Carter and probably Harry. Jason could hear Harry now: 'Only spivs wear things like that, m'boy. Spivs and queers. Which are you?'

Jason blinked again and remembered the shape by the stairs: ten, perhaps twenty metres from his flat. *His* flat.

He left the kitchen and went out of the front door onto the walkway, leaning on the balcony and looking both ways: nothing.

On the far side of the complex, out of sight, someone was revving a motorbike again but there were no signs of anyone moving anywhere within the area.

Jason pulled his front door closed with a quiet click and then walked quickly towards the stairs at the far end. When he got to the top, he heard a pair of voices muttering, their barely audible tones catching the hard concrete walls and echoing upwards. He pressed himself against the front of the flat that was next to the stairs and tried to listen to what they were saying. Were they talking about him? He tried to ignore the hum of the motorbike on the far side and closed his eyes.

'Greeeeeeeeeen, Greeeeeeeeeen.'

It was two men's voices, a low murmuring: a whisper on the breeze.

'Greeeeeeeeeen, Greeeeeeeeeen.'

Jason spun around the pillar at the top of the stairs, peering down at the two figures standing on the landing halfway between the ground and first floors. The taller man was wearing a grey athletic top with the hood down. He was a few years older than Jason with short gelled spiky hair and a dark goatee. The other figure was a kid – fourteen or fifteen, jeans around his arse, thick fake-gold chain around his neck, baseball cap, American sporting top, probably basketball, which was five or six sizes too big for him. He glanced up at Jason, raised his eyebrows towards the other man, and then put an envelope in his pocket and hurried away down the stairs.

The hoody man pocketed a twenty-pound note and straightened his top, peering up at Jason. 'Something I can help you with, bro?'

'What are you doing?'

'Y'know – bit of this, bit of that.'

'Why are you doing it here?'

'Freezing out there, innit? You know what it's like, bro.'

He thrust his hands into his pocket as if to prove the point. Jason looked closer at him. There was a small scar over his left eye and another around the corner of his mouth. He'd tried to style his goatee to cover it up but the smudge of purple was still clear if it was looked for.

The hoody began shuffling on the spot. 'Is there a problem or owt?'

Jason just stared at him, listening to the wind howling through the entranceway. It had picked up in the past few minutes in the way it did around the city. One minute could be pleasant and springlike, the next a gale was howling.

The man took a hand from his pocket and began scratching his head, looking from side to side. 'We serve the same master, don't we?'

Jason eyes suddenly locked to the other man's with such ferocity that the hoody took a step backwards, making his heel clip the wall.

'I don't have a master,' Jason replied, barely moving his lips.

'Okay, bro, look – sorry, wrong word. My bad.'

'Stop calling me "bro".'

'Okay, sorry.'

Jason nodded towards the empty stairs below them. 'Who was the kid?'

'I don't know his name.'

'What did he get?'

'Just some chang.'

'You're selling coke to kids?'

'It's not for him – it's for his dad.'

Jason took two steps down the concrete: 'Did he ask about me?'

The man reeled back, shaking his head. 'I don't understand.'

'It's a simple question.'

'Why would he ask about you?'

'That's what I'm asking you.'

The hoody took another small step away, confused. 'No, I mean I doubt he even knows who you are . . . I only know because, well, your brother . . .'

'You know Chris?'

'Not really. Not well. He's just someone from the estate, ain't he?'

Jason moved forward another couple of steps so he was halfway down the flight. The man's gaze flickered towards the empty staircase heading out of the flat complex but centred back on Jason, who took another step.

'How do you know it's for his dad?' Jason asked.

'What?'

'The kid who just left – how do you know he was buying for his dad?'

'Oh . . . right . . . well, I suppose . . . it doesn't matter really, does it? He had the money and we've got the—'

'There is no "we".'

'All right, bro, look—'

He didn't get a chance to finish the sentence because Jason lunged forward and thrust his palm upwards into the base of the dealer's nose. He felt the satisfying splat before he'd even pulled back. Noses were always best if there was a clean shot. In a proper fight, it was always a tangle of arms and legs and everyone just tried to punch each other – as if that was the best way to take someone down.

The dealer's hands shot up to his face as he howled in pain but Jason was ahead of him, stepping sideways and jabbing him three times quickly in the ears. As the man stumbled sideways, trying to get his balance, Jason kicked with all of his weight into the back of the man's knees, literally booting him up into the air, even though the hoody was taller and probably heavier than him. With a squelch and a thud, the dealer came back down to the ground, landing on the back of his head.

Everything had taken less than ten seconds but without getting his hands dirty, Jason had utterly incapacitated him.

A trickle of dark red oozed from the top of the man's head as he rolled sideways with an agonised groan. Jason stepped across the blood, arched backwards and kicked with all of his might a little under the dealer's ribs. Jason only ever wore trainers or something similar that he could run in – never heavy boots – but the impact was enough to send the man spinning down the lower flight of steps.

With a mixture of thumps and squishes, the dealer rolled and bumped his way to the bottom, landing with a wail of pain before turning onto his back. Jason stepped carefully after him, avoiding the splashes of blood and the sealed bags of powder and pills that had fallen from his pockets.

The dealer stared up at Jason, eyes rolling back and forth, his face covered with blood and snot. He tried to stretch a hand out but it flopped uselessly by his side. 'No, bro . . .'

Jason lifted his foot, holding it a little over the man's head as it rested on the sharp edge of the bottom step.

'No . . .'

13

Jason jarred awake as a spiky tendril slid along his back. He twisted to either side, wondering who had touched him, but the room was empty. He was out of breath, gasping and choking on his own tongue. This was *his* room, his bed, his home. He peered around the space: folded clothes, door shut, phone charging. Just to make sure, he eased the grate cover away from the wall and checked inside, taking out the tub of pills and popping the lid off. It was as full as it was yesterday.

Everything was in place . . . except that it wasn't. The window was open again. He was certain he'd closed it the night before. He had, hadn't he? He must have done – it was freezing outside. There was no way he would have started trying to go to sleep when it was so cold and yet he couldn't remember shutting it on any of the previous evenings.

He latched the window closed, grabbing an elastic band from his top drawer and looping it through the handle before attaching the other end to the catch on the bottom of the window. At least he now knew that if it was open again, either his mum or Chris had done it.

He stared out onto the street below. More kids in uniform were jostling and stumbling their way to school: shouting, swearing, kicking a football, laughing. Being children. Jason wedged himself into the right-hand corner of the frame to try to get a wider view. A cab driver was arguing with someone, with mutual fingers being pointed, while a school bus pulled in behind and beeped its horn.

A normal morning.

Then he tried from the left-hand side, peering around the tight corner. There were a few more kids – but there was also police tape stretching across the road, a lone police car and a white truck with a satellite dish on top. Jason pressed his cheek against the glass, staring at the two officers in bright yellow jackets standing and talking to each other.

He made sure again that the window was firmly closed and then got dressed before heading to the kitchen and filling a glass with water. Jason propped himself on the draining board to see if he could get a better view of the officers but the angle was too tight around the outside wall. He drank the glass of water and then checked Chris's room, knocking gently and easing the door open when nobody answered.

His brother's duvet was half on the floor, the sheet twisted in the centre of the bed and both pillows were covering the alarm clock – exactly as everything had been the previous morning.

In the living room, Jason's mother was sitting slumped against the corner of the sofa as the breakfast television presenters talked about the weather.

'Mum?'

She didn't turn from the screen at the sound of Jason's voice. 'What?'

'I got some food in yesterday. Do you want something to eat?'

His mother yawned and brushed the tangle of hair away from her face. Her eyes were open but there was little life there. 'Like what?'

'There's bread if you want toast. Or cereal? The milk's fresh.'

'Did you get marmalade?'

'Yes.'

'Toast then.'

Jason waited in the doorway for a few moments, watching the screen as the news jingle came on. He wondered if there would be something about the Guptas or the dealer from the stairwell, but the headlines were about the Manchester derby that weekend. All that really meant was that there would be a lot of Japanese tourists in the city for a few days. Harry would hate that.

'Those Japs don't gamble,' he'd say. 'Yanks – they're the ones you want. Or Spicks, Eyeties, Frogs or Krauts. Krauts especially spend a bit of money. Still, give me a dumb Yank over any of those lot. At least they speak English. Show 'em a bit of cleavage and they'll empty their wallet quicker than you can say "mug".'

'Are you making my toast?' Jason's mother still didn't look away from the screen.

'Yeah . . .'

Jason returned to the kitchen, took the bread from the fridge and dropped three slices into the toaster. The fourth slot hadn't worked since Chris had jammed a sausage roll into it in an attempt to warm it up, then tried to wedge it

121

out with a butter knife, causing the electricity to cut out. Their mother had thrown a shoe at him for making the television go off and said she'd kill him if he ever did it again. The fact she'd been threatening that as punishment for any number of minor indiscretions and accidents for the past ten years meant it had been ignored, as with every other time.

Jason filled the kettle up and clicked it on, then leant over the draining board again, squeezing himself against the window pane, watching as one of the police officers began bundling up the blue and white tape. The satellite van had gone, leaving just the two officers. He assumed someone would come knocking on their door at some point later in the day to ask if anyone had heard anything when the dealer had been assaulted in the stairwell.

Something similar happened at least once a month. The woman who lives underneath has overdosed, did you see anyone hanging around? The bloke who lives opposite has put his wife in hospital, did you ever hear them arguing? Someone tried to set fire to the bins at the back, do you have any idea who might have done it? Someone ram-raided an offy and the car was dumped at the back of your flat and burned out, I don't suppose you heard anything, did you? Always the same uniformed officers with a notepad and the look of people who'd already had two-dozen doors slammed in their faces, ready and waiting for the next four-dozen to be closed too. Jason almost felt sorry for them.

Almost.

What was it Harry said about police? 'They're not to be

under-estimated, m'boy, but they're in the force for a reason – they're shite at everything else. If they had an ounce of sense about them, they'd be out there making a living for themselves. There are two types of people – those who do something with their lives and those who try to stop others. All police are the same: they'll talk about upholding the law but really it's jealousy. Envy that you're something and they're nothing. Don't trust a single one of them.'

Jason thought of Natalie and what she'd told him in the car. He knew he shouldn't trust her and yet everything she'd said made sense. Then there was Lucy. She was right too, wasn't she? There was more to life than Manchester. More to life than this.

With a fizz and a plip, the kettle turned itself off and, moments later, the toaster popped too, sending the browned slices into the air.

He smeared them with margarine and marmalade, chose the cleanest mug and then carried everything into the living room. His mother didn't turn from the screen, taking the items from him without a word. The news had ended and the presenters were back on, talking to a writer who looked as if he could have done with a haircut and a shave at any point in the past three months. They really did let any old tramp on television nowadays.

Jason sat next to his mother, watching as she put the tea on the floor and then nibbled at the toast. He couldn't see any alcohol bottles around the room, not that it meant much. There would definitely be some vodka hidden around the flat which she would open as soon as she felt the urge.

'Mum,' Jason said.

'What?'

'Do you remember when I asked you about my window?'

'No.'

'On Tuesday, two days ago, I asked if you'd opened my bedroom window.'

'So?'

'So, did you open it overnight?'

'When?'

'This week – last night, the night before, the night before that. Every time I wake up, it seems to be open but it can't be Chris because he's not around.'

'Why would I open your window?'

'I don't know. It's just . . . I never remember opening it the night before. I suppose I could've done but I really can't recall. I don't remember going to sleep, I just remember waking up.'

His mother finished her first piece of toast and started on the second.

'Mum?'

'What?'

'My window.'

'What about it?'

Jason sighed and leant back into the sofa. His mother was awful when she was in this type of mood. He didn't know if she was deliberately obstructive or if she genuinely didn't know what he was talking about. The number of times they'd had a conversation like this over the years was uncountable. She lived for two things: booze and television.

'You used to sleepwalk,' she said.

The statement came in between bites, completely out of the blue. She hardly ever addressed him unless he'd started the conversation.

'Sorry?' Jason replied. He'd been taken by surprise.

'When you were a kid – you'd sleepwalk around the flat. You'd open your door and wander into the living room and just stand there. You scared the wee shite out of me so many times. I'd turn around and there you were, eyes blank, staring ahead. The first time, I screamed so loudly, that old bat next door came knocking because she thought I was being attacked. In the end, I'd just tell you to go back to bed, you'd say "okay" and then go.'

Jason had never known that and she'd never mentioned it before.

'When did I stop?'

'When Chris came along.'

'So you think I'm opening the window in my sleep?'

His mother shrugged and moved on to the third piece of toast. 'Ooh, I like this guy. What's his name?' Jason turned to the screen but didn't recognise the man sitting on the sofa chatting to the presenters. 'Come on, he's that actor, the one with the tattoo on his arm and the face. He was in that thing with the woman. You know the one.'

'I don't, Mum.'

'Pfft, you're a waste of space.'

Jason closed his eyes, knowing he'd lost her again. Was sleepwalking the answer? It seemed so . . . silly. Did adults sleepwalk? Why would he open the window and then go back to bed?

His thoughts were interrupted by the clatter of the let-terbox. The postman never came this early, which meant only one thing.

Jason heaved himself up and went into the hallway, walking to the doormat where the small business card-sized advertising flyer was lying face-up. The garish pink lettering beamed bright against the yellow background, with images of roulette wheels and two people high-fiving around the edges.

VISIT MANCHESTER'S
PREMIER GAMBLING ESTABLISHMENT
Where better to have a night out?

Accommodating:
birthdays, anniversaries, work dos, stag & hen nights
Slots, table games, shows, bingo on the hour, every hour.

Casino 101: Quay Street, Manchester

His presence had been requested.

14

Jason kept his denim jacket's collar up, his head down and hands firmly in his pockets as he hurried along Quay Street. He passed the men on the door of Casino 101, ignoring the bingo corner and making his way towards the rear of the building. It was later in the morning and far busier than it had been the last time Jason had visited. Somewhere, a woman was cackling at the top of her voice but it was still barely audible over the ding-ding-ding of the machines.

The man in the suit standing next to the door at the back coughed, making Jason look up from the floor, before he tapped the code into the wall and opened the door.

'Make sure you knock.'

'Piss off.'

At the end of the corridor, Jason knocked anyway, waited for the 'come in' and then entered the office. He had never really taken to the dark red walls and a dark wood décor. Because of the lack of natural light, everything always seemed so gloomy. More so than usual today, as if the entire room had been drenched in blood. Jason blinked back the previous day's memory of the dealer in the stairwell.

Harry was sitting at the large table as a semi-naked server hunched over, placing a plate of scones in front of him. Carter was leaning on the bar, watching Jason. When

Harry glanced up, Jason could only see one side of his face; the other was half-bathed in shade from the glow of the lamp in the corner.

'Would you like something to eat?' Harry asked.

The server stood up straight, showing off her toned stomach. Her hair brushed across the top of Harry's head and she giggled, before stepping away.

'I'm fine,' Jason replied.

Harry thanked the server and she tottered out of the room, chest thrust in front of her. Jason resisted the urge to turn and watch her leave, looking at the table where Harry had sliced a scone in half and was in the process of buttering it. He glanced up, caught Jason's eye, and nodded towards the seat next to him. As Jason crossed the room, Harry added jam and clotted cream to the scone and then poured tea into a china cup.

Jason slotted in next to him, saying nothing as Harry took a bite and made an appreciative 'mmmm' sound.

'There's nothing more English than a scone with jam and cream,' he said, putting the cake back on the plate and picking up his tea. 'Well, perhaps tea of course and a fried breakfast. Warm beer too, and fish and chips from a proper chippy. None of these fries – proper thick, mushy chips with battered fish and gravy. Christ, I'm making myself hungry just thinking about it.' He leant backwards and rubbed his belly. Harry certainly wasn't fat but he didn't have the same trim physique as when Jason had first met him.

Harry took another bite, the jam and cream oozing between his teeth before he licked it away, and then he turned to Carter and nodded. In an instant the background classical music was booming around the room. Harry took another bite, drawing Jason's gaze and not letting it go as he swallowed and then began to speak. Jason had to shake his head and shuffle forward in order to hear anything.

'There was an unfortunate incident yesterday,' Harry said.

'Really?'

Harry nodded, eyes narrow, still not letting Jason go. 'Someone who works for me, a young man named Philip Porter, was beaten unconscious.'

'That sounds nasty.'

Another nod. 'Fortunately, I hear there's no brain injury and that there shouldn't be any lasting damage. He's awake this morning and has been able to eat and drink.'

'Lucky him.'

Harry took another bite, licked his lips, and then polished off the rest of the scone. He picked up a satin-looking napkin from the table and dabbed at his face before – finally – turning away from Jason and picking up his teacup. Jason took the moment to peer over Harry's shoulder towards Carter, who was still leaning on the bar. He was facing Jason and Harry but there was only indifference in his eyes. Given the volume of the music, he certainly wouldn't be able to overhear anything they were saying.

Harry leant slightly closer. 'From what I understand, it happened just a short distance from your flat. In the stairwell, in fact.'

'Really?'

Harry reached out, pressed his thumb and forefinger into Jason's chin, and moved his head around until they were eye to eye again. It wasn't forceful, just enough to let him know what was expected. They were less than half a metre apart: so close that Jason could see the wisps of new grey hairs growing on Harry's chin and the liver spots on his cheeks.

'What happened?' Harry said.

It wasn't a question – it was a straightforward demand. Jason held the stare but he could see in the older man's eyes that he already knew. It felt as if his mind had been read.

'He was selling drugs to kids,' Jason replied.

Harry nodded shortly, leaning back, picking up his tea, sipping it and then putting it down on the saucer again with an inaudible scrape.

He stared into Jason's eyes: 'Did you see him?'

'Yes.'

'How old?'

'Fourteen, maybe fifteen.'

'And do you have a particular problem with that?'

Jason broke the gaze and took a breath. He answered in the way he never replied to Harry: with a shrug. He didn't know why he'd attacked the man in the hoody. Perhaps it was the fact he was selling to kids but he couldn't get past the whispered 'Greeeeeeeeeen's he'd heard.

Or *thought* he'd heard.

Harry turned again and with the merest flicker of his hand, Carter silenced the music. 'Join us,' Harry added, turning back to Jason.

Carter obeyed, scraping a chair around until the three of them were sat in a triangle, with seemingly neither Carter nor Jason knowing where to look. Harry glanced from one to the other and took a bite from the second half of the scone he'd cut.

When he spoke, he chose his words very carefully, speaking slowly and making sure he spent equal time looking at both Carter and Jason. 'You know I have no children. Barbara, bless her, was never able to conceive. I've known for a long time that I'd have no natural heir but that means I've had to find . . . *contentment* . . . from other places.' He turned until he was facing Carter. 'You're like my first-born. It's unfair to say favourite – I love all of my children equally.' He turned back to Jason. 'You are one of my children, too, Jase. It's always so horrible when a child lets you down. Some day perhaps one of you – perhaps both – will understand the pain of having to discipline your own children. It hurts you far more than it ever hurts your children.'

Jason glanced nervously towards the door but Harry broke into a smile, reaching out with his empty hand and patting him gently across the face. Jason could smell his aftershave and see the engraved lettering on the man's white-gold watch: H.I. For a moment, he held his hand there, whispering something under his breath that Jason didn't catch.

When he removed his hand, Harry put the remainder of the scone into his mouth with the other and turned to the table, pushing the silver tray containing the plate and teapot away.

Without being asked, Carter crossed to a filing cabinet in the back of the room and brought across a rolled-up sheet of paper. He opened it out on the table in front of

Harry and then placed the teapot, plate, tray and milk jug in the corners to stop it rolling up again.

Jason scanned the paper, recognising the road network of Greater Manchester. The page was so large that it took in everything from Bury in the far north to Wythenshawe in the south, plus Walkden and Urmston to the west, with Oldham and Hyde to the east. From the slightly brown hue of the paper, it looked as if it had been created before Jason was born. There were all sorts of roads drawn on in pen and pencil with neat copperplate capital letters to identify each new addition.

Harry ran his hand across the page, tapping Quay Street, where the casino was, and then angling away. 'You've been doing a terrific job as my personal courier, Jason.'

'Thank you.'

'You're an expert carrier and never fail to deliver the messages I ask you to. You're fulfilling all of that promise I saw in you those years ago.'

'Thank you.'

Harry pointed to a street in Stretford, off to the west of the city centre but well within the M60 ring road. 'There is a row of shops here and I really need you to deliver something there for me. Do you think you can do that?'

'When do you need it doing?'

'Like any good delivery – as soon as possible.'

Jason pushed forward and memorised the name of the street. He hadn't seen it previously but knew the rough area. It wouldn't be hard to find. He nodded an acceptance.

Harry smiled thinly, eyes narrow as he purred the reply: 'Good boy.'

15

Jason leant against the wood, resting his head in the corner, trying to block the other voices out. Sitting on the floor in the back of a van was uncomfortable enough as it was, so quite why someone had fitted reinforced chipboard to the floor and walls, he really didn't know. The van bumped into a pothole and hopped out again, sending the four of them in the back bouncing into the air. It didn't seem to interrupt the conversation going on around him.

'. . . so Rachel, like, she finally gave it up on Friday night. I got her pissed enough that she didn't care where I stuck it. She squealed a bit but was enjoying it by the end. Afterwards, I—'

Carter's retort rattled back from the driver's seat. 'For God's sake, will you keep your stupid, pathetic lives to yourself? No one cares about Rachel, Racquel, Renee, Reena, Rhonda, Rosalin, Rose, Rosie, Rosemary, Roxanne, Ruth – or any of the other tarts you've got on the go.'

Carter stuck his head between the two front seats, looking away from the windscreen and making the van swerve to the left. He fixed the guilty party with a stare that could silence a crying baby and raised his eyebrows, wanting an answer.

'Sorry, like,' came the reply.

With a shake of his head, Carter turned back to the road, muttering a string of swear words under his breath.

The man who'd spoken pulled the balaclava down over his face, apparently wanting to hide from everyone around him just as the van rattled into another pothole and lurched upwards with an unhealthy-sounding growl.

The rest of the journey passed in silence. Jason spent his time examining the men, wondering if he could trust any of them. He already knew Carter but the other three were new faces, though they seemed to know each other and were apparently familiar with what was happening. Jason had been wondering a lot about the size and reach of Harry's influence. When they'd first met, he made Jason feel like his only son. Then there was Carter, who had apparently been around for a while. He felt sure there were others, too, people with different skills. Below Harry's 'sons', there were people like those sitting across from him.

'Everyone needs foot soldiers,' Harry had once told Jason.

It seemed he had foot soldiers all over the city but Jason doubted they even knew who they were working for: they were disposable hired hands. If they messed up and got arrested, they didn't know anything other than some bloke on the estate/park/market/pub had offered them a few quid.

'What did the bloke look like?' the question would come.

'Normal dark hair, normal height, normal dark clothes, no scars, no facial hair, nothing out of the ordinary.'

Harry had people for all jobs – even if that meant looking like a complete nobody.

Jason could guess who the three people opposite him were just by looking at them. The fact they were all in their late twenties or early thirties was the easy bit but there was more to it than that. The oldest had mousy black hair and a scar from his eye to his ear. The love-hate tattoos etched across his fingers meant he had probably been in prison, even if only for a short period. It wouldn't have been for anything serious, perhaps theft or an assault. Harry wasn't stupid – there was no reason to draw attention to whatever they were doing by using someone well-known to authorities.

As it was, Jason had no idea what they were doing. He had simply been told that Carter would collect him. He'd picked the other three up from a pub car park in Moss Side and then they'd been on their way.

The next man – the one who'd spoken – seemed to be friends with the first. He had short ginger hair and matching freckles. From the scabs on his knuckles and the way his nose bulged to the side, Jason guessed he was no stranger to a scrap.

The final man was a little smaller than the others, still older than Jason but definitely in his twenties. He didn't seem to know the other two and hadn't said a word since getting inside, spending his time staring at the floor. There were no scrapes or scars visible and when they'd got changed into the dark trousers and tops, Jason hadn't noticed any tattoos or piercings. He was a trickier one to figure out. Obviously he could be a petty thief or someone else with a minor criminal record but Jason sensed he was probably a bit of a nobody. Perhaps someone who was skint and had made it known he was looking for work?

For those unfamiliar with how the game worked, it might seem that bringing in an outsider made it more likely they would talk if the police somehow got involved. The opposite argument was far truer, though. If someone with no previous record could be persuaded to do something they weren't proud of, something utterly out of their comfort zone, then it could be permanently held over them.

There was no chance he'd been chosen by accident. Jason wondered if he was educated, or perhaps he'd recently been made redundant from a professional job. Perhaps he was an estate agent or some sort of legal clerk? People would be surprised by what others would do for money if they were struggling to pay rent or a mortgage. He might be out of work now and falling in with the wrong crowd. He'd do one job, perhaps two, pocket the money and then try to forget it had ever happened. A few months later, he'd get a job offer and go back to his career as if there had never been an interruption. The difference would be that the moment Harry wanted something, Carter or someone else would be sent to make the request. Before he knew it, the man would be doctoring legal documents or playing with housing surveys.

The man glanced up, caught Jason's eye and then immediately returned to staring at the floor. Jason knew from that fraction of a second that this was his first time doing anything like this. He'd been shocked when Carter had told them to strip and made them all change into the dark clothes. He would be worried by the balaclavas too.

Jason almost felt sorry for him.

The van dropped down a gear and began to slow, before finally stopping. Jason had no idea where they were but Carter's face appeared between the seats again. Beyond him, through the windscreen, there was darkness. He nodded at the trio opposite Jason. 'Right, you three, piss off outside and stay out of sight. I'll be out in a minute.'

Obediently, the ginger man slid the door open and climbed out, followed by the other two. It slammed into position again and Carter turned to Jason. 'You all right, kid?'

'Yeah.'

'It's a bit different tonight.'

'Why?'

'You know who Richard Hyde is, don't you?'

'Not really. I've heard the name.'

Carter checked his watch – plain and plastic – then turned back. 'I suppose you'd pick it up sooner or later. Look, you can't have failed to notice where we do most of our *work*?'

Jason shrugged. 'Hulme, Moss Side, Trafford, Rusholme, Longsight . . .'

'Yeah but what do they all have in common?'

Jason tried to think but nothing sprang instantly to mind. 'They're all dumps?'

Carter snorted with what was almost laughter, even though his expression didn't change. 'C'mon, kid. You're smarter than that.'

'I suppose they're all next to each other.'

'Right, and . . . ?'

'They're all south . . . ?'

Jason asked it as a question, not really sure but Carter nodded approvingly. The fact he was talking so much made it clear how important the evening was – recently he rarely said anything unless Harry specifically asked him a question.

'Exactly – they're all to the south of the city centre. There's an unwritten rule that Hyde keeps his business to the north and we keep ourselves to the south.'

'Who decides what's north and south?'

'Well, it's pretty obvious if you look at a map. Basically, anything below Mancunian Way is fair game for Mr Irwell. Anything above that is Hyde's territory.'

'Who decided that?'

Carter checked his watch again and tutted. 'No idea, kid. If you want to ask, be my guest. All you need to know is there's a general . . . *respect* . . . between the two of them – but every now and then one of them tries it on to see if the other's watching.'

'Right.'

'That's why tonight's more important. This ain't some kids mucking around or some prick on a street corner selling gear he shouldn't be.'

'Okay. Where are we?'

'Longsight. Our friend Hyde has been a right naughty bastard and is doing business where he shouldn't. Whatever happens in there, just go with it.'

'I will.'

'And keep an eye on Eddie.'

'Is he the smallest one?'

'Yeah – don't worry about Ginge and Smackhead, they're sound. Just don't let Eddie shit himself and we'll be fine.'

'Okay.'

Carter reached into the footwell and pulled out his balaclava. 'Right, let's do this.'

Carter put his foot through the fire exit, sending shards of imploding wood scattering across the floor. With a thump of their boots, he led the other four thundering into the kitchen of the pizza shop.

It was almost midnight and the takeaway was closed but the remaining staff members came rushing to the back at the sound of the boom. Smackhead and Ginge wasted no time, grabbing two of the men in uniform and slamming them into the metal counter, before wrestling them to the floor. Carter dashed through to the front, returning with a slightly older man who had dyed black hair and was wearing a white shirt. Pinned to his chest was a badge with 'Nigel: Manager' written on. Before he could even speak, Carter punched him hard in the stomach, making him double over.

Ginge and Smackhead had kicked their duo into submission and were standing over them triumphantly as the two men writhed on the ground.

While everything was going on, Eddie was standing close to the busted fire exit, his balaclava-shrouded head darting nervously from one side to the other. Jason crossed until he was standing next to the door, blocking it in case anyone had ideas about leaving.

With the manager bent over trying to get his breath back, Carter spun until he was facing the largest of the pizza ovens. For a moment his hand hovered around the dials but then he shrugged and turned them all to maximum. He focused back on the manager, heaved him up by the scruff of the neck and then wrapped his fingers around the man's throat, backing him into the wall opposite.

'Evening, Nigel,' he growled.

The man coughed, eyes bulging, until Carter released the pressure. Nigel slumped towards the sink next to him, spluttering.

Carter cracked his knuckles. 'Where are you, Nigel?'

The man looked at the pair of workers bleeding on the floor. 'I, er . . .'

THWACK!

Carter slapped him hard across the face. 'Don't get smart, Nigel. It's a simple question. Where are you?'

'Manchester?'

THWACK!

'Didn't I tell you not to get smart? Try again?' Nigel was cowering, trying to cover his face, but Carter reeled back. 'Put your hands down and tell me where you are.'

Slowly, Nigel dropped his guard, leaving himself unprotected, not that he could offer much resistance anyway. He was in his forties or early fifties, slightly overweight, unshaven and generally the type of person who had probably been bullied for large parts of his life.

'Longsight?' he whimpered.

Carter raised his hand as if to slap the man again, with Nigel instinctively raising his hands to protect his head.

'Didn't I tell you to put your hands down?'

Nigel peered through his fingers, expecting the blow that hadn't come. Slowly, he dropped his hands. There was already a smear of blood on his bottom lip.

'Longsight – exactly. Now, tell me, is that in *north* Manchester, or *south* Manchester?'

'South . . . ?'

Carter nodded approvingly. 'Exactly.'

Eddie was bouncing on the spot. He risked a glance at Jason and then continued staring at Carter and Nigel.

'Give me your hand,' Carter commanded.

Nigel was shaking. 'Pardon?'

'Hold out your right hand. Either do it or I'll rip your arm out of the socket.'

Gradually, Nigel extended his arm, trembling with fear as he peered into the eye holes of Carter's balaclava.

In a flash, Carter reached forward, grabbed Nigel's outstretched arm and dragged him across the kitchen towards the pizza oven. Nigel realised what was going to happen a moment before it actually did, screaming in fear as Carter pulled the door down and pressed the manager's palm onto the baking-hot surface of the oven.

Jason struggled to watch as Nigel's flesh sizzled, with Carter using one hand to press the man's arm down, ensuring he couldn't pull it away, and using the other to cover his mouth. Eddie made a squeaking sound, before catching himself, while Ginge, Smackhead and the two other workers were silent.

Hisssssssssssssss.

The smell of burning flesh was already filling the room before Carter finally pulled Nigel away from the oven, dropping him on the floor and wiping his hands on his trousers. Before anyone else could speak, he picked Nigel back up and dragged him over to the sink, thrusting the man's hands under the cold tap, again covering his mouth.

Jason watched as strips of skin disappeared down the sink with the reddened water; the spit of doner meat at the front of the shop suddenly seeming a lot less appealing.

After a minute or so, Carter stepped away, allowing Nigel to fall to the floor, sobbing to himself and staring at what was left of his hand.

'Can you hear me, Nigel?' Carter asked, moving around until he was in front of the man.

Nigel didn't reply, continuing to moan quietly to himself. In the back corner the other two workers were sitting against the table, nursing bruises and cuts but silently watching what was happening. Eddie hadn't moved since Carter had pulled Nigel away from the oven.

'Nigel, I haven't got time to mess around. Can you hear me?'

'Yes.'

'I've got a message that I need you to pass on for me. Will you do that?'

'Yes.'

'Are you listening carefully?'

Nigel's voice was a whimpering sob. 'Yes.'

'Tell Mr Hyde that Mr Irwell says he should stay away from the south of the city. Can you remember that?'

'Yes.'

'Repeat it back.'

Nigel rolled onto his side with a groan. Slowly he repeated the message word-for-word.

Carter turned to the two workers propped up against the table. 'What happened here tonight, fellas?'

One of them made the error of replying first: 'Er . . .'

'It's not a hard question. You don't need me to tell you the answer, do you? What happened here tonight?'

'Nothing.'

Carter nodded at the one who hadn't answered.

'Nothing.'

'Exactly – *nothing* happened here tonight but you won't be coming back here to work tomorrow. Got it?'

They answered in unison: 'Yes.'

Carter spun back to Nigel, crouching and twisting the man's face until they were looking at each other. 'What happened here tonight, Nigel?'

'Nothing.'

'Perfect. Now don't forget that message because you really don't want to see me again. Give my love to Sarah and the girls.'

16

Jason shoved his front door open and headed straight to Chris's room. His duvet, sheet and pillows were all in the exact same spot as almost thirty hours ago. The last time Jason had seen his brother was when they'd argued in the kitchen almost two days ago. He knew he had a job to organise and carry out for Harry but there was something nagging him about the fact Chris still wasn't home. Even though he stayed out frequently, all of his clothes were still at home and he almost always dropped by, if only to get changed and go back out again.

In the living room, Jason's mum was giggling to herself. At her feet was an open third-finished bottle of vodka. On the television was a talk show, the subject scrolling across the bottom read: 'I've got male and female genitals – deal with it'. Jason half-thought about sitting down to watch it before he remembered what he was doing.

'Have you seen Chris?'

His mother didn't look away from the television. 'Nope.'

'He's definitely not been home?'

'Nope. More toast.'

Next to the vodka bottle was the plate from the morning, still covered in crumbs. Jason picked it up and headed

144

into the kitchen, just as he'd been asked. On his way back to the living room, he peeped inside his own room just in case. The window was closed, the rubber band still in place – exactly as he'd left it.

After giving his mother more marmalade on toast, Jason returned to the kitchen and tried calling his brother's phone.

It rang three times and then: 'Hi, this is Chris. I'm probably shagging or something. Leave a message.'

Jason hung up and tried again: engaged. He waited another minute and tried one more time.

'Hi, this is Chris. I'm probably shagging or something. Leave a message.'

This time Jason did leave a message: 'Chris, it's me. Mum's worried about you. Where have you been? If you still need the money then we'll sort something out. Call me.'

He hung up and sat staring at his phone, willing it to ring.

It didn't.

Jason bounced through the double doors at the front of the Swan and Packet and scanned the pub. Considering it was a weekday afternoon, the place was well-populated. In one corner, four men were crowded around a circular table playing dominoes. Pints of murky, frothy ale had massed to one side, at least three per man, with a tap-tap-tap of plastic on table as they went around the circle placing their tiles.

In the opposite corner, more men were huddled around a table peering up at the small television fixed to the wall that was showing horse racing. 'C'mon, y'bastard. Go, go, go, gooooooo.' A man with wild grey hair jutting off in all directions rose to his feet excitedly, windmilling his arms, before slumping back into his seat as the race concluded. 'Bah – what a shithouse.' Jason turned as the man kicked the table leg, sending an empty half-pint glass spinning across the table and landing – intact – with a hollow clatter on the carpet.

Jason crossed to the bar, where a weary-looking woman with a face like a chipped paving slab was using a tea towel to clean out an old-fashioned tankard. She was watching the men under the television and spoke to Jason without looking up. 'What can I getcha, love?'

'Have you seen Chris around?'

The landlady glanced at Jason, noticing who he was, and then back to the table. 'No but Clarkey and his mob were in here last night.'

'Was he—?'

Jason was interrupted by another clang from behind. The landlady pushed herself up on tiptoes, using the bar to support herself. 'What have I sodding told you, Jack? If you can't control yourself, then piss off down the bookies. It's only a horse, for Christ's sake.'

Jack replied with something halfway between a 'sod off' and a quack. His accent made it hard to tell. The landlady shook her head, continuing the conversation with Jason without dropping a beat. 'I told Clarkey I'd boot the lot of them out if they didn't pipe down but he laughed in my face. In the end he left anyway before I kicked shite out of the little bastard.'

'I'll have a word.'

'You do that.'

'But Chris definitely wasn't in?'

'Not seen 'im – else I would've threatened to kick shite out of 'im too. That Clarkey's a right little turd – if your brother had any sense, he'd find a new bunch of mates.'

Jason half-turned, humming in agreement. 'That's the problem – I'm not sure he's got any sense.'

Jason left the pub, crossed the road and negotiated the interconnecting maze of alleys that led to the community housing estate. The red-brick flats, bungalows, terraces and two-up, two-downs were so intermixed that it was like someone had been playing a computer game and simply dropped a random sample of housing types with no particular thought as to the reason why.

Ignoring the kids bunking off who were literally running rings around the dustbin men trying to empty everyone's waste into their wagon, Jason headed to a row of flats. They were built much like the block in which he lived, consisting of two storeys, but someone had tried to give them an air of respectability by constructing arched overhangs above each of the doorways. If it wasn't for the missing tiles, scratched paint and the fact three-quarters of them were covered in dark grime and filth, it would probably have been a nice idea.

Jason knocked on number twenty and stepped back as a cacophony of barking dogs roared through the letterbox. A woman's voice bellowed from inside: 'Get down, Jazz.

Ace, stop shagging your sister. Shut up, Boxer. Boxer! Boxer! Ouch, get off my leg. Jazz, stop jumping. Jazz!'

Eventually the door opened a fraction and a woman's plump face appeared in the gap, wiry strands of dark hair curling away from her chin. 'What?'

'Is Clarkey in?'

The woman opened the door a little further. 'Bastarding dogs.' She turned back inside. 'Ace, I told you to stop shagging your sister. Get off her now – don't make me come in there.' She growled in a way that was far more intimidating than anything the dogs had managed. There was a yelp and then, finally, silence. She turned back to Jason. 'Who are you?'

'Chris's brother.'

She eyed him suspiciously. 'Have you tried the Swan and Packet?'

'He's not there.'

'Probably in the bookies then. Either that or if he's off down some knocking shop. Christ knows where he gets his money from.'

'Have you seen Chris?'

'Last time I saw your brother, he was sniffing around asking for money.'

Jason sighed. 'You didn't lend him any, did you?'

'No, I . . .' She paused. '. . . yeah, the little sod had fifty quid off me actually. That's my grocery money. Reckoned he'd pay it back this morning but I've not seen him.'

With a roll of his eyes, Jason turned to walk away. 'Nice try.'

*

The bookies' shop was a grubby little hole wedged between a boarded-up former sandwich shop and partially burned-out one-time pub that had been converted into a nursery for all of a month before closing down. One of the larger betting chains had tried opening a branch across the street but the daily delivery of dog waste through the letterbox and eventual fire-bombing meant that the message was finally received. Instead, 'BetFrank' was going strong, if by strong that included the soot-covered shop front, rusty blown-over sandwich board at the front, shutter-covered windows and stencilled 'check out our double steak offers' sign, which could have been stolen from a restaurant but probably hadn't been.

The glass front was reinforced with threads of metal running through it and the overhead shutters hadn't been entirely raised, meaning Jason had to duck as he entered. Considering people weren't supposed to smoke, there was a suspicious whiff of tobacco masking the stale sweat inside the packed one-room establishment. Three gaming machines were pressed against the wall immediately on his right, all occupied by men feeding their money in. On the opposite side were banks of televisions, each displaying various horse and dog races. The floor was littered with small slips of paper, with an almost entirely male clientele standing around watching the screens.

At the far end, a purple-haired woman was resting her elbows on the counter behind a sheet of reinforced glass, leaning her head on her hand, rolling her eyes. On the opposite side of the glass, a drainpipe of a man was wagging an angry finger at her.

'You wrote the number down wrong,' he shouted.

The woman didn't bother to stop leaning. 'Sod off, Clarkey.'

'I told you I wanted twenty quid on number five but you've signed off number six.'

'That's not how it works and you know it.'

'If you give me my twenty quid back, I won't put a complaint in.'

'You won't put a complaint in because you bet on the wrong horse and it's nothing to do with me.'

Clarkey spun around to face the rest of the room, throwing his arms wide, apparently hoping everyone else would join him in protesting against the alleged injustice. He was wearing an impossibly tight leather jacket, skinny jeans and brown suede boots with the laces undone, dragging on the floor behind him. With his scraggy unwashed hair and dark eyeliner, he looked like a drug-addled failed rock musician. At least one part of that was true.

A young woman even skinnier than he was stepped forward, putting a hand on his shoulder and flicking her mop of bleached-white hair. 'Come on, Clarkey, leave it. She's not worth it.'

'She's nicked my twenty quid.'

The purple-haired woman behind the counter pushed herself up from the counter and pointed downwards. 'Look, Clarkey, I've got a panic button under here. You can either take your mates and get lost, or I'll press it and we'll see what happens. Up to you.'

Clarkey took a step backwards, still gesticulating. 'This is robbery.' He spun in a circle, addressing everyone. 'She's stolen my money – she'll steal all of yours too.'

One of the other punters muttered something that ended in 'off' as Clarkey allowed himself to be dragged towards the door by his white-haired friend and another man, equally as thin. Jason stepped to the side and allowed them through, before following them into the car park.

'That bitch nicked my twenty quid,' Clarkey complained as the woman smoothed his hair down.

'I know, babes, I know.'

Jason stepped into the circle they'd formed, finally being noticed. Clarkey's attitude changed in an instant, batting his girlfriend's hands away and standing up straighter. 'How ya doing, Jase?'

'All right – I'm looking for Chris.'

'Not seen him, pal.'

'When was the last time you did?'

Clarkey started counting on his fingers, then looked up. 'What day is it?'

'Thursday.'

He began counting again. 'So, yesterday was Wednesday, then it was Monday, no – Tuesday, er . . .'

'I last saw him on Tuesday afternoon,' Jason said. 'Did he come round yours?'

Clarkey turned to the woman: 'Babes?'

'Yeah, we were out on Tuesday night, weren't we? He had a right strop on.'

Clarkey didn't seem so sure but nodded anyway. 'Yeah – Tuesday night, that's right.'

Jason turned to the woman. 'What was up with him?'

She shrugged. 'Dunno, he was going on about money and his prick of a brother.' She paused, glancing at Clarkey before settling back on Jason. 'Oh, is that you?'

Jason nodded. 'Any idea where he was yesterday?'

Clarkey replied: 'Last I heard he was going to Kat's house.'

'I knew I should have tried her first.' Jason turned to leave before stopping himself. 'I heard you were kicking off in the Swan and Packet last night . . .'

Clarkey shrugged. 'We were only mucking about.'

'You know who owns it, don't you?'

Suddenly, Clarkey was unable to look anywhere other than at his still-untied shoes. 'Aye, well . . .'

'So you know starting a ruck's a really bad idea, don't you?'

'I didn't mean anything by it, like.'

Jason caught the woman's eye, hoping she at least had some control over her boyfriend, even though he'd never seen her before. He didn't need to say anything because she gave a small nod to say she got it. 'All right,' Jason said. 'If you do see Chris, tell him to call me.'

The reason Jason hadn't visited Kat's house first was that he hated going anywhere near the place. People might think the Hulme estate he came from was rough but it was nothing compared to the Salford high-rise where his brother's girlfriend lived. The soulless brown block soared into the sky, bathing the surrounding area in a vast, grim shadow. In terms of what went on in the area, Jason doubted it was any better or worse than where he lived – but at least his block of flats was only two storeys high and the sun was occasionally visible.

Well, the clouds.

Here, there wasn't even that: it was just one big chunk of concrete that had been left to deteriorate.

The grim entranceway had the traditional odour of piss, with piles of junk mail dumped in the corners. Jason had only visited the block once before, when Chris had phoned him after falling down a flight of stairs and wanted a lift home. Thirteen floors of hardened concrete steps might seem like a lot but Jason had made the mistake of taking the lift on that occasion and spent twenty minutes hitting the 'emergency' button after it had broken down.

With that in mind, he began the slow trudge up the steps until finally emerging on the floor where Kat lived. Somewhere on a floor above, there was a baby wailing, its cries echoing along the hard granite corridors.

If any couple proved that opposites attracted, then it was surely Chris and Kat. Chris was tall and spindly, while Kat . . . wasn't. She opened the door, all big dark curls, painted black nails, eye-liner and cleavage.

'I ain't seen 'im,' she said by way of greeting.

'Nice to see you too, Kat.'

'Whatcha want?'

'Do you know where he might be?'

Kat gazed past him as if there might be someone more interesting on the floor. 'No – but he owes me forty quid. I'm supposed to be getting my hair done later and need that money.'

'When did you last see him?'

153

She began scratching a fingernail across her top row of teeth. 'Dunno, my memory's a little hazy.'

'Can you at least tell me what he wanted the money for?'

'Dunno, my memory's— '

Jason interrupted her by digging into his pocket, taking out a twenty-pound note and handing it over. 'That's all I've got on me, you'll have to get the rest from him.'

Kat held the note up to the light to check the watermark and then pocketed it. 'He stopped over on Tuesday night.'

'What time did he leave yesterday?'

'He had his community service in the afternoon, so it was probably about midday.'

Jason had forgotten his brother had started doing his unpaid work – a hangover, in all senses, from a drunken night of abusing police officers in the city centre a few months ago.

'Have you heard from him since?'

'I got a text at about two yesterday afternoon asking if he could stay over last night. It was fine by me but I never got a reply and he never came over. I thought it was because he knew I'd want my forty quid back. I tried calling but there was no answer, plus he's got that stupid message about shagging.'

'Do you have any idea what he was borrowing money for?'

'No – but you can tell him he ain't staying over until he pays back the forty quid he owes.'

'Twenty quid now.'

Kat eyed him with a knowing grin. 'Whatever.'

17

By the time Jason got back to his flat, it was two o'clock – twenty-four hours since Chris had sent the text message to Kat, which was almost exactly the same time Jason had been kicking the drug dealer down the stairs. Without checking on his mother, Jason went into his brother's room and began hunting through the mounds of crap. Underneath the bed, hidden in a sock, was a small polythene bag filled with cannabis and there was a crumpled ten-pound note in his brother's pillowcase, which Chris had almost certainly forgotten about. A box of imported cigarettes with Cyrillic script was at the bottom of the wardrobe but there was little else other than clothes, shoes and pages ripped from pornographic magazines.

Jason returned everything to more or less where he'd found it, including the money, and then went through the tortuous procedure of calling the probation office for information. After being passed from one person to the next, he finally got through to Chris's officer – only to be told information couldn't be given out over the phone and that they closed in an hour.

Luckily, the local probation office was perfectly placed on the border between Hulme and Moss Side, barely ten minutes' walk from the flat.

As Jason walked around the corner towards the office,

he saw a pair of workers standing outside, smoking and chatting while cowering from the wind. After asking to speak to his brother's probation officer, Jason was then left in a cramped, tiled waiting room as, seemingly, nothing happened. Littering the walls were posters featuring impressive-sounding statistics about falling crime levels and the success of various schemes but they completely washed over Jason. Nothing on any of them would come anywhere close to what he knew about.

Eventually, a man with receding dark hair and glasses blustered into the room, precariously carrying a stack of cardboard folders under his arm. He introduced himself as Keith, apologised for the wait, leant in to shake Jason's hand and then had to rebalance himself to stop everything falling onto the floor. After an inelegant hopping display, he used one knee to hold the folders, shook hands, and then invited Jason to follow him.

The probation office was a warren of corridors, closed doors, posters, ringing phones and muffled chatter. Keith made small talk over his shoulder as he walked, commenting that 'winter's just around the corner', saying that it was 'always so depressing when the nights start to come in' and lamenting the fact that he didn't understand 'why it always has to be so cold all the time'. Jason ummed and erred in all the right places, knowing he still needed information from the man, but also beginning to understand why re-offending rates were so high. Faced with such inane chatter, those convicted of drug offences would be straight back on the gear the moment they got out of the door.

Filing cabinets ran the entire way around Keith's office,

with motivational posters pinned above them, showing off slogans such as 'Don't put off until tomorrow what you can do today', plus 'Dream big and dare to fail'.

Keith balanced the folders on the edge of his desk, moved a stack of lever-arch files away from the spare office seat and then finally sat down opposite Jason. After the formality of double-checking Jason was who he claimed, Keith tapped away on his keyboard and then finally they got to the reason why he was there, even if it wasn't quite what Jason had expected.

'If you're here with an apology, I'm afraid that's going to have to come from your brother,' Keith said. 'I haven't put the report in yet but leaving an unpaid work assignment part-way through without telling anyone is a serious matter.'

Jason kept a straight face. It was the first he'd heard of it but the lie came naturally. 'Chris only told me his half of it, so I don't feel I have all the facts for you – but I do know he's sorry. Perhaps if you could tell me exactly what happened, I'd be able to fill in a few of the gaps.'

'He is old enough to do this himself – he's eighteen.'

'I understand, but he's immature for his age. It's not easy at home right now.'

Keith pursed his lips and typed on the keyboard some more, before turning back to Jason. 'Hmm, your mother, yes. Some of that did come out in the initial report . . . well I suppose it can't do any harm. Sometimes in the more *complicated* cases, we do involve family members. Chris is lucky in the sense that he has people around him. It's not like that for many of the people we deal with.'

'I can imagine.'

Keith typed something on the keyboard and then looked up. 'Chris Green was doing unpaid work at Clarendon Park yesterday. I don't know if you know it but it's in Salford. He was on clean-up duty: litter-picking and general tidying, those sorts of things.'

'Were you there?'

'I'm office- and court-based – but there are always people supervising. As far as I can understand, everyone was given a fifteen-minute break and he simply disappeared. We tried his mobile phone but there was no answer. There were no other phone numbers on record, so when the day was complete and he hadn't returned, that's when the breach of conditions was referred to me.'

'But you haven't reported him back to the court?'

Keith shook his head. 'Not yet. I do try to give first offenders a little leeway but it's a two-way thing. I was hoping he'd be back here today to explain himself. Sending his older brother doesn't quite cut it, I'm afraid – especially as he's still not answering his phone.'

'What will happen if you report him?'

'That somewhat depends on what I write. He could end up having extra hours added to his unpaid work, or perhaps having an extra punishment – such as a curfew. The fact he hasn't been in contact doesn't bode well, I'm afraid.'

Keith did seem genuinely concerned. He rubbed his forehead and sighed, fixing Jason with a concerned gaze. Jason didn't really know how to respond – this was largely news to him.

'Can I tell you something in confidence?' Jason said,

peering over his shoulder as if making sure there was no one there.

'Of course.'

'I don't know how much you already know but we've been having a few problems with our mother. She's been . . . *ill*.'

Jason purposefully added the pause, Keith's eyes narrowing before he offered a short, knowing nod.

'Chris has been looking after her,' Jason added. 'I don't want to speak for him or try to make excuses but sometimes she calls and then you have to rush away.'

Keith hummed under his breath before replying. 'We're not the rigid totalitarians some might think. We do have a degree of discretion. For instance, this is your brother's first breach of his first terms – but I need to speak to him. It's admirable you've come to stick up for him but it's still on his shoulders. If he explains all of this himself, then I'll see what I can do.'

'What is it they were doing in the park?'

'I'm not sure how that's relevant.'

'Oh, it's not. I suppose I was just wondering how he slipped away.'

Keith pursed his lips but answered anyway. 'There's a copse of trees and bushes close to the nursery near to the road. It needs cleaning out every six weeks or so, so they were there. I suppose he simply walked away.'

'What time did he leave?' When Keith raised his eyebrows, Jason clarified: 'I'm curious what time Mum would have called him.'

After another check on the computer, Keith answered.

'He was there at half past three, gone by quarter to four. I should say, it doesn't matter *when* he left; even if it was only five minutes before the end of his work period, it would count as a breach.'

Jason said he'd make sure Chris got in contact, knowing he was going to have to find him first.

Depending on the time of year and day, parts of Clarendon Park would sit in the shadow of the tower block where Kat lived. Jason knew that if his brother had simply skipped out from his unpaid work, that's where he would have headed. The fact Chris had gone missing part-way through his community service was worrying – he could be stupid but not *that* idiotic.

He had been arrested in Manchester City Centre two nights after his eighteenth birthday for refusing to go home quietly after a drunken night celebrating. From what Jason had heard, the police had been quite reasonable. Chris had hurled a takeaway pizza at a girl outside a club for no apparent reason and then got into an argument with her boyfriend. When the police had turned up, they'd given him the chance to get in a taxi and go home quietly. Instead, the alcohol had done its talking and Chris had told them where to go. They'd promptly showed him exactly where *he* could go – the local nick and then magistrates' court. Usually first-time offenders would get away with a slap on the wrists or a fine – but Chris had opted not to talk to the duty solicitor and then sworn at the magistrates.

Jason had only found all of that out afterwards when Harry had asked about his brother's court appearance, having read it in the *Manchester Morning Herald*. When asked, Chris had pleaded his innocence, blaming his friends, the girl at whom he'd thrown the pizza, her boyfriend, the police, the magistrate for 'looking at me funny' and anybody else who wasn't him. Despite that, he had seemed chastened enough not to want to go through it all again – especially with the realisation that he was going to have to work picking up other peoples' rubbish and not be paid.

By the time Jason had walked back to his flat and then driven to Clarendon Park, the school run was over just in time for the commuters' rush hour to begin. Considering Keith had said the people on community service had been cleaning out the grove close to the nursery, there was a noticeable amount of rubbish nearby. Jason stepped over the small pile of fag ends next to a drain and then began the grim task of kicking his way through the densely packed mix of trees, bushes, long grass, mud and general litter. After around fifteen minutes, he realised he was getting nowhere, so retreated back to the edge of the park.

It was only when he stopped to take in the place properly that Jason realised he'd missed the obvious part of what Keith had told him. Chris might have been clearing out that area at some point but he was on a break at the time he disappeared. Jason moved back to the pile of cigarette butts and turned in a circle. Whether Chris had walked away, or if something more sinister had happened, it had occurred without him being seen by anyone else cleaning up. That meant there was only one direction in which he could have gone – towards the nursery.

Jason followed the muddy trampled-down grass to the pavement and then began searching around the clipped, tidier bushes that lined the edge of the park. He had only been searching for a minute when he saw the dark plastic mobile phone slightly hidden under a branch. It was unquestionably his brother's, with a zigzag crack across the screen and endless scratches across the back.

He picked it up and jabbed the buttons, unsure how that particular model worked, but soon made the screen come to life. With just twelve per cent battery remaining, the first problem was guessing his brother's four-digit unlock code. He first tried the day and month of Chris's birthday, then one two three four, four three two one and nine nine nine nine. When none of that worked, he tried to think of the way his brother's mind operated. Chris wasn't stupid but he was forgetful, which meant there was only one other easy option. They lived at flat fifteen, so he typed one five one five into the phone and the device sprang to life, revealing the mass of missed calls from Jason, Kat, Clarkey and an unknown number that was, presumably, the probation office.

The top text message set Jason's heart racing, the message clear, simple and sent on Tuesday: 'Prince of Wales, 9 p.m. Bring the £.'

It wasn't so much that the Prince of Wales was a guest house known in select circles as a place where illicit merchandise could be bought that worried Jason – it was the fact that it was close to Cheetham Hill in the north of the city.

The *north*.

Unless Kat had specifically lied to Jason, which he doubted, Chris had missed that meeting at the Prince of Wales – with the reason he needed money now apparent.

18

Jason parked in the shadow between two street lights opposite the Prince of Wales Bed and Breakfast just as the sun dipped over the horizon, bathing the city in a murky haze of fading daylight. The front was a mess of peeling paintwork and damp-riddled wooden beams over the porch: the sort of place where even a one-star review on a ratings website would be generous.

He had to wait for only ten minutes before the first man hurried along, reached the end of the B and B's path, looked both ways along the street, and then headed inside. Three minutes later and he re-emerged, again checking both ways, and then bustling away, hands in pockets, bobble hat pulled down.

The clientele over the next forty-five minutes wasn't that varied: almost entirely men who wore hats or hoods, stayed for two or three minutes, and walked away incredibly quickly. It was barely long enough for breakfast, let alone time to take a kip.

After a few moments of inaction, Jason got out of his car, crossed the road and headed inside, instantly reeling from the smell of wet dog inside the porch. The main reception area was little better, with creased, peeling wallpaper, a dirty dark red carpet and a scratched wooden counter. A balding middle-aged man entered from a side office seconds after Jason rang the bell on the counter.

He glanced at Jason, then at the front door, before asking what he wanted.

'Are you the owner?' Jason asked.

'I'm the manager. What do you want?'

'What have you got?'

The man had a dreadful comb-over, with strands of black hair greased to his scalp. As he tilted his head, a wisp separated itself from the rest and hung limply. 'We've got rooms for thirty quid a night.'

'What else?'

'You get cornflakes, milk and toast included in the price, plus a wake-up call if you want one. Keep the noise down, check out by eleven – that's it.'

'What else?'

There was another pause before the man replied: 'Who's asking?'

'Chris Green's brother.'

The manager shot an arm down under the counter but Jason had already anticipated the move, pouncing across the counter and wrenching the man's arm to the side. He was stronger than he looked but Jason had the momentum, sliding across the wood and thumping him into the wall behind. Usually he would keep his knees low in order to land on the target and keep himself on top but this time the luck wasn't with him. As Jason leant backwards, the empty wooden bookshelf on the wall above creaked, rattled and then fell, almost in slow motion. The corner caught him on the temple, immediately opening a cut.

Jason was trying to clear his head but the manager swung around, hitting him in the mouth with a flailing fist. The blow wasn't hard but with the shelf pinned across his chest, Jason didn't have a chance to deflect it, taking the full force and tasting blood. The manager swung again but Jason ducked, feeling the rush of air as the fist brushed his nose. He was trying to shake the collapsed shelf away but the manager was still scrambling towards the underside of the counter. Jason scragged the collar of the man's shirt at the same time as he noticed the sawn-off shotgun slotted into a compartment purpose-built beneath the reception desk.

The sight of the weapon gave Jason a rush he had rarely felt before. Suddenly it wasn't just a minor scrap, he was fighting for his life.

There was a scratching sound as the manager's shirt started to rip but Jason had enough of an angle to wrap his hand around the back of the man's neck, squeezing as hard as he could. Avoiding a thrash of arms and hands, Jason finally managed to brush the bookshelf away, punching the manager in the back of the head and then scrambling to his knees. This time he was unable to avoid the flying elbow that smacked him in the same spot as where the shelf had hit him.

In an instant, any pretence of calculated, skilled fighting was lost as Jason and the manager began rolling in the small gap between the counter and the wall. Jason took an elbow under his ribs that made him wince but countered by thrusting his head forward and feeling the implosion of the man's nose breaking. Blood spattered into Jason's eyes but he blinked and got lucky as his vision cleared. As he stumbled to his feet, Jason cracked a knee into the manager's pelvis and then grabbed the gun, stumbling backwards against the wall but keeping his balance and covering the man with the weapon.

The manager's face was a mess of smeared blood, his nose squat and spread across his face. He was trying to catch his breath, holding his arms to his sides before spitting a tooth onto the floor and shaking his head.

'I hope your brother's worth it – you've just got yourself killed, pal.'

He would have sounded more threatening if he wasn't trying to speak with a broken nose.

'I'm the one with the gun.'

'Do what you want – you should do your homework about who owns a place before you try to rob it.'

'I'm not robbing you – you're the one who reached under the counter.'

The manager shuffled backwards slightly, keeping his arms out wide but moving into a sitting position. He half-spat, half-coughed a mouthful of blood onto the floor and groaned.

'So what do you want?'

Before Jason could answer, the door squeaked open and a thin woman entered. Her long black hair hung around her shoulders and she was wearing a dark woollen hat, heavily made-up eyes peeping under the brim. She first noticed the manager peering over the top of the counter and then swung around just as Jason pointed the gun at her. As she ducked for cover, the manager leapt up, angling his shoulder into Jason's knee with a roar of triumph, pain and fury. Off-balance, Jason fell into the wall, but used it to springboard himself forward, crunching the handle of the gun into the back of the manager's head with a solid clunk. As he slumped to the ground, his grip slipped and Jason stepped clear.

On the other side of the counter, the woman was shrieking but Jason held the gun by the barrel out to the side one-handed, not pointing it at anyone.

'Stop screaming!'

Her mouth closed, eyes darting to the manager and back to Jason. Considering there was a gun in the general vicinity, she didn't seem as frightened as her screeches made out.

'I don't 'ave no money,' she said, accent local and thick.

'What are you here for?'

'Er . . .'

Jason blinked away a drop of blood that was dribbling around his eye. 'I'm not going to shoot you – but just answer and save us all a lot of messing around.'

'Just after a bit of candy.'

'What do you do with it?'

She sneered at him: 'What do you think?'

'I mean is it for yourself or are you selling?'

'What's it to you?'

'Just answer.'

'You a Fed or something?'

Jason held his arms out again, indicating the blood stains on his clothes. 'What do you think?'

The woman didn't seem sure but she eyed the shotgun and answered anyway: 'Bit of this, bit of that.'

It was exactly what Jason was afraid of. There was no way his brother had a bad drug habit, else he would have noticed. That meant this place wasn't just selling to the odd junkie, it was a full-on wholesaler.

The manager groaned as he rolled onto his back, clutching his head. Dark red-black blood clung gloopily to his fingers. His words were still only partially audible through his shattered nose. 'Oh, don't worry – your brother's got himself in big-time.'

'How much does he owe?'

'Two and a half.'

'I've got the money . . .'

The manager started laughing before stopping himself, cradling his ribs and moaning. 'It's too late for that.'

'How much do you want?' Jason asked.

'You know where you are, don't you? You know whose gear he was selling and then not bringing the money back? He's lucky he's still got kneecaps.'

Jason flipped the gun barrel up, took out the two cartridges and tossed them on the floor. 'Where is he?'

'No idea – he could have helped himself by turning up on Tuesday night. If he's gone missing, well . . .'

Jason glanced towards the woman but she was biting her nails and not even looking at him, as if this was something she saw every day. Maybe it was.

This was typical Chris.

Jason turned back to the manager: 'If I find out you're lying, I'll be back.'

The man grinned through bloodied teeth, the gap in the front showing the roof of his mouth. 'And I'll be waiting.'

Jason walked through the front door and tossed the gun into the dark shadows of the yard, where it bounced and clattered into the fence. Behind him, the manager's mocking laugh was seeping into the night. 'Richard Hyde's not a man you want to owe money to.'

19

Jason's watch showed five past eleven when he finally pulled up outside the gates of the only place he thought he could go. Harry owned a large house in the village of Astley to the west of the city. As Manchester had expanded, Astley had become a suburb on the commuter belt. From what Jason had found out, it was where Harry had grown up. Rather than taking all his money and buying an enormous mansion, or purchasing land and having someone build him a dream home, Harry had simply bought the largest property in the area. Jason had only been there once before, when he'd been left in the back of the black car as a teenager while Harry went inside and returned shortly afterwards, not wanting to talk about anything.

The route to Astley was easy enough but Jason couldn't remember where the house was and spent over an hour driving in and out of every road until finally finding what he was pretty sure was the correct one.

Harry's house was set back from the road, steeped in the night's darkness, almost hidden except for the large set of metal gates and high, thick walls that ran around the property. It was the gates that Jason remembered the most – thick black metal prongs with vicious spikes on top. As a teenager, he'd peered through the tinted glass, wondering what type of idiot would try to break into Harry Irwell's house.

Jason got out of the car and approached the gates, peeping through a gap towards the large building masked by the gloom. He pushed the gates but they were locked, so he tried phoning Harry's mobile. As he stood, the night breeze whistled along the deserted street, making him shiver in his thin denim jacket. His arms ached and there was a dull thudding in his head from where the shelf and the manager had hit him.

After three rings, the line went dead – not even an answer machine – so Jason pressed the buzzer fixed to the wall next to the gate. Underneath the button was a speaker and a faint humming noise sizzled out before it went silent. There was no way Jason could keep phoning Harry, let alone pressing the call button. If Harry was out for any reason and his wife, Barbara, was home alone, Jason didn't want to think of the fury he'd face for scaring her.

Feeling a little lost for ideas, Jason walked along the pavement to the spot where the wall stopped and turned ninety degrees but there was no easy way in – which he supposed was the point. Jason returned to the gates, more slowly this time, looking for footholds or anything else that might get him over. Harry could ignore someone calling him, or ringing the box outside of the house – but it was unlikely he'd overlook the doorbell.

Either way, Jason was doing something incredibly stupid – but then it was already a night for it. How much worse could it get when he had already beaten up one of Richard Hyde's minions and pointed a gun at him?

For a few moments, Jason stood staring through the gates at the house but it was clear there was only one thing for it. Although the gates only had one horizontal bar – at the very top – the thick brick pillars they were connected to offered something he could press his back against. Slowly, and very wary of the bulbous row of spikes running along the bottom of the gate specifically to stop people climbing them, Jason began to shimmy upwards. He pushed back against the bricks, resting his feet on the railings, and used his hands to pull himself up. Usually, it wouldn't have been too hard but his arms felt so tired from fighting that they were struggling to support his weight.

A third of the way up, Jason stopped to catch his breath. He was barely higher than if he'd jumped and tried to cling on but the metal was rough on his palms and the adren-aline that had surged through him in the guest house had long since worn off as he'd got himself lost.

Five more reaches and heaves left him almost at the top but there was a cut in the webbing between his thumb and finger from a loose metal splinter. It wasn't just Jason's arms that were hurting now either – his shoulders were on fire, his neck aching from the strain. He also realised that he'd not thought about getting down on the other side. It was at least a two-metre drop, probably more, yet there was nothing on which to lower himself, except for perhaps the railings that were already tearing his hands to shreds.

After another stop to catch his breath and think about how ridiculous this was, in so many ways, Jason stretched up and pulled himself high, grunting in exertion, before finally managing to twist his body. He wedged his fingers onto the sandstone ledge on top of the pillar. There was hardly any room as there was a giant stone sphere, but just enough that Jason could pull himself up so his lower half straddled the gate. The spikes were dangerously close to his crotch as he balanced with both feet in the same spot on the gates' horizontal rung.

On the other side was the driveway but behind the wall was a row of bushes that would probably have been the old border. Of the two options, Jason aimed for the one he thought would be less painful, flinging himself sideways and landing with an agonising thump across his back and arse as he fell into the tangle of grass and hedge. For a few moments, he lay still, staring up as the clouds drifted across the sky, masking and unmasking the stars. It was a strange type of pain that was surging through him. Aside from the scrape over his eye, Jason doubted there would be a serious mark on him, yet everything ached. He tried to push himself up but ended up collapsing again, so simply lay still: watching, breathing, and cursing his brother for being so bloody stupid.

Finally, Jason climbed to his feet, thinking that if a person was ever going to burgle Harry, they would need not only a death wish – but a sodding big ladder and a blow-up slide. He stumbled his way up the driveway but had to cover his eyes as the blazing, bright white security lamps lit up the area like floodlights over a football pitch. The drive ended with a turning circle, where the black car with the blacked-out windows that Jason knew so well was parked next to a smaller white Audi that Jason had never seen before. He assumed it was Barbara's, waiting, peering up at the windows of the house, wondering if the lights would have disturbed someone.

Nothing.

As with car and burglar alarms, security lights were largely useless because everyone ignored them. With alarms, no one ever thought, 'Oh the Smiths opposite are being burgled,' they just assumed one of them had drunkenly stumbled home late and forgotten the code.

With security lights, for the most part, people were so incompetent at fitting them that they flared on when a car drove past half a mile away. Jason suspected that Harry's security lights were more to stun anyone who might have got as far as he had. Any stray cat would likely set them off, so he probably ignored them, as any sensible person would.

The lights did at least show how majestic the house was. Two white pillars were attached to a Roman-style porch roof, covering a wide brown oak front door. It wasn't a mansion, but Jason guessed it had six or seven bedrooms from the number of upstairs windows. Downstairs, tall, wide windows offered a sweeping view of the manicured garden and water feature. It was expensive without being wildly extravagant, which pretty much summed Harry up.

Jason paused at the front door, wondering if he should try phoning again or simply ring the doorbell. Given the time and locked gates, he doubted Harry ever had unexpected visitors at this hour of the night. Feeling the chill, which only made the aches worse, Jason tried calling Harry again.

One ring, two rings, three rings. Dead line.

There really was nothing else for it – he'd come this far,

been this stupid and now all Jason could do was ring the doorbell. The small ivory-textured disc to the side of the door offered a satisfying old-fashioned ding-dong that echoed through the house and out onto the porch.

Behind, the floodlights switched themselves off, leaving Jason in darkness again. From inside there was no obvious movement through the frosted side window and no sound.

Jason suddenly had the creeping thought that he'd got the wrong house. He spent all his time being careful, planning ahead, not leaving himself open to trouble and then he'd found out his brother had a problem and everything had gone out of the window. He turned around again, seeing Harry's black car and reassuring himself. Definitely the right house.

Dinnnnnnnng-donnnnnnnng.

Still nothing. Jason peered around the overhang up towards the windows.

'Harry!'

He counted to thirty before ringing the bell for the third time and shouting Harry's name. After getting to nineteen, a light snapped on inside.

Jason felt his heart pumping – he had definitely crossed a line and there was no going back now. He stepped away from the front door as he heard footsteps and then a heavy bolt and a chain. The door swung open a crack but Jason couldn't see who it was.

He whispered loudly: 'Harry, it's Jason.'

With a creak, the door was opened fully, revealing Harry in a tartan check dressing gown that was tied tightly and came down to his knees. He had one hand in his pocket but removed it as he saw who was in front of him. His hair was usually neat and meticulously parted but now the grey strands were limp and unstyled. In the dim light from the inside, his wrinkles seemed more pronounced – like those of the ageing man he was, not the almost mythical figure Jason knew.

'Jason?' He sounded confused.

'I'm sorry, I—'

Harry held up a hand to stop him, opening the door slightly wider and turning at a squeak behind him. At the bottom of a winding staircase was Barbara: so much older than when Jason had last seen her. Then, she'd been blonde and stunning in the way some women in the Fifties were, keeping most of her looks and figure but with an air of grace and knowledge it was difficult for younger women to exude. In her dressing gown, her skin was almost as pale as her white hair. She gazed out in confusion at Harry and Jason.

'Go back to bed, dear,' Harry said. 'I'll deal with this.'

She was still staring at Jason, perhaps wondering if she knew him, but she nodded and turned without a word, padding back up the marble-looking stairs.

Harry held the door open. 'You better come in.'

The floor was white and hard, similar to the stairs. Harry closed the front door and immediately led Jason through a side door into a room with red walls and a matching wooden border that was very similar to his office at the casino. His slippers were woollen with a brown criss-cross pattern, barely making a sound as he patted along the floor.

Around the walls were bookcases filled with hardbacks,

except for one side that had photographs on the wall. Jason only noticed he was staring at them when Harry spoke.

'That was taken many, many years ago.'

The picture showed a much younger Harry sporting a slicked-back dark quiff and bushy sideburns, wearing a brown suit with wide flares. Barbara was in her wedding dress, looking stunning, as they both saluted the photographer with a glass of champagne.

'Different days,' Harry continued. 'Before this place, before anything really.'

Jason turned to see Harry standing next to a large globe. He flipped the lid open, revealing a drinks cabinet. He held up a thick crystal glass. 'Do you want something?'

'I've got to drive.'

Harry nodded but reached into the bowl, tugging out three bottles one after the other, scanning the labels and then choosing a whisky.

'I'm usually dead to the world by half eleven,' Harry said, not elaborating but leaving the message clear.

'I'm sorry, I—'

Harry turned with the unscrewed bottle in his hand. He nodded at Jason's clothes. 'What happened to you?'

Jason peered down to see the smeared blood on his denim jacket. He didn't know if it was his or the bed and breakfast manager's. 'That's sort of why I'm here.'

Harry spun back to the globe, poured himself a generous measure, and then waved Jason across to two leather-backed armchairs. He eyed Jason again. 'For God's sake, don't get blood on the material. Barbara will blow her top.'

Jason took off his jacket, folded it over so the worst of

the blood was covered, and then laid it carefully on the floor.

'It's my brother . . .'

Before he could finish, Harry tutted and looked away towards the large curtains. 'Is that something you really need to bring to me at this time of night?'

'He's missing.'

'You're sure he's not just run away with a girlfriend, or gone on holiday?'

'There's more . . .'

Harry tutted again. 'Oh, Jason . . . how can two siblings be so different? You don't stand out, you have a good head. Your brother . . .'

'I think he owes money to Richard Hyde.'

Harry didn't react, other than smacking his lips and taking a drink of his whisky. He held the liquid in his mouth, taking a breath through his nose before swallowing. Jason watched the side of his face, looking for anything – a sign that he was angry, furious even. Instead there was only calm.

After swallowing, he pursed his lips and nodded slowly. 'That's an awkward situation. Does Mr Hyde know he's your brother?'

'I really don't know.'

'How much?'

'Two thousand, five hundred. I've got the money.'

Harry had two more mouthfuls, each time holding the liquid in his mouth before swallowing. Without a word, he stood and crossed to the drinks cabinet, pouring himself more and returning to his seat.

'You're smart enough to know that it's not about the money.'

'I know.'

Another mouthful. Another pause. Harry's voice was slightly croakier when he responded. 'When did he go missing?'

'Yesterday afternoon – Wednesday. He missed an appointment to pay the money back on Tuesday. He's been gone for thirty-odd hours.'

'I'll make some inquiries.'

Jason couldn't stop himself breathing out in relief. Harry and Richard Hyde might have a rivalry but there was respect too. They could be in the same room without violence, or even threats. There had even been photographs of them in the local paper shaking hands or posing near to each other at various civic functions.

Jason pressed his hands on the arms of the chair ready to push himself up when Harry spoke again. 'Has my delivery been made yet?'

'I got sidetracked because of Chris. I haven't forgotten.'

Harry continued staring towards the curtains, the lip of the glass touching his mouth. 'You do remember I requested it be made as soon as possible?'

'I know.'

'It's important to me.'

'I know.'

He finally turned to face Jason, their eyes meeting for the first time since Jason had been invited in. There wasn't anger there, simply a matter-of-fact gaze of stone.

'I'm afraid my inquiries may have to be delayed until my delivery has been made. I always said that brother of yours would get you into trouble.'

20

Jason pressed his foot down on the accelerator as he passed the fifty miles an hour sign. The revs blistered through the engine as the speedometer touched fifty but not beyond. The vehicle was unfamiliar, the steering not as responsive as on his own, but the acceleration was ridiculous. With his, he would practically have to stamp on the pedal to make it shoot forward; with this, the merest nudge of his foot made it surge ahead. For trying to stay under the speed limit and not be noticed, it was a nightmare.

In the passenger seat, Chris was apparently unable to sit still, wriggling like a child ready to ask how much longer the journey would take. 'Wow, man – did you hear that guy's knee pop?'

Jason didn't want to have this conversation but was resigned to it. 'I also heard him tell us everything we asked,' he said sternly. 'There was no need to hit him.'

'I thought that's what we were supposed to be doing?' Chris replied. 'You said he owed money, so we were giving him a reminder it was due. Bang!'

'How do you think he's going to be able to get that money together if he can't walk?'

'I dunno, man, I just thought he was looking at me funny—'

'You had a ski mask covering your face and you were twirling a baseball bat with the top sawn off. How do you think he should look at you?'

Chris didn't reply for a moment and when he did, there was clearly no regret in his voice. 'I just think that noise was cool. Like a sort of splat and a pop. How much do you think we'll get paid for this?'

Jason stopped at a red traffic light. The road was deserted in all four directions. 'We'll get what we get. You don't deserve anything.'

'Why not?'

'Because I didn't give you a signal to hit anything, let alone shatter the poor bastard's kneecap.'

'I thought he was—'

'Looking at you funny is not a reason to hit someone. You have to judge a situation. Some people need that threat, some just need a talking to. For some, you need to talk about their families, others are more worried about themselves. You want them to pay – if you put them in hospital, they can't. It's about judgement.'

'All right, I'm sorry. What else do you want me to say?'

Jason didn't reply. The light turned green and he eased away into the night. It didn't matter whether Chris apologised, it would be Harry that Jason had to speak to the following day. This was a simple job, one he'd done plenty of times over the past couple of years, yet this time had been a complete disaster. Jason didn't need to wait to know that the man would end up in hospital. He'd tell the nurses he'd fallen down the stairs, or something similar, but there was no way he'd be able to continue going about his business. That meant the money he'd promised would be with them before the weekend had no chance of appearing, which meant Harry would be angry at Jason – all because of stupid Chris and his lack of judgement.

That was only part of the story, of course, because the only reason Chris had been there in the first place was because of Jason.

Stupid, stupid, stupid.

The roads were eerily quiet, a smattering of stray animals and pub kick-outs staggering home. Jason kept half an eye on the speedometer, making sure he was under the limit just in case there was a police car waiting around the corner. They were still in their dark clothes and needed to switch those and the car before he'd feel safe.

In the passenger seat, Chris was still wriggling, but because of the lack of anything to look at through the window, he was now hunting through the glove box.

'Will you sit still?' Jason snapped.

'Sorry, I'm just . . . do you wanna go out after this, for a few drinks, like?'

'You're only sixteen!'

'There are a few places in town that don't bother about ID.'

'I don't care. If you're going to drink, do it round your mates' or somewhere else. It's bad enough at home, what with Mum . . . as she is.'

'I was only saying – it's been a good night, so we should celebrate.'

'It's *not* been a good night – you messed up.'

Jason was so angry, he was driving over the limit and had to ease off the accelerator.

Chris was peering out of the window again, not wanting Jason to turn and catch his eye. 'It wasn't *that* bad.'

'All you had to do was stand there and look menacing. You're a big enough lad, it should have been easy.'

'There's not much I can do now.'

Jason didn't reply. His brother did sound suitably chastened but that didn't change the fact that everything was going to have to be explained to Harry. Perhaps they'd get lucky and the bloke's injury looked and sounded worse than it was.

'Soooooo,' Chris said, drawing the word out, 'how much do you think it'll be?'

'I told you – it'll be whatever it is.'

'Don't you get told how much it is before a job?'

'We're not flipping burgers in McDonald's.'

'I know, I just thought—'

'It's a shame you didn't think back there.'

Chris didn't miss a beat. 'I just thought you might discuss an amount.'

'Don't worry about it. You'll get what you get.'

A short pause and then: 'What are you going to spend yours on?'

'I've not thought about it.'

'But you must have a few quid. You never seem to spend very much.'

Jason ignored the insinuation. Chris didn't know about his savings, no one did. If Chris knew about the six-figure amount, then he'd constantly be asking Jason for money, wanting to waste what was being put away for their own good. Jason wanted to take them away to Crete: both Chris and their mother, if possible. His mother at the very least. That's if they could get her off the sofa onto a plane.

'I know what I want,' Chris said.

Jason wanted to ignore him but the question slipped out. 'What?'

'Clarkey reckons his mate's cousin has this second-hand Ferrari for sale—'

'How much do you think you're getting? It'll be hundreds, nothing more.'

'I know but this is the start, isn't it?'

Jason didn't know how to let his brother down gently. This could have been the start, but it would now be the last job with which Chris was involved. With Harry, people only got one chance. Mess up and you were done. Complain and someone would remind you *why* you were done. Keep complaining and, well . . . people didn't do that. Jason wondered if his own lack of judgement in using Chris meant that he was now 'done' too. He'd only find out when he next saw Harry, or Carter.

'Anyway,' Chris continued, 'Clarkey's mate's cousin doesn't want that much for it because it needs a load of work doing. He'd probably take a few hundred up front and then—'

'You're not buying a Ferrari. You're too young to drive anyway.'

'I know but there's that aeroplane place out the back of

the rugby stadium. I'll be able to drive around there and then I can take my test when I'm old enough.'

'Are you listening? You're *not* buying a Ferrari, whether it's in pieces or not. You're *not* buying any car. You're not having anything that any other sixteen-year-old might not have.'

Chris went silent for a moment as Jason pulled into the back alley where the garages were. He got out of the car, opened the garage door, and then reversed in. With the garage door pulled almost closed, the pair of them stood in the narrow gap between the vehicle and the wall. Jason ordered Chris to change back into his own clothes and drop the dark things he had been wearing in a bin bag.

'What's going to happen to the clothes?' Chris asked.

'Stop asking questions.'

'It's not a hard one. Is there some laundrette somewhere where everyone takes their balaclavas, gloves and black trousers to be washed?'

'Just get changed and shut up.'

Chris did as he was told, with Jason changing too. Outside, he locked the garage door, put the bin bag into the back of his own car, and then they set off to head to Hulme. Chris wasn't that far away with his guess. Sometimes, if a job was particularly gory, they'd burn everything. Other times, he'd throw the dark items in with his normal wash and take it to the laundrette. Most of the people there were so desperate not to get into a conversation that they'd bury their faces in a magazine or book and not worry about what anyone else was up to.

As they neared home, Chris seemed unable to let it go. 'So how much do you think we'll get?'

'I told you – don't worry about it. You'll be paid and that's it.'

'But how much would you usually get for something like this?'

Jason risked a sideways glance away from the road towards his brother. 'I thought I told you what the first rule was?'

'I know, you said don't ask about any other jobs.'

Jason turned back to the road. 'So why are you asking?'

'I'm trying to work out how much I'll have.'

'Well, don't. Just leave it in a bank account and use it if you need it. Don't stand out, don't make it obvious.'

'How much do you have?'

'I told you not to ask.'

'But you've been doing . . . things . . . for ages. Say you got five-hundred quid a week for, like, five years, that's . . .'

Chris started counting on his fingers but Jason did the mental arithmetic without thinking – £130,000, which was a fair bit less than he actually had. Not only had he been doing jobs for Harry for longer than five years, it was, on average, more than five-hundred a week.

It wasn't long before Chris realised he didn't have that many fingers. '. . . I dunno, you'd have, like, two million quid or something.'

'Do you think that if I had two million, I'd still be living in that flat with you and Mum?'

'I dunno, you must have loads though. Why don't you buy a decent car, or something?'

Almost to illustrate the point, the suspension bobbed down and then up over a pothole, sending them bouncing out of the seats.

'Don't stand out,' Jason said.

'That's pretty boring. I think I'm going to make a list of things I want. A new phone would be good, then there are these sunnies that Clarkey's got . . .'

Jason zoned out, knowing there was no point in arguing. Using Chris had been a bad idea – *his* idea – but it wasn't one he'd repeat. All he could hope was that Harry realised it was an honest mistake and that was the end of it. One day, Chris was going to get him into some real trouble.

21

NOW

Jason gasped for breath, sitting straight up in bed, feeling the sweat on his brow coupled with the icy spider creeping along his back. Somehow, he was hot and cold at the same time. He twisted his way out of the bed covers, taking in his bedroom. The window was open again, allowing the freezing air in. The rubber band he'd looped around the handle was sitting neatly on the windowsill. Had he opened it the night before? Had he done it in his sleep? He couldn't remember.

Five past ten: somehow Jason had slept through the night and woken up later than he ever usually did. Outside the window, there were no kids, no old men kicking footballs, just one woman leaning against a lamppost having a conversation on her mobile phone. Was she someone Jason knew? She was black but it was hard to see anything else because her hood was up, her coat was tight and she was wearing gloves. She didn't peer up towards his flat either, so if she was watching him then there had to be someone else involved, telling her on the phone that he was in the window and she shouldn't look up, or else she'd give herself away.

Jason pulled the window closed and looped the rubber

band back into place. He found three more in his top drawer and stretched them all around the handle on the side and the catch at the bottom.

Something was seriously not right in his head.

It was just a woman on a phone, yet he couldn't shake that feeling of being watched. Knowing he was becoming suspicious simply made it worse, because it gave everything a second level – he was paranoid about being paranoid.

And what was going on with his window? It was nothing, insignificant, and yet it could only be him opening it. Why would he do so – and then why would he forget?

His clothes were folded tidily, as always, even though he couldn't remember doing it, but Jason went through his wardrobe to find something warmer than what he'd laid out. His bloodied top and jacket were hanging over the radiator, having been washed and scrubbed – something else he didn't remember doing when he got in. If he was a heavy drinker, at least he'd have an excuse, but the gaps in his memory were worrying. More than worrying.

What was going on?

He stared at himself in the mirror. Aside from the graze over his eye, he'd come out of everything at the guest house miraculously well. There was a slight darkening of skin around his shoulder joint but there were no other marks on him and the aches he'd felt at Harry's now seemed like a dream.

In the kitchen, Jason had a full glass of water, before checking his brother's room just in case. It was still empty and hadn't been slept in.

With no advertising card on the doormat, Jason headed

into the living room, where his mother was partially awake, leaning her head on the crook of the sofa where the arm met the backrest, watching the news.

Jason sat next to her, asking if she was all right, but the only thing she'd say was that she wanted more marmalade, toast and tea, so he returned to the kitchen. By the time he arrived back with a plate of toast and a steaming mug, she was asleep again. Jason put the food on the floor in case she woke up, covered her with a blanket, listened to the newsreader say how police were still looking for any witnesses in the Gupta blaze case, and then turned the television off.

Harry wasn't going to help him find Chris, neither was his mother – meaning he'd have to try something else.

Jason kept one eye on his rear-view mirror as he drove across the city from Hulme to Longsight. He parked on a quiet residential street close to the speedway stadium and waited, watching anyone who went past. Aside from the odd mother with pram, the morning was quiet. When he was almost certain he hadn't been followed, Jason got out of the car and did a lap of the estate, using all of the cut-throughs and shortcuts he knew about, sometimes running, sometimes walking, before finally emerging onto the main road. If anyone had managed to trail him, then they would have done a stunning job to remain unseen.

The cafe was a throwback greasy spoon: the type of place Harry would eulogise the loss of. 'All these chain coffee shops with their mocha-this and latte-thats, they're draining the soul out of our city, Jason, m'boy. Who else is going to take it back if not us? You can't trust the council – they're busy taking back-handers for planning permission.'

Jason liked places like this for another reason – because of the van and lorry drivers who passed through, no one paid anyone else a blind bit of attention. The regulars would have their smiles and 'usuals' from the owner but he could be as anonymous as he wanted – no CCTV, no one keeping debit card receipts. It was cash only, accept it or sod off to Starbucks.

After ordering a full English and tea, Jason slipped into a back corner booth, away from the windows. At one point, the place had been done up like an American diner, but it didn't look as if it had been renovated any time recently. The leather seats sagged, the tables were covered in brown films of grease and spilled teas, with the black-and-white checked floor a mass of chipped and missing tiles.

Jason's food arrived just as the door jangled and Natalie walked in, dressed completely differently from the past two times he'd seen her. Like a chameleon, she had adapted to the place where he'd asked to meet her: loose jeans, jumper, hair tied back. She would stand out only because she was naturally pretty, not because she'd gone out of her way to.

After a small nod of acknowledgement in his direction, Natalie approached the counter, ordered, paid, and then slipped into the booth opposite Jason.

'Nice of you to call,' she said, fixing him with a stare.

'It's not what you think,' he replied.

'You said in the car that you'd never call but here we are.'

'My brother's gone missing. He got himself into a bit of trouble and . . .' Jason glanced away from her towards the window, not wanting to seem too vulnerable. '. . . I'm not sure where he is or how to get him back.'

'Isn't that something your master can deal with?'

'I don't have a master! Why do people keep saying that?'

Natalie didn't reply instantly but there was a hint of a smirk on her face. Jason didn't know where his outburst came from – he didn't usually let his emotions show, let alone snap at people.

A young man in a white chef's smock broke the silence by shuffling out of the kitchen and approaching the table, two plates in hand. 'Two Englishes,' he said, plonking a plate in front of each of them, then turning to the counter and picking up two cups of tea, placing them on the table too. With a grunt that sounded a little like an 'all right?', he disappeared back into the kitchen.

Natalie picked up a slice of toast and dipped it in her egg yolk, seemingly happy to wait for Jason. He had asked her to come, after all.

Jason picked up his fork and stared at the plate, still not wanting to make eye contact. 'He can't do anything to help Chris.'

'Who can't?'

'You know who. Do we have to go through this?'

Natalie took another bite. 'Why can't your master do anything?'

Jason tensed his free hand under the table, keeping control. 'Because my brother owes money to Richard Hyde.'

'Ah.' She finished the first piece of toast, picked up her knife and fork and sliced into the black pudding. 'So what do you think I can do about it?'

'You're police, aren't you?'

'When did Chris go missing?'

'Wednesday afternoon – almost two days ago.'

'So report him as a missing person. Tell them where he was last seen, who with, all that type of stuff. Someone will crack on with it.'

'You know I can't do that.'

'Why not?' Natalie peeped up at Jason. 'Genuinely, why not? Your brother's not into anything he shouldn't be, is he?'

'Don't make me spell things out. He's in trouble and I'm coming to you for a favour.'

Natalie returned to her late breakfast, slicing into a sausage. 'That's an interesting choice of word.'

'What, "favour"?'

'It implies this is all reciprocal but from the conversation we had in the car, you made it very clear you didn't want anything to do with me. We spoke about your master but you refused to even name him. I asked you about some of the things which he might be involved with and you wouldn't reply. I spelled out what I might be able to do for you if you were to talk to me and my colleagues about the things you knew but you said you weren't interested.' She jabbed a fork in his direction. 'If you're looking for a favour, don't you think you should be offering me something?'

Jason suddenly wasn't hungry. His phone started to ring and he snatched it out of his pocket, hoping it might be

Chris, before remembering that he had Chris's phone too. Lucy's name flashed but he let it ring out.

Natalie's knife scratched across her now almost empty plate as she nodded towards the phone in Jason's hand. 'Problems?'

Jason pocketed it again. 'Is there anything you can do to help?'

'Report him missing.'

'I can't!'

Natalie ate the last of her egg before putting her cutlery on the table. 'What do you want me to do? If you won't report him missing, nothing can formally happen. It's not like I can get a search team together on the basis that your brother owes someone a few quid. The best I can do is go through a few channels and come back to you. That might take the whole weekend and he could be back by then.'

'Anything could happen over the next few days.'

Natalie slurped the remains of her tea, before returning the empty mug to the table. She'd polished everything off, with Jason barely touching his food or drink.

'So report him missing,' she said, rubbing the remaining toast crumbs from her hands onto the plate and shuffling sideways, ready to leave.

'Isn't there anything you can do?'

Natalie shrugged, standing and reaching for her jacket. 'If you want to work together, it's a two-way thing. That means you do something for me, I do something for you. I told you in the car what I wanted. Now, if you'll excuse me, I've got work to do. If you want a serious conversation, then you've got my number.'

22

For the few moments after Natalie had left, Jason had the idea of calling her back, asking exactly what she wanted to know, telling her the truth about Harry Irwell, and then letting her and her people go away and find his brother. It would be the ultimate madness, throwing aside everything he'd worked for in order to get his brother back – and that was *if* the authorities genuinely could do something, which he wasn't convinced of.

His other idea was to go to Harry and say that the police had been onto him – some smart, intelligent woman who acted as if she knew a lot – and that they were asking about his boss. So far, he'd said nothing but he was wondering if Harry could get Chris back now so that he didn't have to talk to Natalie any longer. That would only bring more awkward questions though – why had the woman targeted Jason? How had she found him? Jason didn't know the answers to either of those. Then he'd have to go through his meetings with her, line by line, as Harry and Carter dissected whether he'd given anything away. Then they'd wonder why he'd called her and become suspicious whether there was a deeper relationship there. Before long, Jason would be on the outside at best, at the bottom of the canal with rocks tied to his limbs at worst.

The job that Harry wanted doing couldn't be completed

until it was dark; but in another twelve hours, it could be too late for Chris, not to mention the fact that Harry had said he'd only make inquiries then, which would be the start, not the end, of any search.

Jason tried to eat but his stomach was hurting, suspicion creeping through him that the man in the booth closest the window had been watching him and Natalie the entire time. Perhaps he'd taken photos on his phone and sent them off to Harry, Carter or someone else?

Jason sat tall in his seat and stared in the man's direction, noticing the boy and girl opposite him, each eating beans on toast. Were they his cover, or was it just a father taking his children out for lunch on a Friday? Why weren't they at school?

With a blink, Jason tried to forget them. It didn't matter – no one in here did, and he had to stop seeing demons in corners. No one had followed him, his car wasn't outside and nobody knew he was here, except Natalie – and she only knew because he'd called her.

But he still had a major problem that neither Harry, Natalie or anyone else he knew could help him with. That left just the one person he could go to.

The wipers rattled across Jason's windscreen. Murky grey skies and a vicious wind had rolled in as he'd been inside the cafe and mulched leaves and rubbish were whipping across the road.

He stopped at the traffic lights, the red burning into the now-afternoon, and stared at himself in the rear-view mirror. He looked a mess and needed a proper shower.

BEEEEEEEEEP!

Behind, the small Punto honked in annoyance and Jason blinked, realising the light was green. How long had he been staring at himself?

With a judder, the engine stalled and cars started to indicate around him. Finally he got going just before the light returned to amber, pulling onto the A62 and heading towards Failsworth, then past the ring road to the outskirts of Oldham. Jason had never had the need to come this far north and east of the city before. It was still in the wider Greater Manchester area but eight miles away from the city centre, ten miles from his house.

At first the buildings became more spread out but then he hit the rows of garish yellow-, pink-, green- and black-fronted takeaways on either side of the road. On the few occasions Harry had talked of this district, he'd always spoken of the 'Pakis' and the 'terrorists' that ran it. Jason had been expecting minarets and an exclusively non-white crowd of people and was surprised to see the type of red-brick community housing similar to that in his area. Along the sides of the roads and in the cars around him, the ethnic mix wasn't too different to what he was used to either, leaving him wondering if Harry was genuinely mistaken about the type of community this was, or if he was deliberately trying to portray it in a bad light.

Jason followed the signs to the centre and then navigated the complicated mess of lanes until following more arrows towards the out-of-town retail park. The huge units were a mix of boarded-up fronts and backlit store signs but the car park was almost deserted: a large stretch of empty, drenched tarmac. He did a full lap of it, making a mental note of the quickest way to get to the exits just in case.

He parked close to one of the traffic islands that separated the shops and restaurants from the huge building that backed onto the main road. As the drizzle continued, banging off his car's roof and dribbling across the windscreen, Jason stared towards the flashing lights and neon strip that ran around the roof of the Crown Casino. He knew that the size would be carefully measured to fit within gambling laws, with designated spaces assigned to gaming tables and machines. It was amazing how much knowledge he had picked up about planning and gambling rules, simply by being in the room when Harry and Carter discussed things.

A handful of people parked their cars and rushed through the rain to get inside. Jason knew this was a stupid idea but what other option did he have?

He pulled his jacket over his head and dashed towards the casino entrance, only looking up when he was under cover. His eyes skimmed across the upper walls and ceilings, looking for the security cameras and trying to remember where they were. If he was going to do this, he had to do it properly, so he made a full lap of the floor, ensuring he was filmed in as many places as he could be. Intermittently, he stopped, peering closely at one of the tables, or a slot machine, then he entered the restaurant and paid for a cup of tea using his debit card. If anything bad was to happen, he wanted to make sure there was a trail left to prove he had been here.

After paying for the drink, Jason did a lap of the eating

area, finding the table in the centre that was covered by the most cameras.

Then he waited.

He'd only had two sips when a thick-set, barrel-chested man dressed like a penguin in a sharply pressed dark suit and a bright white shirt emerged from a door disguised as part of the wall. Jason weighed him up quickly: the ear-piece, thick fingers and square jaw. A fight between him and Carter would be interesting to watch.

The man headed straight for Jason, stopping on the other side of the table. 'Your presence has been requested.'

Without replying, Jason put his almost-full cup down and stood, following as the man returned the way he'd come, leading the way through the concealed door. The tunnel beyond was dark, with faint overhead bulbs showing the way but not throwing any light on where they actually were. Jason continued following until they emerged through another hidden door into a bright corridor. The suited man turned, walking to the end and then knocking on a door.

'Come in.'

Inside, Jason had to do a double-take at the wood panelling, dark walls and large oak table. Aside from the slightly different shades and layout, it could be Harry's office in the city centre.

Richard Hyde sat behind the desk, sipping from a china cup. As he glanced up at Jason, he placed the cup delicately back on its saucer, twisting the handle to make it perpendicular to the edge of the table. He was wearing a smart pinstripe suit with a pink tie in a thick Windsor knot. His hair was darker and thicker than Harry's, swept sideways at the front. Jason stood awkwardly, looking down as Hyde slightly adjusted his rimless spectacles, peering over the top and then nodding to the seat opposite.

Jason sat, taking in the rest of the room: a bar in the corner, a large window with the curtains half-pulled, a chandelier. The similarities to Harry's office were uncanny, with the wide bank of monitors built into the back wall the only major difference. Each screen was showing a different angle of the gaming floor and Jason could see the ones pointing at the spot in the canteen where he'd been sitting minutes earlier. At Harry's place, the monitors and record-ing equipment were in a separate room.

Hyde's eyes were a sharp, focused brown: 'You want the king, you get the jester.'

Jason didn't know how to reply, so he remained silent. The suited man stood behind him, his presence intimidat-ingly close.

Hyde adjusted his glasses so he was looking through, rather than over, them. 'Can't Mr Irwell do his own dirty work these days?'

'I'm here for me.'

'Are you indeed?' Jason shrugged as Hyde pursed his lips. 'Brave boy. What do you want?'

Jason nodded backwards towards the suited man. Hyde's eyes flicked upwards and then he nodded.

A moment later, with a small click of the door, they were alone.

Hyde took another sip from the cup and then re-aligned it on the saucer. 'So, to what do I owe the pleasure of this unexpected visit?'

'I'm here for Chris Green.'

'Who?'

'My brother.'

This time, Hyde shrugged, which didn't seem quite right given his expensive suit. His glasses had found their way to the end of his nose again and he was watching Jason un-blinkingly over the top. 'What about him?'

Jason reached into his jacket pocket and took out the money that had been in the boot of his car. He had drawn the rest out from the bank after talking to Natalie. He placed two thousand-pound bundles on the table and then took two more piles from his inside pockets. 'This is your two and a half, plus one and a half interest. I want him back.'

Hyde stared at the money and then took another sip of his drink. After glancing up at Jason, he took his glasses off, licking his lips, eyes narrowing. Jason was trying to read the man's face. It didn't seem as if he was deliberately draw-ing things out but it was almost an entire minute before he responded. When he did, it wasn't what Jason expected.

'What do you think is going on here? Is this some sort of trick?'

'Why would it be?'

'If this is Mr Irwell's idea of a joke—?'

'I told you – I'm here for me.'

'Yes, you said . . . your brother . . . except I have no idea who Chris Green is, nor why you're offering me a pile of money. If you want to gamble it, there's an entire floor out there.'

Jason straightened himself, trying to remain calm, not

wanting to crack or get angry in front of the other man. 'I want him back.'

'So you said but I don't know why you think I have him. Maybe you should start at the beginning?'

Jason took a breath. 'We each know about the Prince of Wales . . .'

'It's a guest house in which I have a stake.'

'My brother has some debts there and he went missing two days ago.'

Hyde peered down at the money again and finished off his tea with a slurp. At first he lined up the handle parallel to the table as before, then he twisted it until it was at a ninety-degree angle. He nodded approvingly. 'It might surprise you to learn that I don't know every in and out of what happens around this city, although I heard that someone did quite the number on the manager of the establishment you mention.' His eyes narrowed, focusing on Jason, who had to look away. 'I could use someone like that – someone with the front to march into the lion's den, so to speak.'

'I don't know what you're talking about,' Jason said.

'How is Mr Irwell? Keeping well, I trust?'

'He's fine.'

'It's dangerous times out there – we all know what happened to Nicholas Long and his son with his city-centre empire. This is all a complicated game, a dangerous game – but a game nonetheless.'

'I'm only interested in what you know about my brother.'

'Then I'm afraid you've come to the wrong place. I can

make a few inquiries but I'll tell you man to man that I know nothing about this.'

Jason stared at him, looking for a hint of a lie that he couldn't see. 'Could someone else be acting without your say-so?' he asked.

A small smile slipped onto Hyde's face. 'I might not know every minute detail of what happens in the city but I would know that. If your brother *is* missing, then it's nothing to do with me.'

'The Prince of Wales manager said—'

'I don't care what he said. I'm telling you that what you think happened is not true.'

Jason tried to suppress a shiver, not knowing if it was from a draught, or if it was something deeper. He stood abruptly, accidentally knocking over his seat and then struggling to disentangle his legs from the chair's. He lumbered towards the door before Hyde's low, calm voice sounded.

'Mr Green.'

He turned, one hand already on the door. 'What?'

'You forgot your money.'

'Keep it – he owes it regardless of anything else.'

Hyde smiled again, fully this time. 'How much do you know about me, Mr Green?'

'I . . .'

'Not much, I suppose – only what you've been told. My children were sent away when they were young because I didn't want them being drawn into anything. That was my decision and I've had to live with it. I might be many things but I don't get involved when it comes to other people's families. If you leave a picture of your brother, I'll ensure it's circulated and that none of my people will deal with him in future. I'll even ban him from my gambling and betting establishments if you want. Say the word and I'll extend that to pubs and clubs as well. As for his debts, the slate is clean. We'll call it a show of respect from me to you because it takes some countenance to come here in the way you have.'

Jason watched for a hint of deception but there was nothing. He maintained eye contact, squeezing the money back into his pockets and then turned to leave. This time he wasn't called back.

23

Jason remembered hardly anything of the drive home. The road, other cars, traffic lights, rain and pedestrians were simply a backdrop as he reran the conversation with Richard Hyde over and over in his mind. Was there something else he should have asked? Had he missed a hint at what was going on? And what did Hyde mean when he'd asked how much Jason knew about him?

It was true that all Jason's information came from what Harry and Carter had spent years talking about – but could the reality be so different to what he knew? Or what he thought he did?

Hyde controlled business in the north of the city with Harry working in the south. Every now and then, they might encroach on each other's territory and a message needed to be sent. Was Hyde implying that wasn't true? If so, what had everything been for?

The rain summed up Jason's mood as he arrived home. Schools were beginning to empty for the weekend but the streets were clear aside from a handful of uniform-clad children kicking their way through puddles. Jason parked and hurried up the stairs to his flat. He had the key pressed to the lock when a wave of déjà vu fluttered through him. He glanced towards the stairs at the opposite end of the balcony, hearing a low moan. The image of the dealer he'd beaten dropped into his mind again: was he somehow back, slumped in the stairwell, groaning for mercy?

Jason walked slowly towards the sound, listening for another hint of the groaning but there was only the rattle of the rain on the roof.

As he peered around the corner of the concrete, down towards the landing between the two sets of steps, the first thing Jason saw was the blood spots on the wall. He'd not been to this end of his apartment block since he'd kicked the dealer down the stairs. It wouldn't be much of a surprise if it hadn't been cleaned since – and yet the marks seemed so red. So new.

He moved down the stairs quickly just as the rain became harder, until it felt as if it was rattling even the concrete.

'Jaaaaaaaaaaason . . .'

It sounded like the elements were whispering his name.

He turned at the midway point on the stairs, seeing a flash of the dealer's crumpled body at the bottom, but things were different this time. A third of the way down, another body lay, curled into a ball, a vague moan seeping into the drumbeat of the torrent.

'Chris?'

The shape turned slowly, head rolling across the sharp corners of the concrete. Chris's face was a mess of cuts and grazes. Blood had dried underneath his mashed nose, with a long slice arched over his eyebrow. Along his hairline, deep red liquid had scabbed, matting the hairs together. Jason crouched at his side, not knowing what to do.

'Chris?'

His brother groaned and stretched his left arm out, cradling his right across himself.

'Can you stand?' Jason asked.

Chris's eyes opened, the lids and lashes sticky with blood.

His reply was a croaked whisper, almost drowned out by the rain lashing the building. 'Don't know.'

Jason sat on the step and gently wrapped an arm around his brother's back, slowly standing and doing his best to pull Chris to his feet. They stumbled towards the wall but Chris latched his left arm around Jason's upper back, leaning on him for support. Step by slow, agonising step, they made their way to the top, Chris moaning each time he had to raise his leg. Progress along the walkway was even slower, Jason stopping each time his brother squealed in pain.

Finally inside the flat, Jason was relieved to hear the gentle snoring coming from the living room: at least that was one less thing he'd have to deal with. He lowered Chris carefully onto his bed and then disappeared into the kitchen, pouring a glass of water and filling the washing-up bowl with lukewarm water, before taking a flannel and painkillers from the bathroom.

In the bedroom, Chris was laid flat on his back, staring at the ceiling. Jason carried everything in and then sat on the bed next to his brother.

'Where does it hurt?' Jason asked.

'Arm.'

'I'll take you to the hospital if you need it.'

'No.'

'You might have a broken arm, or ribs, or—'

'No!' Chris's voice was more forceful this time, more like his usual one. He gradually shuffled his way up the bed, resting his head on the pillow until he was almost sitting. His right arm was still wrapped across his front. 'Too many questions if we go.'

Jason pressed three paracetamol tablets into Chris's left hand and held up the glass of water. 'At least take these. They'll help a little.'

Chris did as he was told but seemed to struggle swallowing, chewing and grimacing instead as he sloshed water down his top. In the end, Jason held the glass for him, trying his best to angle the liquid into his brother's mouth. Their efforts were so poor that even Chris started to smile, before stopping himself and saying how much it hurt.

Jason wet the cloth and dabbed gently at the areas of dried blood on his brother's face.

'You're going to have to take your clothes off,' Jason said as he rinsed the flannel out in the water.

'I don't think I can lift my arm.'

'I can cut them off if you prefer?'

'No – Kat bought me this shirt. She'd go mental.'

It was only a simple-looking grey T-shirt underneath a ripped jacket but Jason helped ease the tops off, slowly raising his brother's arm and supporting his head. Underneath, Chris's torso was a mass of black, purple, blue and yellow. Jason didn't know much about medical matters but from the grimaces, the pain was in his brother's shoulder, rather than his arm.

Jason ran his fingers across Chris's chest and abdomen,

but the only other sharp flinch came as he touched the top of his brother's ribs on the right-hand side. Other than that, it was more a constant grumble of discomfort.

In the kitchen, Jason emptied the ice-cube tray into a tea towel and returned to the bedroom, telling his brother to hold it to his injured shoulder as he continued to wipe the blood away from Chris's face.

Perhaps surprisingly considering he rarely did what anyone told him, Chris did exactly as was asked.

'What happened at the park?' Jason asked.

'How do you know I was there?'

'I visited your probation officer.'

'Oh.'

'He seemed okay . . .'

Chris instinctively tried to shrug but winced as he forgot about the injury. He wriggled the tea towel on his shoulder. 'What does it look like?'

'Like a rainbow.'

'This is going to take some explaining to Kat.'

'You've got to call your probation officer too. He said—'

'I will.'

Jason paused, wondering if his brother was ready for a full-on interrogation. The last thing he wanted was another argument. 'So,' he said slowly, 'what happened?'

Chris grimaced again as he tried, and failed, to fidget into a slightly more comfortable position. 'This is cold,' he said.

'It's ice, what do you expect? It's for the swelling – not that it'll do much if there's a broken bone in there. I don't think it's dislocated if that's any relief. If you're lucky, it's just bruised.'

Chris closed his eyes. 'It's not much relief.'

'You're wheezing slightly, so you might have a rib or lung injury. You should really—'

'I'm not going to the hospital.'

Jason didn't want to keep pushing it. Getting his brother looked over by a doctor was going to invite uncomfortable questions for them both. 'So, what happened at the park?'

'Let it go.'

'I don't want to let it go – tell me.'

'What good is it going to do?'

'Not much but I still want to know.'

Chris sighed, wriggling the tea towel and opening his eyes again, staring at a spot somewhere over Jason's head. 'I was litter-picking close to these bushes. They give you these stabby stick things—'

'Is that a technical term?'

Chris grinned, winced, then grinned again. 'You spike all the rubbish and put it in these bags you carry around. We were on a break, so I'd nipped away from the others to have a fag. I was wandering along the road near the nursery using my phone and there was this grey van parked there. This guy leant out of the driver's window – I thought he was going to ask directions or something, then the next thing I heard the side doors opening and it all went dark.'

'How do you mean?'

Chris temporarily released the tea towel, reaching for the glass of water and taking a drink.

'I don't really know. Someone grabbed my arms and I think they put a hood over my head. Someone was holding my mouth too. There must have been at least three of them.'

'Did you recognise the driver?'

'No, it was too quick.'

'What happened?'

Chris took a breath and looked away again. 'The ice is melting.'

'It does that – stop changing the subject.'

Jason couldn't remember seeing his brother cry but Chris's Adam's apple began to bob and he was blinking rapidly. Neither of them spoke as he composed himself. When he replied, it was as if the moment had never happened. 'They put cable ties round my wrists and ankles.' He rotated his left wrist to show the slim fleshy scars cut into the skin. 'I think I was in this cage-type thing in the back of the van. The ground was hard and cold but I kept bumping into what felt like chicken wire.'

'Did they say anything?'

'No – the exhaust was loud, plus it kept bumping up and down. When it stopped, someone pulled me out of the van and there was this sliding door sound. When they removed the hood, I was in what I think was a garage. There was this sort of carpet on the walls and ceiling, then see-through plastic sheeting covering it. I thought . . . well, you only have sheeting like that for one reason.'

Jason gulped. 'You're here though.'

Chris removed the dripping tea towel from his shoulder, offering it to his brother. 'Just about.'

Jason took the towel and threw it in the washing-up bowl. 'How many were there when they took your mask off?'

'Just two. There must have been more before that but I suppose they drove off. They both had masks on.'

'Did either of them say anything?'

'No one said a word the entire time.'

'I know about the Prince of Wales.'

Chris twisted slightly on the bed, sitting up fully, not wanting to have the conversation. 'Oh.'

'I know how much money you owe.'

'Not much use now, is it?'

Jason felt uncomfortable, knowing that if he'd given his brother the money when he'd asked for it, this could have been avoided. 'What were you doing at the B and B?'

'This and that.'

There was that phrase again. Jason wanted to ask for clarification but there was no point – he used it himself to evade the truth and so did his brother.

'Was it them who took you?'

Chris started to shrug again but caught it in time to stop himself recoiling. 'I guess so. I told you: nobody said anything. I kept saying I'd get the money but no one replied. They just, well . . .' He pointed towards his damaged shoulder. 'What day is it?'

'Friday.'

'They kicked shite out of me for a bit, then blindfolded me again and cable-tied my hands behind my back. I heard the sliding door, which is why I think it was a garage, then it was quiet. They put this plastic cylinder thing in my mouth that I couldn't get out, so I couldn't shout. All I could do was bumble around in the dark. In the end, I just gave up and lay down. They'd come back every few hours and start again.'

Jason didn't say it but it seemed to him as if whoever had carried out the beating knew what they were doing. The isolation and the sheeting were there for the scare factor but they hadn't seemingly caused any serious damage. If they'd wanted to kill or severely injure Chris, they could have done. It was the same thing he'd explained to his brother when their assignment had gone wrong – by smashing the man's kneecaps, they'd stopped him being able to get the money he owed. Whoever had beaten Chris hadn't made the same mistake.

Richard Hyde had told him he had nothing to do with this, which, coupled with the fact none of the abductors had asked Chris for money, left an awkward question: if Hyde was telling the truth then who had taken his brother? And why?

'You could have just given me the money,' Chris said, out of the blue.

Jason didn't want to tell him anything about Hyde. 'You wouldn't tell me what it was for.'

'I'm your brother – isn't that enough?'

'Perhaps I know what to do with money better than you – maybe I'm trying to do things for your own good?'

Chris pointed at his pulped face. 'Was this for my own good?'

24

With Chris asleep and his mother drinking and asking for toast in front of the television, Jason thought about getting his team together to complete Harry's task. It wouldn't take much organising but he wasn't in the mood for what was needed, let alone the fact he was unhappy that Harry had refused to help find Chris.

He wanted to get away from the claustrophobia of the flat, his mother's requests and the increasingly overbearing sense that he was trapped by them.

At least he had somewhere to go.

Lucy opened the door with a grin. In one hand she was holding a cereal bowl, which she raised into the air. 'You hungry?'

'For cereal?'

Jason stepped across the threshold, closing the door behind him and feeling the heat as before, like standing in front of an open oven. Lucy took another mouthful and turned, talking over her shoulder: 'What's wrong with cereal?'

'It's almost seven in the evening.'

'What's your point?'

'I've never seen anyone eating cereal at teatime before.'

Lucy grinned, thrusting the spoon into the air. 'You've never lived!'

She was wearing a red skirt that ended just above her knee and a loose T-shirt with a logo on the front that Jason didn't recognise. Her hair was in a loose ponytail, swinging from side to side as she walked. Lucy put the bowl and spoon down in the kitchen and led Jason into the living room. It was set up as it had been before: the chair in the centre and the easel in the corner. They assumed their positions with Jason draping his jacket over the sofa and putting on the hat that had been on the seat waiting for him.

'Sorry I couldn't come over earlier,' Jason said. 'I was working and it was busy.'

Lucy was twirling the paintbrush around, mixing something he couldn't see. 'I had nothing on this evening anyway, plus there's never anything on TV on Fridays.' She glanced up, catching his gaze, her eyes more green than blue compared to the last time he'd seen her. 'You look tired.'

'Mum's not been well and I think my brother's caught it.'

'Oh, do you live with them?'

Jason had been so caught up in creating the first lie about why he could be tired that he'd spilled the truth about one of the other things he'd been concealing.

He replied with something that wasn't quite a lie, though it stopped him from sounding completely pathetic. 'I'm trying to save money – it's so easy to blow it all on rent or a mortgage but I figured that if I saved as much as I could, I might be able to get something that's actually quite nice.'

Lucy began dabbing her brush on the canvas. 'Sounds sensible – but I couldn't live with my parents any longer. The odd weekend back at home is enough but it's impossible to relax.'

She shifted on her seat, leaning in closer to the canvas and opening her legs slightly. Jason tried to stop himself from looking but the pull was too much. His eyes jumped down to her thigh and then quickly away again. He couldn't see anything, not really, but felt a wave of excitement he wasn't used to. Was she flirting with him? Trying to see how he might react? The paintbrush continued to zip across the canvas, her top half out of sight. Jason risked another glance, lingering on the creamy colour of her skin.

With a slight adjustment, her legs were closed again and Jason turned his gaze back to the wall where he told himself he should have been looking the entire time.

It was only when Lucy poked her head around the side of the easel that Jason realised she had been talking to him.

'Sorry?' he said.

'I asked what you've been up to since Wednesday morning.'

'Not much – just work and looking after Mum.'

He felt a dribble of sweat slither down his back. It was warm but this felt like something else he wasn't used to: nerves. From the sofa, something buzzed in his jacket pocket.

'You should get that if you need to,' Lucy said.

Jason reached across and picked up his coat, taking his phone out of the pocket and checking the screen – no message. Confused, he realised he still had his brother's phone in the other pocket. He checked the front but didn't unlock it, even though he knew the code. Now his brother was safe, it felt more of an invasion of privacy than it had before. He put it away again and threw the jacket back onto the sofa. When he looked up, Lucy had been watching him, paintbrush angled as if in mid-flow.

'Do you have two phones?' she asked.

'One of them is my brother's. He dropped it and I forgot to give it back to him.'

Her eyes narrowed slightly before she turned back to the canvas. 'I went out with this lad – Martin – who I later found out had two phones. There was his main one which everyone had the number for, then a pay-as-you-go one which he kept to himself. It was in my first year here. We were never in each other's pockets, so we'd go out with our own friends, but I found out that he'd chat up other girls and if they were remotely interested, or drunk enough, I suppose, he'd give them that number.'

'How did you find out?' Jason asked.

Swish, swish, swish of the paintbrush.

'His best friend told me. I say "best" but how good a mate could he have been?'

'Why would he do that?'

'He was trying to cop off with me. We were at some house party and were the last ones standing after everyone had either passed out or gone home. He put a hand on my leg and I pulled away, saying I didn't want to. Then he said I shouldn't be so loyal because Martin wasn't to me. After that, the whole story came out. I don't really know how I missed it – most of his friends knew, apparently, then he'd have both phones out in lectures or at his flat: texting me from one, his other girlfriends from the other.'

'What happened to his friend?'

Lucy stopped painting and peered around the canvas. Her knees parted slightly again but Jason forced himself not to look. 'Are you asking if I shagged him?'

'No, God, no. I just meant—'

Her head bobbed back behind the canvas again. 'It's okay, I know what you meant.'

It was a good job she did, because Jason wasn't sure. In fact, he probably had been about to ask in a non-direct way whether she'd slept with Martin's friend. When he glanced down, her knees were touching once more.

'It really is my brother's phone,' he said.

Swish, swish, swish.

Lucy paused before replying. An agonising, judgemental silence on a statement Jason hadn't needed to make.

'You don't need to answer to me.'

Jason opened his mouth to respond but stopped himself. Despite everything he'd done over the past few years, even the past twenty-four hours, he knew he had no idea how to talk to the opposite sex. Had she told him the two-phone story simply because he had a pair, or was she testing him in some way? As the silence continued, her brushstrokes shortened.

He was beginning to panic that he had to say something in order to not seem evasive. 'Have you had many boy-friends?' he blurted out.

Swish, swish, swish. Lucy put the paintbrush down and dabbed her finger into one of the pots next to her. 'I'm only twenty-two – how many boyfriends do you think I've had?'

Ick.

Jason really had a talent for talking himself into trouble. Too high and she'd be offended, too low and she might think he thought she was ugly, or fat or something. She wasn't either but this was getting ridiculous. What counted as a boyfriend? Holding someone's hand and hanging around with them when you were both twelve, did that count? Did a couple of nights out mean two people were seeing each other, or was that something more casual?

'Er . . .'

Lucy bent to pick up her pot of water from the floor. As she did, her T-shirt flopped down, showing off a red bra that left Jason open-mouthed and blank at what he was supposed to be answering. Was she doing this on purpose – or was she simply comfortable in her own home, wearing her own clothes, and he was taking advantage?

She swilled her finger in the water and began dabbing at a different colour. Jason forced himself to focus on the wall behind her.

'If you don't want to guess, how about you tell me how many girlfriends you've had.'

Jason tried to think of a number that wasn't too high but blabbed out 'a few' before he knew what he was doing.

'How many's that?' Lucy peeped around the canvas and must have noticed something in the way he was sitting because she didn't turn back to her painting instantly. 'You can tell me the truth.'

'I suppose no one, really . . .'

Jason could feel her staring at him but refused to stop watching the wall over the top of her head.

'You've never had a girlfriend?'

'Not like that.'

'But you've—'

'Yes.'

'Right . . . sorry.'

Lucy disappeared behind the easel again and Jason let go of his breath, risking a glance at her and then returning to gazing at the wall. He shouldn't have snapped – better yet, he should have come up with a number. How hard was it to say 'two' or 'three', or something that made him sound like a normal person without being some ridiculous lothario when he clearly wasn't? Or, worse, a complete loser?

Lucy dabbed her finger in the water and picked the brush up again.

'I've only had two boyfriends if that makes you feel any better. They were both dicks – both cheaters. I told you about Martin but I was also seeing this lad called Ewan when I was seventeen. I thought we were going to be together forever – marriage, kids and all those other stupid things you think when you're in love for the first time. In the summer before my A levels, a whole bunch of us went off to Leeds for the festival. I was sharing a tent with Ewan but there were probably a dozen of us in total. We all camped in a circle and lit a fire in the centre. On the first night, we all ate, drank, sang and generally had a laugh. The next day, we'd gone down to the arena but my best mate, Susanna, said she was feeling ill and was going back for a kip. A bit later, Ewan said he was going to get some warmer clothes from his bag. He'd only been gone for a few minutes when I realised I'd left my phone in the tent too. By the time I got back there . . . well, you can guess the rest. It turned out they'd been at it the whole time we'd been together.'

'That's pretty shite.'

'For the best though. She got pregnant about six months later off a bloke who works at a petrol station. Ewan failed his exams and now works in some cafe. Last time I was home, I went in there and got him to make my drink. He was asking how I was, so I told him I was having the time of my life in Manchester. Bit of a lie, like, but close enough.' She paused and then laughed. 'Not that I'm stalking him or anything.'

After a few more swoops of the brush, Lucy put it down and stood, taking a step back and examining the painting.

'Happy?' Jason asked.

'It's coming along.'

'Can I see it?'

'Only when it's done.'

She sat again and dipped her thumb in a pot of dark paint. 'So why haven't you had a girlfriend then? You're not *that* disfigured.' She peered around the easel, grinning.

Jason found it hard not to return the smile. This time, the reply came naturally. 'Not found the right person, I suppose. Anyway, what about you? If you dumped that Martin in your first year, that's, what, two years back?'

She returned to the picture. 'Uni guys are all tight jeans and stupid hair. They're either going around quoting poetry, or – worse – writing it, or they're going on about football all the time.'

As she twisted her body, Lucy's T-shirt hung limply again, showing Jason the full outline of her red bra and a tantalising glimpse of what it was covering. Her eyes were fixed on her work and Jason couldn't resist any longer, tracing the curves with his eyes. It was only when she tugged her top back up that he realised she was watching him and that he must have been looking for far longer than he thought.

Jason's gaze darted back to the wall.

Lucy put the paintbrush down and reached into her pot of water, rinsing her fingers. She dried them on a cloth and then stood, holding her elbow. 'I think I need a rest. I'm not far from being finished.' She walked around the easel and then plucked the hat from Jason's head, spinning it onto the sofa. 'I probably need one more session if you're free some time next week. I'm busy this weekend.'

'I'm sure we can sort something.'

He reached out for his jacket.

'You leaving?' Lucy asked, taking a step backwards.

Jason hadn't thought it through: the motion to leave was instinctive because Lucy had finished what she was doing and he no longer felt useful. This was what he was always like when he'd finished a job – in, out, don't hang around.

Before he knew it, Jason was standing at Lucy's front door, jacket on, ready to leave. She stood in front of him, hair half tied back, half undone, a smeared hint of black paint on her chin.

'Shall I call you when I'm free?' Jason asked.

Lucy nodded but things felt awkward. Did she want him to stay? Should he say something? Try to kiss her? Wait to see what she did?

Why was it so difficult?

After a moment of not being sure, Jason turned and opened the front door. Uncertain what else to do, he patted her on the shoulder, which only confused things further. One hurried 'goodbye' later and he was on his way, wishing he had the ability to read minds.

25

Jason slept well, dreaming of Lucy and Crete. Suddenly the two were entwined in his mind. He wasn't just saving for himself, Chris and their mother: she was there too, even though he didn't really know her. There was something so real about her that he could barely focus on anything else. He hadn't lied when he said he'd been with women in the past but they had almost been dreams: drunken fumbles and paid-for regrets where he might as well have kept his eyes closed because none of it quite lived up to what he thought it could be. He couldn't remember any of their faces, yet he could blink and Lucy's shades of blonde hair and bluey-greeny-whatever-colour-they-were eyes were in front of him.

As he awoke to the chill of his bedroom, the window open again, it had all fallen into place. *She* was the adult: boyfriends, broken relationships and plans for the future. He was the petulant child still searching for a substitute father's approval.

Jason stood at his window and picked up the four elastic bands from the sill. It could only be him opening the window. He'd left a pair of socks in front of his bedroom door that would have been moved if anyone had entered. He must be sleepwalking and, for whatever reason, opening his window at the same time. There was no other explanation. Did that mean there was some deep-seated anxiety about which he needed to worry? It was certainly an odd thing to do.

He resisted the Saturday-morning urge to contact Lucy, making a different call instead. Not long after, Jason was sitting in the cafe, watching the door and nursing a black coffee – or Americano as the server had semi-sneered at him. He checked the clock above the door but it was still two minutes to ten.

The previous evening was on a constant loop in his mind: the hints of flesh, the fact Lucy had told him about her previous boyfriends and the look of what he was now certain was disappointment when he said he was leaving. He hadn't imagined it, had he? Hadn't just enjoyed the surreptitious glances when he didn't think she was looking? Perhaps she'd worn the skirt for him? And the T-shirt. And the bra . . .

With a rattle of the bell over the door, Natalie breezed in, perfectly on time, glancing quickly towards the brown leather armchair Jason was in and then approaching the counter. She was dressed for a Saturday-morning run: leggings, trainers and a tracksuit top with her hair in a tight ponytail. Moments later, she was opposite him with a bottle of water.

'Fallowfield today, is it?' she asked. 'Are we doing a tour of Manchester's breakfast establishments?'

'I've been thinking about what you said.'

Natalie's features hardened. 'With your brother?'

'No . . . I . . . he's back.'

'Is he okay?'

'To a degree.'

She nodded. 'There wasn't much I could do. I asked a few questions but no one who might have been close to the situation knew anything about Chris Green – or anything like that. No one had heard of him.'

It took Jason a moment to realise what she'd implied. 'You have people inside Richard Hyde's setup?'

Natalie took a sip from her bottle of water and smiled slightly. She obviously wasn't going to answer but, if true, it backed up what Hyde had told Jason in person – it wasn't him who had arranged for Chris to be abducted and beaten.

'Do you have people inside . . . *Harry's*?'

Jason could barely bring himself to say the name. Natalie continued watching him without reply, the bottle close to her lips. The cafe was a hive of noise: the whoosh of the espresso machine, the chatter of people nearby, the tinkle of the main door. At the counter, someone was asking about the WiFi password; behind Jason a mad-sounding woman who probably needed a sleep was telling her boyfriend/husband about how pregnancy was giving her a craving for marshmallows and millionaire's short-cakes and that it was his sole responsibility to provide them for her; in the corner a pair of children were building something that looked decidedly phallic out of Lego.

Natalie spoke in a slightly raised whisper. 'Can you think of any other reason why someone might want to harm your brother?'

Jason shook his head. 'Not apart from what I told you.'

'How about you?'

He frowned. 'What do you mean?'

'Doing something to your brother might be a way to get to you.'

Jason thought of the poor Gupta family, shuddering as he remembered their fate, even though it wasn't down to him. There were others before, of course – people for whose misfortune he did deserve the blame. That didn't really make sense either, though. Why now? Why would somebody go after his brother and not him?

Slowly, that icy spider skulked along his back as it had done every morning that week: a creeping realisation that there was someone he'd disappointed recently. Someone he had gone against. Someone powerful.

Chris had disappeared an hour after Jason had kicked the dealer down the stairs, sending a flurry of pills, powders and crushed leaves across the concrete with him. He remembered finding Chris in the same spot he'd left the dealer. Was there a symbolism there? A message?

Harry?

Natalie noticed the shiver, putting her water on the table and eyeing him carefully. 'Something I should know?'

Jason shook his head, listening in to more of the conversation behind him. The woman's boyfriend/husband was sitting in apparent silence as she complained about the state of the canteen at her work, pointing out how the tea from the machine was 'glorified piss with a bit of milk in it'.

He was brought back to his own conversation by Natalie clearing her throat. 'Is there a reason why you called me here?'

Jason sipped his coffee to give him a moment to think.

There was a reason but he couldn't think of a way to put it into words that didn't make it sound so . . . real. He lowered his voice unnecessarily. 'What is it you want from me?'

'I've already told you at least once.'

'Things were different then.'

Natalie sat up a little straighter, staring Jason up and down. From the confused scowl on her face, she didn't seem happy. 'What changed?'

Jason didn't know how to reply. He could mention Lucy, talk about what had happened to Chris, or even go on about his meeting with Richard – but the truth was that *he* was changing: questioning what he wanted from his life.

Natalie leant in, speaking so softly that Jason almost missed it. 'Are you trying to play me?'

'You came to me in the first place, remember.'

She rested against the back of her chair again, biting her bottom lip. Behind, the man was talking about a house he'd seen in Swinton and how it needed a bit of work but that they'd be able to get a good price for it. It was utter normality – buying a house, moving in, having children. That was what people did, wasn't it?

Jason looked up to see Natalie still watching him, as if he was a fascinating new pet that she didn't quite know how to talk to.

She nodded her head slightly, motioning for him to lean closer. Her words were crisp and chosen deliberately but almost lost among the voices around them.

'I want enough to get Irwell off the streets.'

'What about Richard Hyde?'

'What about him?'

'Are you going after the pair of them, or just . . . Harry?' Jason still struggled to say the name.

Natalie was shaking her head. 'Who said anything about a pair? There's more to this city than just those two: Harry Irwell, Richard Hyde, Christian Fraser. Until a short while ago, there was Nicholas Long too. I could go on. There's Thomas Braithwaite out in Liverpool. You might be tied up in your own little world but this is a big place and sometimes you have to knock the dominoes down one at a time.'

Jason pressed back into his seat, thinking about what she'd said. Perhaps he was too wrapped up in Harry's empire to see the wider picture.

Natalie waved him forward again. 'If it's any consolation – and I can't say any more than this – we do have a plan.'

This time, Natalie picked up her water and rocked back in her own chair, letting Jason consider what she'd said. He sipped his coffee, which was thick and strong.

'You know who Nicholas Long was, don't you?' Natalie asked, just loud enough for Jason to hear.

He nodded.

'He died in a puddle of his own piss. That's how all these types go out eventually – face down, soon to be forgotten.'

'Harry's not all bad,' Jason replied.

'How do you know that?'

'He does . . . good things. He saved me.'

Natalie nodded but was clearly unconvinced. 'Remember Jan Erikson?' she asked.

Jason couldn't meet her gaze, finding a spot on the door just above the coffee chain's logo and staring at it.

'Jan was a Danish national who came here with his girl-friend – a beautiful blonde girl named Helena. They did a bit of travelling and a bit of studying. Helena wanted to be a poet, Jan an artist. He died after taking two amphetamine tablets that were contaminated with some sort of cleaning powder. Helena ended up brain-dead in a coma. Those pills were bought in the park right next to your estate. The kid who sold them was arrested but never spoke a word about where he got the tablets from.'

Jason tried to block her out but Natalie continued speaking.

'What about Irma Sylha? She didn't come into the country legally, so it was probably in the back of a cramped, hot van hoping the customs officers didn't ask the driver to stop. Either that, or hidden under the back seat of a car, struggling to breathe. Her family in Albania say that she thought she was coming to Britain to work as a nanny: she'd even been shown photographs of the children she was going to be looking after. A nice middle-class suburban family with twins. It didn't turn out like that, of course. As far as was pieced together, the moment she got here, her passport was taken and she was forced to work in a flat as a prostitute. All the money she made was taken and, accord-ing to another girl who was freed, they were injected with something that was most likely heroin or methadone to ensure they couldn't leave. When one of her clients got a little too excited and choked her to death, she was dumped in a ditch on the side of the road, either by him or more likely by the people controlling her. The media only knew the correct name to report because Irma's passport was discovered among a pile of three-dozen others as part of a drugs raid.'

Jason didn't remember the name specifically but he did recall something about the case from the morning news as his mother dozed on the sofa. If Natalie was saying that was linked to Harry then it was the first he knew of it – but that was no different to the Guptas' house being set on fire. Jason would be doing a job for Harry in one area of the city, with another group doing something completely separate across town. He didn't know if Harry was into prostitution and people-trafficking. It was never the type of thing he'd ask.

Or want to know.

Natalie leapt on his discomfort and suddenly he couldn't hear anything other than her whispered tones. 'How about Liam Argyle? One of his friends was getting married and he was on a stag night at Casino 101. He ended up on a run of bad luck, losing game after game, bet after bet. His friends told him to give it up: to go and have a drink with them and forget about it. Except that he didn't – he kept going until, according to one of his friends, he'd cleaned out the joint savings account he shared with his wife-to-be. Of course, she was less than impressed, except that it didn't stop there; day after day he returned to try to win his money – and her – back. No one ever turned him away, or refused him credit. We don't even know how much money he owed by the time he hung himself from a light fitting in the house that was just about to be repossessed.'

Jason did know this name because it had been in the papers and on the news a couple of years previously. It had sparked a debate about gambling and whether it was Liam's fault, the casino owner's, the council's, the government's or society's in general. Harry had produced paperwork to show that Liam had lost less than a thousand pounds at Casino 101, putting himself as much in the clear as he could. No one had access to the business accounts to prove any differently, with the only other person who knew for sure stone cold in the morgue. After a day or so, everyone had gone back to complaining about the weather and things had carried on as normal for everyone except Liam's friends and family.

'You can't say that's entirely Harry's – or anyone else's – fault,' Jason said.

Natalie finished her water. 'If it was isolated, I'd agree. I can find you a list of more Irmas, Jans, Helenas and anyone else you want to talk about.'

'No.'

She nodded, knowing he'd say that. 'So what is good about *Harry Irwell*?' She practically spat the final two words. There was something personal there. Natalie quickly corrected herself, regaining her professionalism. 'Jason?'

'I don't want to talk about it.'

'This isn't you, Jason. I can see it.'

'What do I get if I can help you?'

'That partly depends on what and how much you provide me with. Safety would be the main thing.'

'What if I wanted to go abroad?'

She clucked her tongue. 'That can be arranged . . . within reason.'

Jason finished his coffee as the door tinkled again, bringing him back into the room and making him aware of everyone around him. Suddenly the place felt too open. 'I want to see something in writing,' he said.

'That shouldn't be a problem – but I'd want something from you to prove you're not some low-level goon who doesn't know anything.'

'Like what?'

'That's up to you.'

'It's complicated – there is no inner circle. The only person that knows everything is Harry.'

Natalie stood, picking up the empty water bottle and leaning over the table. 'It's up to you then, isn't it? You called me this time, remember? Call me again when you have something useful and then we can talk about your paperwork.' She straightened her top and lowered herself down to eye level, giving Jason nowhere else to look. 'Bring me Harry Irwell, Jason. You do that and I promise your life will change forever.'

26

Jason jumped awake, shivering from the cold but feeling sweat on his forehead. He had deliberately left his window open the night before, knowing that it would somehow end up like that by the morning anyway. He peered across his bedroom but the window was exactly as he'd left it, latched on the third notch. The sound of a Monday morning drifted through the gap – car engines, children chattering, footsteps, the splutter of a bus pulling away.

As he closed the window, Jason had a flashback to the night before: vague dreamlike memories that didn't seem quite real. His hands felt sore as he clenched and unclenched his fists, observing the grazes across his knuckles. Harry's message had finally been delivered to the shop in Stretford. Sunday evenings were the perfect time for things like that: fewer cars, fewer people, hardly any staff and only a handful of convenience shops allowed to be open. The final part of a weekend always felt like the zombie apocalypse had hit and the only people out and about were too blind to see what was happening around them. Jason liked it, giving him the anonymity to do what he needed.

After a drink of water, Jason checked on his brother, who was sleeping in his room. The covers were strewn around the edges of the bed and the floor, Chris's arm cradled across his chest in the makeshift sling they'd created from bandages. The kaleidoscope of colours was really beginning to come through on his upper body and around his eyes – if there was one thing the Green family did well, it was bruise. His mother spent years proving that when they were younger and now her children were showing the same tendency.

Chris hadn't left the house since Jason had found him on Friday afternoon, though Kat, Clarkey and the rest of his friends had come over to keep him company the previous evening, which was probably why he was now sleeping off a hangover.

He wasn't the only one.

In the living room, their mother was passed out in her usual position: one arm hanging off the sofa, blanket half covering her, empty bottle on the floor, television on. Jason watched the news headlines but the Guptas seemed to have dropped off the radar, with the agenda back to dogs who could walk on their hind legs and a soap star's upcoming wedding. Jason hunted for the remote, found it wedged underneath the sofa, and then turned the television off, enjoying the moment of silence before his mother groaned and rolled over. He watched her from the back of the room, not daring to move in case she woke up properly. Some days he could deal with the temper swings but he didn't think he could even handle one of her good moods today. He thought of the other two women in his life: Natalie and Lucy. Both potentially offered a way of escaping a life he hadn't previously realised he was unhappy with.

With a snort and a cough, his mother was on her side

again, scratching at the material of the sofa like a frightened hamster before settling.

Jason crept out of the room, easing the door closed behind him and then turning to face the doormat where the advertising flyer for Casino 101 was lying exactly where he knew it would be.

Jason waited by the door at the back of the casino as the suited man ignored him. It was a different security guard than usual but then they all looked the same to Jason: big blokes, big chests, big arms, limited vocabulary, not much hair.

'Are you going to let me in?' Jason asked, one hand already on the handle, waiting for the security guard to tap in the keycode.

The man continued staring across the games floor, replying in a low, gruff voice. 'He ain't here.'

'Harry?'

'Mr Irwell to you.'

'Where is he?'

No reply.

'I was asked to come here,' Jason persisted.

The man remained unmoving, lips together, eyes steady ahead. Somewhere behind Jason there was a ding-ding-ding of money dropping.

'Are you going to let me in?'

'Nope.'

Jason pressed down on the handle anyway, knowing it wouldn't open but wanting to make a point. That was lost as the guard spun, wrapping his sausage fingers around Jason's wrist and squeezing.

'I said no. Are you going to make me throw you out?'

His grey eyes bored into Jason's, letting him know that slinging him out on the street was the preferred option. This wasn't the first time Jason had visited the casino only to find Harry not there – but it was the first occasion his presence had been requested and then he'd been left unsure what to do next.

Jason yanked his hand away, thinking about retaliating. With a bit of luck and planning, he probably could over-power the man, despite the size difference, but doing that on the floor of Harry's casino in full gaze of the cameras and punters would be one of the stupider things he might do.

Muttering 'monkeys in suits' under his breath and with no better way to maintain his pride, Jason headed to the exit. Phone calls to Harry and Carter went unanswered – not that Carter had picked up any time recently. Jason didn't even know if he had the correct number any longer. The one stored in his phone was something from the old days when Carter used to be more directly involved in operations. Now he simply shadowed Harry: a lingering, menacing presence over the man's shoulder.

It was only when Jason marched into the squalling wind that it dawned on him what he might have missed. With a sigh and a loss of dignity, he turned and headed back through the casino, returning to the door at the rear. This time he kept his distance from the door and its guard.

'Did he leave a message for me?' Jason asked.

The grey-eyed statue barely moved his lips. 'Who?'

'You know who.'

'He did actually.'

'Why didn't you tell me that before?'

'You never asked – you wanted to barge through the door, then you ran away ready to cry.'

Jason bristled, wanting to fire something back but knowing the suited man had information he needed. He thought about playing the 'Harry wanted to see me' card again but he'd already said that. This was the exact kind of brinksmanship and competitiveness that Harry would enjoy watching anyway – plus it was true that Jason had tried to go through the door without asking the questions he probably should have.

'What was the message?' Jason asked.

The man moved for the first time since Jason had returned, scratching his head exaggeratedly. 'It's hard to remember. I'm only a monkey in a suit, after all.'

'Are you going to tell me?'

His gaze flickered sideways towards Jason and then away again. 'You gonna stop being a little shite when you come here?'

Jason took a closer look at him, realising he *was* the same man he'd seen many times – he'd just cut his hair slightly shorter. The slow truth was dawning on Jason that he was the person who'd been a dick all those times: barging his way in, not acknowledging the man on the door, not even knowing his name or noticing what he looked like.

'Yes,' Jason said, defeated.

'Fine – he told you to meet him at the Empire . . .' The guard turned, standing a little straighter. '. . . and the next time you touch that door without waiting, I'll snap your sodding arm off. Got it?'

The Empire was a cross between a lap-dancing bar and a private members' club. During the day, it was occupied by men in suits hosting business meetings in a far more appealing environment than their offices, as well as retirement-age, suit-wearing men who wanted to get away from the wife for a few hours. In the evening, the clientele was much the same but there were naked women and marginally more alcohol.

Jason had only visited once previously – when Harry had invited him along for an evening treat the night after he'd turned twenty-one. Jason had hated the experience, sharing nothing in common with the other men to whom he'd been introduced and not getting anything from the girl with the empty eyes who had dragged him into one of the side rooms. She'd told him it was fine and that it happened to everyone but Jason couldn't escape the feeling that it would somehow get back to Harry and that he'd be disappointed. Now, that fear and the eagerness to please seemed ridiculous.

After ringing the bell for entry, Jason entered a tall-ceilinged reception area with long lines of sparkling floor tiles, more wood panelling and elaborate chandeliers. If there was a mucky-faced girl in a maid's uniform somewhere, it could have been something out of a period drama with which TV companies endlessly bored everyone.

A short, bald man was scowling behind a reception desk, unimpressed at Jason's trainers, jeans, T-shirt and jacket. He was wearing a suit so brutally pressed that the shoulders had corners that could qualify as dangerous weapons. 'Can I help you?' he asked.

'I'm meeting someone,' Jason replied.

The man's eyebrows rose in a 'no-you're-not'-way.

'Are you now?' he said.

'Harry Irwell.'

His brows shot back down again. 'Oh . . . What's your name?'

'Green. Jason Green.'

The greeter typed something into the computer in front of him and nodded shortly, still not happy. He pointed at a leather-bound book. 'You'll have to sign in – then you can follow me.'

'I'm not sure he'd be happy with me putting my name in that book.'

After a moment in which Jason thought there might be an argument, the man nodded crisply. 'You better follow me then.'

He led the way through identical-looking corridors, walking quickly and not checking over his shoulder before stopping in front of a towering oak door. He rapped sharply and waited for the 'come in', before pushing inside, standing as tall as he could by the door and slightly bowing his head.

'Sorry to intrude, Mr Irwell. There's a Mr Green here for you.'

He stepped to one side as Jason entered the room, marvelling at the soaring mural on the wall in front. It showed a king he didn't recognise astride a horse, raising a sword in the air as an army stretched across a sweeping wide valley, lush with grass and trees.

'Beautiful, isn't it?'

Jason turned to see Harry sitting in a chair with a back so high that it seemed like a throne. Light flooded in through two floor-to-ceiling windows, with more wood panels lining the other walls. Harry was by himself, wearing a warm-looking grey wool suit, puffing on a cigar – even though the smoking ban probably meant it was illegal. Jason couldn't stop the smile from creeping onto his face. Of all the illicit acts Harry might be involved in, it was the smoking that Jason immediately associated with being criminal.

Harry didn't appear to notice the smile, using the cigar to point at a far more normal-looking chair to his side. 'I hear your brother is back with you . . .' he said.

'Yes.'

'How is he?'

'Not too bad.'

Harry puffed on his cigar, holding it in his mouth and breathing out the smoke in one long plume before moving on. 'Thank you for last night's delivery. It seems as if everything went to plan.'

'I think so.'

'The usual reward should be with you already.'

'Thank you.'

'I have something else for you . . .' Harry caught Jason's gaze and raised his eyebrows, wanting the question to be asked. Jason remained silent and so he eventually continued. 'This is a collection, Jason – but it has to happen tonight. I know it's short notice, so I'm happy to increase the rate.'

Jason had little option other than to accept, especially after taking so long to do the previous job. 'Okay.'

'Do you know Whitehill Industrial Estate?' Harry asked.

'I've heard of it.'

'There's something I need picking up from there. You know the usual drill.' Harry waved him across, waiting until Jason was close enough to feel his breath brushing his ear and smell the taste of cigar before whispering the time and place. 'You'll need some of your better associates,' he added.

'Okay.'

Jason started to move away but Harry reached out and grabbed his arm, squeezing so tightly that he couldn't stop himself from squealing slightly.

Harry released him but there was a glint in his eye. 'I heard you made an interesting pit-stop on Friday.'

For a moment Jason thought he was talking about the cafe and Natalie but then he realised Harry meant Richard Hyde's casino. Perhaps it wasn't just Natalie and her people who had eyes in both camps.

Jason straightened his sleeve and stepped away. 'I needed to get Chris back.'

Harry's reply was firm and assertive. 'I thought you came to me with that? Came to my home? I told you I would make inquiries.'

'I know, but—'

'Don't you trust me, Jason?'

'Yes, but you said—'

'I said I would make inquiries, yet you went to Oldham anyway.'

Jason wanted to look away but Harry had him locked in an unflinching stare.

'I was . . . worried about Chris,' Jason stammered.

Harry waved him forward again and Jason obeyed, stepping towards the chair without thinking. Harry patted him on the shoulder. 'You must feel quite vulnerable in that flat of yours. You, your brother, your mother, cooped up in the same place with all of those problems going on around you. Assaults, muggings . . . wasn't one of the shops around the corner from you firebombed not too long ago?'

Jason stepped away, not replying.

Harry took another puff from his cigar as Jason edged closer to the door. 'I'm just saying you should make certain you're careful in a place like that. You're one of my greatest assets, Jason. One of my sons. We should be able to trust each other. We do, don't we?'

'Yes.'

Harry bowed his head slightly. 'That's such a relief to hear, m'boy.'

27

TWO YEARS AGO

The pain burned through Jason's body: flaring along his sides, grating his upper torso and pounding into the backs of his eyeballs. He'd been hit before, beaten even, but never like this. His torturer knew exactly what he was doing, carefully targeting the areas that would hurt the most but never going too far. There would be bruises, perhaps even cuts, but nothing worse than what someone might get from tripping on the top step and taking a self-inflicted tumble.

The next blow sliced across the top of Jason's back, catching him a little under his shoulderblades. He arched backwards in agony, making the manacles that were joining his hands to the ceiling jangle like a set of keys. He slumped to what would have been his knees if the chains weren't holding his weight. Instead he was caught halfway between standing and kneeling, letting the metal hold him up and spitting a mouthful of blood onto the cold, hard floor.

Carter moved back into his eyeline, expression perfectly neutral. He could have been having a conversation about what to have for tea, shopping for socks, eating dessert, or winning a sporting event. His features barely ever changed. Jason had no idea if he was enjoying inflicting the punishment, or if he was simply doing a job. He was wearing a see-through plastic cover over the top of his actual suit. Across the arms were spattered flecks of blood.

Jason's blood.

Carter stepped towards Jason without a word and punched him in the side, slightly towards his back where the kidney was. With a groan, Jason swung away on the chains and then drooped forward again. Carter didn't smile, didn't laugh, didn't do anything other than wipe his fist on the see-through material and step away.

Jason closed his eyes, thinking he could hear the ding-ding-ding of the casino machines somewhere nearby. Perhaps they were overhead, or down the corridor? He had no idea – the room was like the inside of a concrete block: grey, no windows, cold. All that was different was the wooden door.

Ding-ding-ding-ding-ding.

Someone had hit the jackpot . . . or maybe the sounds were in his head.

Thunk!

Carter hit him again, this time in the stomach, stealing Jason's breath and making him want to double over, even though he couldn't. Jason didn't open his eyes, but couldn't stop thinking of the room: a concrete tomb used to hand out who knew how many punishments. He'd never been here before, never even heard of the place. The blindfold and van journey meant he didn't even know where he was.

There was a gentle squeak of the door, footsteps, and then silence.

'Jason . . .'

The voice echoed slightly in the cramped, closed room. Jason opened his eyes but it took a few moments for his vision to clear and the shape of Harry to blur into view. He was dressed immaculately: spotless three-piece suit, shiny shoes, fingers touching as if he was praying, wedding ring glinting from the overhead strip lights. Carter wasn't in sight.

Jason tried to answer but was still struggling for breath and only ended up coughing more blood into his mouth, dribbling it down his bare chest.

'I'm sorry this had to happen, Jason. I did try to warn you about using your brother. I said he was unreliable, that he didn't have what you had, but you went ahead and opted for him anyway.'

Harry stopped, waiting for the reply, but Jason could only cough and gurgle. Harry nodded and Carter stepped into view with a plastic container of water. Jason drank the liquid as Carter tipped the flask for him, continuing to pour even when Jason tried to pull away. The water slopped over his chin and upper body, making him feel even colder before Carter eventually stopped.

Jason coughed again and then finally answered. 'Chris wanted some money and was struggling to find anyone who'd hire a fifteen-year-old. He hated school and I was trying to help.'

'That's admirable but I still told you not to.'

'I know.'

Harry's voice was methodically, hypnotically, calm. 'I heard he bought an expensive watch, clothes, flashing himself around.'

'I tried to stop him.'

'Then our man couldn't pay what he owes because of what that idiot did to his knee.'

'I *tried* to stop him—'

'Not hard enough.'

Jason slumped in the manacles. 'I know I messed up.'

'What am I supposed to do now, Jason? Do I let our friend off his debts because his knees are shattered and he can't do anything?'

'I don't know.'

Harry was striding back and forth, his footsteps the only sound echoing around the concrete room. 'If I do that, what sort of message does it send to others? Say one of our other friends who owes money gets wind of this and throws themselves down the stairs. I can hardly demand what I'm due if they have no means to make it back, can I? What sort of precedent do you think that would send?'

'I—'

'A very bad one, Jason. That's the position you've put me in. Do I accept that our friend is in an unfortunate situation caused by you and let him off, or do I ask some-one else to send out a more . . . *refined* . . . message that people must pay what they owe?'

'I'm sorry . . .'

Jason's eyes had closed again, the weight of the past week taking its toll. It really had been a careless idea to use Chris for anything and Harry had told him not to.

Harry was getting louder: 'I didn't want to do it, Jason, but you made it happen. I had to have that message sent and it was done last night. Our friend might not be able to pay his debts at all any longer but there's a bigger picture. He might be out of the picture but everyone else suddenly seems keen to make amends because they don't want the same to happen to them. I suppose in some ways I should thank you for the mix-up.'

Jason moaned, this time not because of his own pain.

'But we still have a problem with your brother,' Harry added.

'He won't say anything.'

'Oh, I know he won't.'

Jason's eyes shot open again. 'You haven't . . .'

Harry put his hands on his hips and stared. One second. Two. Silence. 'What do you take me for?'

Jason stammered an apology but Harry was on a roll.

'I *know* he won't say anything because I'm going to let you deal with him. I know what you're capable of and how persuasive you can be. I don't care what you say or how you phrase it but the message should be simple: no fancy shite, no showing off and no more working with you.' Harry's voice had risen to a steepling inferno of fury. He breathed deeply through his nose and for a moment, the tiniest fraction of a second, Jason thought it might be all over. That Harry would give Carter the nod and this room would be the final thing he ever saw. Eventually, Harry breathed out, his air of calm returning. 'Got it?' he added.

'Yes.'

'Chris is not as smart as you. You know the type of people I like to work with, don't you?'

'Yes.'

Crunch!

Jason swung to the side as Carter's fist pounded into his opposite kidney. It was so unexpected that he screamed in agony. As another blow came, this time to the back of his knees, it felt as if his body was being twisted, mangled into scrap. He slumped forward, stars spinning in the darkness of his closed eyelids.

Ding-ding-ding.

When Jason awoke he was sitting in Harry's office, fully dressed with a cup of tea and two chocolate biscuits in front of him. At first he thought he was dreaming but then the smell of blood caught in the back of his throat and he began spluttering. As the retching got the better of him, Jason realised his ribs, neck and back were aching; his shoulders were stiff, head thumping.

Then he remembered the concrete room and Carter's fists. He spun but the office was empty apart from Harry on the other side of the table.

'How are you feeling?' Harry asked softly. A concerned father.

'Tired,' Jason croaked.

'I'm sure I can arrange for someone to take you home.'

That sounded good but Jason didn't reply. His memories of the past few hours were melding into one, like a television programme where the plot jumped from one time period to another. He'd been walking through the park; and then CUT he was in the concrete room; and then CUT Harry was there; and then CUT he was here. Was that the order or had he forgotten something?

'Jason . . .'

He jumped slightly, wondering if he'd fallen asleep for a few moments. With a groan, he pushed himself up until he was sitting straighter.

'Does that sound good, Jason?' Harry asked. 'We'll take you home and you can get some sleep.'

'Okay.'

'It's such a shame, my son. I hate to see my children squabbling and fighting. Perhaps you should drink your tea first? It'll make you feel better.'

Jason stared woozily down at the milky brown liquid. It did seem incredibly appealing. He took a sip and then another, feeling a slight spinning sensation.

'I hope you've learned your lesson, Jason. Remember where I found you – you're better than that.'

28

Jason stared at the figure on the computer screen: £330,420. He had been paid five thousand for the Sunday-night job – a little more than expected, especially considering how long he'd taken to do it. Still, it didn't seem like much compared to Harry's implicit threat against Chris and his mother.

It wasn't news that Harry knew where his flat was, or what his living arrangements were, but he'd never made his thoughts so clear in the past. The incident with Carter in the concrete room two years ago seemed like it had happened to someone else at the time, even though the bruises were real. It had almost slipped from Jason's consciousness in the months since. It was a dream, a second-hand story, except that Jason knew it had definitely happened and Harry had now reminded him of what he was capable.

A familiar face appeared over the top of the monitor and Jason hastily closed the browser window as Lucy walked around the bank of computers and sat next to him. She was dressed as she always was at the library: hair tied back, smart almost secretarial skirt and blouse. Jason had swiped his card without thinking of her – checking in at the library the day after a job was habit, Lucy or no Lucy.

'I didn't think I'd be seeing you today,' she said with a twirl of her hair.

'I had a couple of things to check.'

'Are you coming over later?'

'I don't think so – work's busy today, probably tomorrow too.'

Lucy tilted her head, as if wanting to ask why he was using a library computer if he was so busy but she didn't. 'How was your weekend?'

'Quiet, mainly looking after Mum. You?'

'I went out with a couple of people off my course. Nothing ridiculous: just a burger and a few drinks. There was some football on the telly so we went back to one of the other's girls' houses and watched some chick flick. It was shite.' She nodded at the screen, smiling. 'What's the temperature in Crete?'

Jason typed the web address in from memory. Sunny, twenty-one degrees, no breeze: beautiful. He turned back to Lucy but she wasn't looking at the screen. Instead, she reached out and took his hand in hers, running her fingers across his knuckles and making him wince.

'You haven't been fighting, have you?'

Battling the urge to pull his hand away, Jason shook his head. 'I was fixing a cabinet in our kitchen and the whole thing came tumbling down.'

'Oh – I didn't know you were good with your hands.' She giggled and Jason wondered if she was flirting.

'I'm not,' he said, 'hence the falling down.'

He held his knuckles up to emphasise the point but

Lucy had tilted her head to the side and was smiling slightly at something he'd missed.

'You really don't know when someone's joking, do you?'

The grin remained as she continued: 'I've been touching up a few odds and ends on your painting. I'm really pleased with it. The edges are all sorted, it's just a few details now.'

'I'd really like to see it.'

Lucy squeezed his arm as she stood. 'You will. Now, we're in a library – what books do you like?'

Jason clicked the button to log off the machine and stood too. Lucy was already around the other side of the computers.

'I don't know,' he said. 'I told you I don't really read.'

'Have you *ever* read a book?'

'When I was a kid.'

'What did you read then?'

'One of the lads I knew at school used to bring comics in. We'd share them around.'

He thought she was going to mock but she shrugged. 'We've got a big selection of comics nowadays. It's all the rage – though pretentious types call them "graphic novels" because they don't want to use the word "comic". Do you want to see what I've been reading?'

'Not more art books?'

Lucy grinned wider and Jason was pretty sure she *was* flirting. 'Don't be cheeky,' she said, 'come on.'

She turned, striding across the floor. Jason followed, apologising to an old woman he nearly sent flying in his eagerness not to let Lucy get away. She was waiting on the corner of a long walkway with shelves on either side.

'Do you often assault old people?' Lucy said.

'Not usually on Mondays.'

She smiled and took his hand – properly this time, interlocking her fingers into his. He felt a spark tingling along his arm. 'Come on,' she whispered. 'And no knocking over pensioners.'

Jason allowed her to lead him along the aisles until she stopped in front of a row with colourful spines. She sat on the floor, tugging him down with her, and picked a book off the shelf.

'Travel guides?' Jason said.

'I like looking at the pictures. I know you can search on the Internet but there's something about seeing it on a page that feels . . . I don't know – better.'

Jason tried to read the word on the front. 'Gala-p—'

'Galapagos. They're a bunch of islands not far from Ecuador, filled with different types of animals. They're amazing.' Lucy flicked through the pages, finding photographs of penguins, turtles, enormous tortoises, birds and too many other things to name. Then she showed him books about Indonesia, the Rocky Mountains, Malaysia, Thailand. Places Jason had never heard of, let alone thought about visiting.

Lucy leant her head against the row of books behind, with three books open on her lap. 'I want to go there and paint these things. My mum will go mad, I know she will, but if you don't do it when you're young, when are you going to?'

Jason was looking at pictures in the Australia book, marvelling at the rock structures and bright colours. 'I've never really thought about it.'

'Don't you want to see the world?'

He turned back to the book, not knowing how to reply.

'Jason?'

'I'd like to see the sun a bit more.'

She giggled, closing the top book. 'Wouldn't we all?'

Jason hurried across the road into the newsagent. Every time he visited, there seemed to be someone different working there. This time it was a Goth girl with short black hair, a ring through her nose, two more through her lip and at least ten in each of her ears. She tutted as he bought his ten scratch cards and turned to the ice-cream freezer. Hearts, diamonds, clubs, spades, reds and blacks: nothing – not even enough to buy another card. So much for a one-in-five chance of winning.

He returned to his car around the corner, watching and waiting for a sign anyone could be watching. It wasn't necessarily a surprise that Harry was aware he'd gone to the casino in Oldham, yet Jason wondered exactly how he knew. He was pretty sure he hadn't been followed, so the only other option was that Harry had someone within Hyde's organisation working for him. That person would have recognised Jason, which was a little worrying in itself. He went out of his way not to get a reputation, with most of his work being done in the shadows and under the cover of a balaclava. He couldn't be that widely known because the manager of the Prince of Wales hadn't recognised him and the police had never come knocking on his door.

In his rear-view mirror, Jason watched a man walking his dog along the pavement. He didn't know dog breeds but it was something brown, black and big. The owner was whistling absent-mindedly as he bobbed along the street and then tied his dog to one of the bike racks outside the newsagent before heading in.

The rest of the road was quiet, nothing moving except for the tornado of grit, dust and rubbish whipping in between the vehicles.

'Don't you want to see the world?'

Was Lucy actually asking if he wanted to go away, or was it a general question? Not being able to read her made their relationship — if it could be called that – all the more interesting. Jason didn't get her jokes or know if she was flirting or being herself. He had no clue whether she was innocently asking what his interests were, or trying to talk him into a round-the-world trip. They barely knew each other and yet, if she asked him outright, he didn't think he'd say no. Not that he'd definitely say yes, either. He simply didn't know – which was a confusion he wasn't used to.

His city of black and white had become a colour chart of greys.

Convinced he hadn't been followed and that there was no way anyone could be listening in to his conversation, Jason took out his phone and called Natalie.

She answered on the second ring. 'What?'

'You told me to call if I had something useful.'

He heard a scrabbling noise, perhaps her reaching for a pad and pen. 'Do you want to meet?' she asked.

'Is there a chance someone might be listening in to this?'

'I can't do much if MI5 are bothered with you but I wouldn't bet on it.'

'Oh . . .'

'I'm joking, Jason. No one's listening in.'

He had one final look in the mirror and then took a deep breath. There was no turning back now. 'There's going to be a robbery tonight,' Jason said.

A pause. 'Is your master going to be there?'

'No, that's not how it works.'

'But you're going to be involved?'

In the confusing mist of Harry's threats and Lucy's girlishness, Jason realised he'd not thought the conversation through. 'I'm not sure I should say.'

'Fine – I'll do a bit of guessing and you can correct me if I'm wrong. Do you have any sort of recording of your master, or anyone, asking you to do something you shouldn't?'

'No.'

'Are the goods going to be delivered somewhere that could be tied to your master?'

'No.'

'So what do you have?'

'I, er . . .'

Natalie was angry. 'You have nothing – again. I told you to only bother me if it's with something to show you're not a low-level goon, but that's exactly what you're proving. If you want someone to end up on your shoulder tonight watching your every move, making sure nothing happens, then you're going the right way.'

'Don't do that.'

'Why not?'

'Because if I'm nicked then all this comes to an end. I can't give you information if I'm sitting in a cell somewhere.'

'You're not giving me information anyway.'

Out of the corner of his eye, Jason saw the man emerging from the newsagent, newspaper under his arm, ice lolly hanging from his mouth, despite the autumn chill. He untied his dog and started walking back the way he'd come, though the animal seemed more interested in the lolly than in trotting home.

'What can I do to prove myself?' Jason asked.

'Get me information.'

'I'm trying.'

'Fine – then sabotage things tonight.'

'I can't.'

'You've told me there's going to be a robbery, which isn't something I can put to one side and forget. There are people above me, channels through which I have to go. They're going to say you're a nobody and that I was mistaken in even thinking you'd be useful. You've offered me nothing, wasted my time, and now you're going out on a robbing spree and expecting me to turn a blind eye.'

'I'm not.'

'Forget it, Jason. If there are reports of anything serious happening overnight, there'll be someone knocking on your door before you're even out of bed.'

29

Jason sat in the driver's seat of the van wondering how he'd got himself into this mess. He had to decide what he *actually* wanted, not just do things without thinking them through. That level-headedness had got him this far and kept him – for the most part – on the right side of Harry. Now he'd somehow ended up in the middle of Harry and Natalie: both wanting their own result, both offering their own threats. Harry's veiled piece of intimidation was more a general reminder that Jason should tread carefully but Natalie's was far more direct.

From the darkness behind, there was a dim flash of light. 'What have I said about phones?' Jason snapped irritably. 'Turn it off.'

'It's Carly,' one of the men said, 'she's got a strop on because we were busy last night and we're busy tonight.'

'I don't care if it's the Prime Minister, turn it off.'

There was a snigger, almost lost in the tinkle of the device being turned off.

'And shut up too – we're supposed to be keeping an eye out. Have you got everything I asked for?'

There was a grumbling from behind and then Kev replied. 'You said bring tools.'

'What have you got?'

'The usual.'

Jason kept his eyes on the warehouse across the road, waiting for the telltale headlights that would indicate they were up. 'Tell me – I want to know.'

'There are two bats, an old snooker cue from my garage and this.'

Jason didn't like the way Kev had said the final word, so he turned, peering into the darkness of the van behind him. In the man's hands was the unmistakeable outline of a pistol. Kev was bobbing it up and down in his hand, feeling the weight.

'Who told you to bring that?' Jason said.

'You said bring the tools.'

'I didn't say bring a gun!'

'So be specific next time!'

Jason turned back to the street but knew he had to ease off. Keeping control of the group was one thing but going out of his way to wind them up was another. It wasn't that he'd never seen a gun, or that he'd never seen people threatened with one, but he could have done without its presence this evening. It only took one clown with an itchy finger and something that made him jump and suddenly everyone was in deep shite.

'Just don't bloody shoot anyone,' Jason said.

'I wasn't planning to,' Kev replied. 'If we'd had a bit more notice, I might have been able to get some proper gear together.'

'The money will be good, just . . .'

Jason tailed off as a set of headlights glinted off the van's wing mirror. At the far end of the road behind, a vehicle had turned and was accelerating towards them.

'Is everyone clear?' Jason asked.

There was a mumble of yeses but obvious tension too. Usually, Jason would take his time planning everything down to the smallest details, providing escape routes, as much background as they needed and ensuring everyone knew what his role was – even if it was to stay in the van and keep his gob shut. This time, Harry's details had been minimal and Jason had not had time to scout the area. Natalie's warning was still ringing in his ears, too.

Under the street lights, Jason could see that the other van was a mucky grey, its lights swinging around as it eased onto the forecourt of the warehouse. Exactly why they were making a delivery at half past ten at night, Jason didn't know, though it was likely there was something not entirely above board going on. Either way, Harry had been right with the timings.

'Get ready,' Jason whispered, watching through the side window as the other van's lights switched off and the doors clunked open.

The grey van was the size of a large Royal Mail delivery vehicle: high sides and a drop-down platform at the back. Inside, there would be plenty of room but if it was full, there would be too much merchandise to transfer to their van, especially as Jason had four other men to carry.

Two men approached the shutters to the side of the warehouse, with one of them knocking loudly on the side. Moments later the heavy metal began rolling upwards and a pair of security guards emerged, wearing padded black outfits and starting a conversation, which Jason took as his cue.

With a flick of the key and a roar of the engine, Jason slammed the van into reverse, wrenched the steering wheel sideways and then jammed his foot on the accelerator. The vehicle growled its annoyance but obeyed, swerving across the road with a squeal and blocking the warehouse's gates. The side doors were already open as Jason stomped on the brake, his partners tearing into action before the four men by the warehouse door knew what was going on.

The forecourt was lit by two white spotlights in the back corner and the mild glow from the street lights. Jason had already spotted the CCTV camera pinned high on the building but there was little they could do about it other than cover their faces with masks and balaclavas. The van's number plate would be recorded, of course, but seeing as they never used the same plate twice, that wouldn't make much difference.

Jason climbed calmly out of the driver's side, trying not to let the adrenaline get to him. Things had happened so quickly that by the time he turned towards the shutters, one of the people from the grey van was already on the floor, blood pouring from the back of his head onto the concrete. He was screaming in agony as one of Jason's men cuffed him in the back of the head, ordering him to be quiet.

Both security guards were kneeling, hands interlocked behind their heads as Kev waved the gun in their vague direction. If he didn't hold the weapon more firmly, he was going to end up blowing his own kneecaps off.

It took Jason a moment to realise that the driver was missing – along with Pete and Gavin. Kev glanced quickly over his shoulder, nodding towards the dark corners of the forecourt where the lights didn't reach.

Shite.

Jason took off, following the line of the building until he got to a stack of wooden pallets. In the murk behind the building, he could hear a struggle. There was a clatter of wood on metal and then a man's voice: 'Ow, bastard.'

Jason ran until he reached a metal mesh fence. At the bottom, Pete and Gavin were swinging a bat and snooker cue upwards in the direction of the driver, who was almost at the top of the fence but had snagged his arm in the loops of barbed wire above.

Jason stepped in front of the other two and peered up at the silhouette of the driver. 'Do you want to come down?' he called.

'What are you going to do to me?'

'That depends on if you come down.'

'I've got kids.'

'Haven't we all – just come down and you'll be able to see them again.'

The man motioned upwards. 'My sleeve's stuck on the wire.'

'So rip it away.'

The man offered a token yank but not enough to break the material and then he peered back down. 'Who are you?'

'Christ, you're not CID, are you?' Jason said. 'What sort of question is that?'

The driver swung his legs, trying to get a better foothold on the wire. He was just out of Jason's reach but if he swung down hard enough, he could probably work a boot into one of them – though he'd probably take a blow from the bat for his troubles. One of them could climb up after him but that meant they could end up cutting themselves on the rough wire – not advisable with all the DNA testing that went on.

Gavin swapped the snooker cue into his other hand. 'I'll get him down.'

'No you won't,' Jason replied. 'Get round the other side and start unloading the van.'

'What are you going to do?'

'Just go.'

Reluctantly, Pete and Gavin slunk back into the shadows, clearly frustrated at the lack of action.

Jason waited until they were alone and then called up to the driver again. 'Where did you think you were going when you started climbing?'

'I don't sodding know. Those two started chasing me and I panicked.'

'If you come down, you won't be hurt. We're taking what's in the back of the van and we'll probably tie you up to stop you calling anyone but that's it. No one's coming after you or your kids.'

'How do I know you're not going to kick shite out of me if I come down?'

Jason shrugged. 'You don't but I can call back my friends with the bats if you want?'

The driver didn't take long to make his decision, wrenching his arm away from the wire until his top ripped. He slipped down the fence and then dropped to the ground, landing in a hunched position like a cat ready to pounce. He glanced towards Jason, weighing him up, but then thought better of it, walking with his head down back to the front of the warehouse.

Kev was there, still waving the gun around, his grip far too loose. The prick was even holding the weapon sideways, probably like in some action movie he'd seen. The two security guards and the man from the passenger's seat of the van were lying face-down on the concrete, hands cable-tied behind their backs. The driver assumed the same position on the ground without complaint and Kev cracked a set of thick plastic ties around his wrists.

At the rear of the grey van, the unloading was going quickly enough. The other three members of Jason's crew were carrying boxes from one vehicle to the other. Gavin stopped halfway across the forecourt. 'It's not all going to fit,' he said.

'I know – just get as many as you can and make sure you leave room in the back for you lot.'

The rear of their van was already stacked a third full with the plain brown boxes that Harry wanted. Jason climbed inside and ripped the corner of one, only to see a pile of polystyrene packing peanuts. The boxes were fairly heavy, so the contents were probably something electrical. On the side of each case was a sticker with Japanese or Korean characters printed on but nothing in English. Jason transferred a few boxes, nervously checking his watch each time. The driver had cost them at least five minutes and he wasn't happy at how brightly lit the tarmacked area was. All it would take was a late-night dog-walker cutting through the industrial estate and they'd have a problem.

Because the boxes were heavy and awkward, the fetching and carrying was beginning to slow with their van a little over half full. At the front of the warehouse, Kev was spinning the pistol around his finger Western movie-style in a way that was only going to end with a bullet blasting into his own stomach. Jason dropped a box into the back of the van and called across that it was time to go. The three who had been carrying the stolen goods slumped, relieved, into the narrow space they'd left in the centre of the stacked boxes, with Kev jogging across the car park and climbing into the passenger's seat. With a slam of the doors and a grunt from the engine, they were off again.

There was an excited hum of achievement in the van, even though nobody was speaking. The job was only half done but the most difficult part was over.

'How's the guy you hit over the head?' Jason asked Kev as they both pulled off their balaclavas.

'He'll live. If he'd shut his mouth, it would never have happened.'

'Did you get their phones?'

'I do know what I'm doing.'

Jason went back to concentrating on the network of roads that led off the estate. The gruff engine lurched as he changed up a gear and then spluttered a throaty cough of annoyance. There was a collective intake of breath from everyone as the engine growled in response to Jason's foot on the accelerator, before chugging and jumping its way along the road. Jason could feel the others watching him as he guided the van into a wide lorry drivers' lay-by, where the vehicle rolled to a halt.

Jason tapped the circular dial on the dashboard. 'It's out of diesel. I don't know why – I filled it up earlier.'

Kev opened his door and jumped down. 'Bollocks, it's leaking.'

They all climbed out, looking in the direction he was pointing back along the road Jason had driven. Behind, there was one long trail of liquid, the street lights illuminating the rainbow reflection.

The five of them massed in the shadows, Gavin asking the question they were all thinking: 'What are we going to do?'

'We're going to have to run for it,' Jason said. 'Split up and make your own ways home. Go the shortest way you can but stay off the main roads. Pick your cars up tomorrow. I'll be in contact.'

Kev nodded towards the van. 'What are we going to do with all of this?'

Jason reached into his pocket and took out a box of matches. 'The only thing we can do.'

'What about the money?' Kev asked.

'I don't know yet.' Somewhere in the distance, a car's tyres squealed. They all stopped for a moment, turning and trying to figure out where it was coming from. 'Go!' Jason shouted.

None of them waited for a second invitation, scattering in different directions as Jason walked backwards and struck a match. If Natalie wanted sabotage then that's what she was going to get. He watched the orange flame flicker against the dark of the night and then tossed it towards the floor, stepping quickly away as the glow turned a pale blue before flashing along the trail of leaked fuel.

By the time the explosion hit, Jason was already across the road, head down and heading towards the woods.

30

Jason stood just out of reach of the security guard at the back of the casino. 'Is Mr Irwell in?'

The same suited man from the previous day nodded. 'Yes.'

'Can you let me in?'

The guard turned, tapped the code into the keypad and opened the door. 'Not that hard, is it? Make sure you knock.'

Jason didn't reply, heading along the corridor and tapping on the door at the far end. Inside, Harry was behind his desk, cup of tea and buttered toast in front of him. Carter was sitting nearby, reading a newspaper, and didn't look up.

Harry was smiling as he sipped his tea, pointing to the seat opposite him. 'Beautiful day, isn't it? Nice to see the sun at this time of year.'

'It's still cold.'

'That it is.' Harry pursed his lips, waiting until Jason had sat. 'There was an interesting story on the news this morning. Burned-out vans, a botched robbery . . .'

Without prompting, Carter stood, crossed to the record player at the back of the room and dropped the needle onto the vinyl disc. The crescendo of violins instantly blared through the room. Harry wagged a finger towards Jason, motioning him forward.

'What happened?' Harry asked.

Jason leant in and explained briefly about the fuel leak. One big unavoidable, unforeseeable, accident.

Harry nodded, fingers touching as if praying again. When Jason had finished, he pressed back in his seat and nodded towards Carter. The music stopped as suddenly as it had started.

'I fancy a bit of a drive,' Harry said, standing and tapping Jason on the shoulder. 'How about you come along for the ride?'

Jason glanced towards the advancing Carter knowing this was an order, not a request. Before anyone could lay a hand on him, Jason stood, sounding as enthusiastic as he could. 'Okay.'

Jason sat in the side seat in the back of Harry's black-windowed car. This was the exact spot in which he'd been sitting all those years ago when Harry had first given him a lift home. The leather still squeaked in the same places and Jason knew where the softest part was. He squished himself into the material, peering at Harry, who was sitting opposite, sipping a cup of tea. In between them, Carter was back reading his newspaper.

In the few minutes since they had set off from the casino, nobody had spoken. Jason thought about breaking the silence but what could he say? He'd already explained what had happened with the van the previous night – Harry either believed him or he didn't.

The windows were too dark to see through but Jason could tell from the way the vehicle had finished stop-starting for traffic lights that they were on their way out of the city. He tried to picture the roads, guessing they were heading through Castlefield to the south of the city, else they would still be sitting at junctions.

Harry was avoiding any attempt at eye contact, focusing on his cup and then relaxing back into his seat and closing his eyes. Jason didn't dare look towards Carter.

As the vehicle sped up, Jason concluded they must be on the motorway or one of the A roads. He closed his eyes, trying to block out the impending sense that something bad was happening. Visions of shallow graves in the middle of nowhere or drowning at the bottom of a river with weights tied to his limbs were swimming through his head. Were the doors locked? Could he throw himself out and survive? If so, where would he go? They could just come back for him and he didn't know where he was.

The only sound was the smooth hum of the engine and the fluttering of newspaper pages. Without making it obvious by patting his pockets, Jason tried to think of what he had on him. His phone, his wallet and a set of keys. Only the keys could do any damage and that was if he was close enough to someone. He ran through Carter's repertoire of violence. He'd seen him in action plenty of times – always methodical and targeted blows, rarely brute force. If he was going to strike, the first thing he'd go for was either Jason's ears or his windpipe – something to throw him off-balance. Then it'd be his legs. If a person couldn't stand, he couldn't run or fight.

Carter was undoubtedly bigger and stronger and Jason didn't particularly fancy his chances if it came to it – but if he could try to anticipate what might happen then he could at least give himself an advantage, however small.

With a lack of anything useful on him, Jason stared into the darkness of his eyelids picturing the layout of the vehicle. The U-shape of the leather seats had a small table in the centre, with Harry's tea on top. Underneath the seat where Carter was would be the metal baseball bat but there was no way of getting to that. In a cabinet to the side of Harry was a selection of glasses and at least one bottle of whisky. They'd be reasonable weapons – but only if the violence began here. If the car stopped and he was ordered out, he could hardly grab the bottle.

Then he remembered the weapon that wasn't.

Harry quite often read his mail in the car, always using a sharp letter-opener to slice across the top of the envelopes. It was a blade in everything but name – typical Harry in that if anyone ever wanted to search the back of his vehicle, they wouldn't find a knife capable of cutting someone ear to ear, they'd find an antique tool used for opening envelopes.

Always a step ahead.

Jason tried to picture where it would be but could only think of the drawers underneath the table close to his feet. He opened his eyes again, trying not to move any other part of his body as he peered around the space. Harry was either asleep or doing a good job of acting like it, with Carter continuing to read. As gently as he could, Jason rubbed the sole of one shoe across the other foot, snagging the loop of his shoelace and tugging. To his relief, the lace slipped through the knot, hanging limply on the ground.

After peeping at Carter again, Jason eased forward, hunching over his feet. He rested his left hand on his shoe, delicately slipping the drawer open with his right.

Jason glanced from Carter to the drawer and then spotted the varnished wooden handle of the letter-opener nestling in the corner. He looked back to Carter, willing him not to glance over the top of the newspaper as he tried to grasp the handle but, in his eagerness, he only succeeded in nudging it deeper towards the back of the drawer. There was only one thing for it, so Jason turned his full attention to the drawer, edging it out a little further, gripping the handle of the letter-opener, twisting it, and then sliding it up his sleeve.

'You all right?'

Harry spoke through a yawn but his words were so out of the blue that Carter dropped the paper, looking over the top to see what was going on. The drawer was almost closed but Jason nudged it the rest of the way with his knees, lodging his thumb in his sleeve to stop the blade falling out.

'Just re-tying my lace.'

Neither of them answered, so Jason did as he said, feeling Carter watching him carefully. When he was done, he relaxed back into the chair, closing his eyes, tucking the whole of his hand into his sleeve and fingering the bottom part of the blade. At least if someone came for him, he'd be ready.

When the car eventually stopped, forty-five minutes had passed. Jason had spent much of the last quarter of an hour getting the letter-opener into his jacket pocket in a way that didn't make it jut out and wouldn't lead to it stabbing his side either. Eventually, he scratched a hole into the corner of the material, meaning it fitted lengthways. He could pull the improvised weapon out quickly if needed but it was indistinguishable in the lining.

Harry was the first person to move, crouching and opening the door before stepping out. 'Jason,' he said, holding the door open.

Jason climbed out, taking in the surroundings as Harry reached back inside. They were parked on the edge of a hard trail that led towards a copse of trees. On either side were stretches of overgrown grass and unclipped hedges. It was some sort of country park but Jason had never visited before and couldn't place it. Overhead, the cold sun blazed high, making the day seem a lot nicer than it was.

When Harry got out of the car for a second time, he was wearing a thick woollen overcoat and had a cardboard tube under his arm. Jason glanced at it but didn't ask what it was as Harry slammed the door and led the way along the trail. At least Carter wasn't coming.

They were back to not speaking as Jason followed Harry along the path deeper into the woods. Despite his shiny shoes and smart trousers, Harry didn't stop as the path became a mud trail. Jason looked for the bulges in his pockets – was there a gun in there? He checked over his shoulder just in case Carter was following after all but the track was clear.

They walked for around ten minutes before the path eventually widened out into a clearing with picnic benches on either side. Birds chirped to each other overhead and there was the faint sound of traffic but otherwise the area was spookily serene.

Harry sat on a bench, with Jason opposite, hands in pockets, cupping the handle of the letter-opener.

In the bright sun, away from the artificial bulbs and dim chandeliers, Harry looked like an old man: the wrinkles deeper, eyes more tired than fierce. Finally, he addressed Jason properly. 'It's a crying shame that last night's collection didn't go as planned,' he said. 'I'm not looking for reasons or excuses but I do have a way for you to make it up.'

He placed the tube on the picnic table between them and popped the plastic lid off, removing a rolled-up sheet of paper and flattening it. It was the map from Harry's office, brown and ancient, roads drawn on and labelled with neat handwriting.

'A friend of a friend, Samuel Yates, is currently residing at the prison.'

'Strangeways?' Jason asked.

'Yes – though he is being moved this evening to Wakefield. I don't know the exact time but it'll be after dark and there's going to be a police presence, as you'd expect.'

Jason let the knife handle go and pressed the fluttering map down, peering at the outline of the prison.

'You can't expect me to break someone out of the prison van . . . ?'

'No – I would like you to slow it down. There are . . . other . . . people involved for the additional aspects. Like I said – friend of a friend.'

Jason stopped to listen to the birds for a moment – this wasn't what he had expected at all. Suddenly the secrecy made a little more sense: Harry suspected someone could be listening into his conversations, he just didn't suspect it was Jason.

'Call me again when you have something useful . . .'

If he hadn't been so paranoid himself, Jason would have been able to activate the voice recorder on his phone. Everything was so quiet here that it would have picked up what Harry was asking. This was exactly the type of thing Natalie wanted, yet it was too late now.

Harry pointed to the map. 'There are a few routes they could take towards the M60. If the prison van hits the motorway, then it's game over. You need to stop it before it gets there.'

'How would you like me to do that?'

Harry tilted his head, telling Jason to use his imagination without actually saying it.

'Anyway,' Harry continued. 'Among the problems are that I can't help you with the direction the van is going to take.' He traced his finger along one of the roads but Jason wasn't convinced.

'Wouldn't it take the most obvious route?' Jason asked. 'If it goes along Bury New Road, it leads directly to the motorway. There are traffic lights but you're going to get lights anywhere you go.'

Harry shrugged. 'You might be right. This is unknown territory for me . . .'

The irony wasn't lost on Jason that Harry wasn't actually planning on doing any of the work himself.

'. . . I was thinking it might go for one of these more indirect routes,' Harry said.

With his finger Harry traced a few roads away from the prison. Jason nodded, though he still regretted not recording any of the conversation.

'What exactly is it you want me to do?' Jason asked.

'I told you – stop it.'

'I understand that but . . . this isn't the type of thing I've done before. Do you want me to drive in front and slam on the brakes, or—'

'I was thinking something a little more destructive than that. You'd have to stop it driving away.'

The picture was finally clear – Harry wanted Jason to crash into the prison van, which would be the easy bit. Hitting it in a way to incapacitate the other vehicle, while still being able to get out of his own, would be the awkward part, to say the least. Not to mention that the van with which he was familiar was burned out on the edge of an industrial estate.

'There'll be friends nearby,' Harry continued. 'Don't stop the prison van too close to the centre and don't let it get to the motorway. Once your bit is done, get yourself away. I'm not asking you to be involved with anything that happens afterwards.'

'You're asking a lot.'

Harry rolled the map back up. 'I know. Last night was small-time, this is the big leagues. This is a large favour for someone else. You'll be rewarded well. Leave behind your clownish mates – this is you and only you. Get things right and last night's mishap and your Oldham visit will be long forgotten.'

Harry dipped his head slightly, letting Jason know that he was serious but Jason found himself reaching for the letter-opener again, checking over his shoulder to make sure Carter hadn't crept up behind them. This wasn't the relationship they used to have – Harry would never have asked for something this big before. Jason wanted to say no, yet the implied threat was there to his mother and brother, not to mention that he still didn't know who had abducted Chris.

Harry reached across and passed Jason a plain white business card. Written neatly on the back was a postcode and a number. 'There'll be a van waiting there for you,' Harry said.

'How much?'

Harry's eyes narrowed. 'Pardon?'

'How much am I getting paid?'

'You've never asked that before.'

'You've never asked me to do anything like this before.'

Harry was sucking his top lip, eyes squinting so tightly they were almost closed. 'Forty.'

'Fifty.'

Jason didn't think asking for more money was a good idea but he didn't want to do the job anyway. When Harry said 'fine', he wished he'd asked for more. Fifty thousand would leave him at three hundred and eighty thousand pounds. If Jason waited things out, that would knock six months off the time it would take to get to half a million but did that figure even matter any longer?

He could phone Natalie and tip her off, even though he still had nothing provable for her; or he could crash one van into another, run for it, and end up with fifty thousand pounds.

As the autumn sun continued to shine, Jason could almost smell the year-round summer of the Greek islands. Twenty-one degrees . . .

31

Early evening darkness made it easy to get around the back streets of the city without being noticed but Jason still preferred the summer. It was one thing to blend into the shadows but he couldn't feel his fingers and every time he breathed it sent plumes spiralling into the atmosphere. It was hardly conducive to getting anything done.

Jason was tired – this was the third night in a row he was out on a job, something he'd never done before. He read the sign at the front of the breakers' yard and then waited as a woman hurried past on the pavement, push-chair thrust out in front, rasping cough echoing along the street. Jason rested against the fence, checking left and right to make sure there was no one else around and then he tugged the padlock that was linking the two gates in the centre. From a distance, it would appear locked – it was only when holding the metal that it became clear the lock's jaws hadn't been snapped together.

As he slipped between the gates, Jason felt his phone rumbling in his pocket. Struggling to get his gloves off, he took the phone out of his pocket in just enough time to see the letter 'N' flashing on the screen. He thought about answering but had nothing to report back to Natalie. He also wasn't sure how she would have taken the news about the van-load of burned-out electrical items. It rang off anyway, so he re-pocketed the phone and walked towards the van parked in the centre of the courtyard.

Close to the gate was a ramshackle Portakabin, with grate-covered windows and mud spatters along the edge. Towering on the other sides were piles of wrecked cars and pieces of scrap metal. As the clouds shifted, the bright white of the moon caught the sharp metallic edges: a cascading waterfall of junk.

The van in the centre looked similar to the one Jason had burned out less than twenty-four hours ago: dark blue, no logos, number plates that were five years old and almost certainly belonged to a different vehicle. With the back empty, it could no doubt get up a fair head of steam.

The doors were open but there was no key in the ignition, perhaps not surprising considering the gates had been left unlocked too. Jason tried the grille at the front of the vehicle but there was nothing except a thin layer of black grime, which he ended up wiping on the ground. He eventually found the keys taped to the underside of the front wheel arch on the driver's side. Jason took a few moments to ensure he knew where all of the controls were and then he opened the gates fully, eased the van out, locked the place properly, and set off for the city centre.

The letter 'N' flashed on Jason's phone again but he ignored it for the second time. Natalie could wait – she was probably only going to bollock him and say that whatever arrangement they had was over. Jason was slumped in the front seat of the van, parked on the side street opposite Manchester Prison's main gates. A van had entered but nothing had come out in over an hour. There was no doubt some-thing was happening, though. Three marked police cars were parked on the road outside, the officers huddling together at the front under a street light and sharing a flask of tea.

Jason's phone began buzzing once more – Natalie again. This time, he turned it off. The last thing he wanted when trying to concentrate was his phone ringing the entire even-ing. He didn't know if he was going to speak to her again anyway. She was offering him an escape but the money he could make this evening offered its own getaway too. He was playing both sides, trying to find a way out but not knowing who was giving him the better option. Natalie wanted something he couldn't offer but there was some-thing different about Harry too. He was expecting more from Jason but showing the stick as well as the carrot.

Jason didn't know if he was being used or doing the using.

In a flurry of movement, the police officers raced back to their cars and, moments later, the gates slowly cranked open. As the white-grey prison van edged into view, Jason started the van's engine, leaving the headlights off.

One of the police cars began moving towards the main road, with the prison van behind and then the final two police vehicles. No sirens, no blue flashing lights, no drama.

Jason had searched the name 'Samuel Yates' on his phone, wanting to know at least something about the man whose escape he was supposed to be aiding. Yates was an accountant who'd been jailed eight months ago for killing his wife. According to the news report, he'd come home early from a business weekend away and found his other half in bed with a man he didn't know. As they'd struggled to get dressed and proclaim some sort of apology, Yates had calmly walked to the kitchen, picked up the biggest knife they had, returned to the bedroom and stabbed the pair of them to death.

Then he'd carved out her liver.

By the time the police arrived two hours after neighbours had reported the screaming, he had polished off three-quarters of a bottle of wine and a third of his late wife's liver, with a side of carrots and broccoli.

Yates's lawyer tried to argue he'd had a mental breakdown, which wasn't beyond the realms of possibility given the meal he'd cooked himself, but the prosecution had said the killings were ruthless and that the decision to take out his wife's liver was a ploy to pretend he was insane.

In the game of Insane or Not Insane, he'd been ruled 'not' and the jury had found him guilty. The judge told him he'd spend the rest of his life in prison.

Except there was more to it than that.

Harry, or his 'friend of a friend', wouldn't be worried about getting a wife-killer out of prison, especially not in such a public way as this. It was the fact he was an accountant that surely mattered. Somewhere along the line, his firm would have been doing business for someone like Harry, who needed a special kind of expertise. Money would be laundered, accounts would be fiddled. Yates would know things. Whoever wanted Yates could hardly sign into the prison as a visitor and ask where their money was, so a little creativity was needed.

Jason really should have asked for more money.

The convoy turned right onto the main road – the exact route Jason had predicted, at least so far. One road, approximately four miles. Harry had told Jason not to do anything too close to the city centre, so that ruled out the first three-quarters of a mile or so, with the final half mile also no good because it was too close to the motorway junction. That left him under three miles to work within.

Jason flicked his headlights on and accelerated out of the side street, pulling onto the main road behind the final police car.

As they were walking back to the car, he'd asked Harry how their 'friends' would know he was about to intercept the van but Harry had said not to worry – they'd be nearby, watching.

The convoy stopped a short distance along the road at a set of traffic lights and Jason checked his mirrors. Directly behind was a dark hatchback. Could that be holding the rest of the gang? Everything about Harry meant don't ask, just trust. There had never been a problem in the past – deliveries arrived when he said they would, people were in the places they were expected to be and even the money turned up regularly. Yet Jason couldn't help but feel he had missed something. It was one thing to have faith in someone saying a vehicle piled high with electrical items would arrive at a certain time, another entirely to trust that there was a group of people out of sight ready to jump in and help.

Still, believing in an unseen force was what faith was all about. Jason just didn't know if he held that conviction in Harry any longer.

Fifty. Thousand. Pounds.

As the lights flickered to green, the police cars and prison van accelerated as one, going at about five miles over the limit. Jason stayed close to the police car at the rear, knowing what he wanted to do and that he'd only have one go at it.

A few hundred more metres and they stopped at the next set of lights. Jason checked his mirrors again – the dark hatchback had gone.

What would happen if he turned around and went home? He'd already got on Harry's bad side by visiting Richard Hyde and then he'd sabotaged the previous night's theft. He couldn't make another mistake, regardless of Natalie or anyone else. She could promise all sorts but she couldn't protect him against a third strike.

He wondered if he'd had such a good relationship with Harry over the years simply because he hadn't messed up very often. Until he'd used Chris for a job, he'd barely even seen Harry's darker side. The incident with Carter in the concrete room had taught him a lesson but not the right one. What it *should* have told him was to forget about his half-a-million target and find a quicker way out. Instead, he'd taken it as a reminder that he had to do a better job.

It dawned on him that he had become everything he'd spent his teenage years trying not to be: he was his mother.

It wasn't the drink, drug or television addiction but Harry was 'Uncle' Graham and he was the broken, battered partner going back for more. How had he not seen it before?

The traffic lights burned green against the night sky and the prison van edged away again, slightly more slowly this time. Jason turned right, waiting until the police cars were out of sight of his mirrors and then hammering the accelerator. At the next junction, he spun left without slowing, roaring along Bury Old Road. Bury Old and New Roads ran parallel to each other, separated by Clowes Park.

When Jason had been younger, everything with Harry had been a bit of a game, then he'd realised it was more serious than he'd first assumed. Even then, he thought the money he was making was going to be his freedom but the only way to truly get away was to pack up in the middle of the night, take his brother and his mother and disappear. He'd been so naïve.

The van barrelled along the road, being flashed by a camera as Jason blazed through a set of red traffic lights.

One chance – fifty thousand pounds and then he'd do what he'd always planned: he'd go. Forget Natalie and her vague promises, he'd take things into his own hands. He'd somehow persuade Chris and his mum they had to leave – even if he had to bribe her with alcohol – and then he'd drive to Dover and get on a ferry. From France, he could . . . well, he wasn't sure but at least he'd be out of Manchester, out of England. Perhaps then he would call Lucy and ask her to visit him. She wanted to travel, after all.

Jason skidded left around the next corner, just about maintaining control but knowing he had to keep the speed up. He would definitely be ahead of the convoy but still had the stretch of tarmac that took him back to the junction with Bury New Road and he was hoping for a bit of luck with the traffic lights.

The speedometer hit fifty, with the traffic lights ahead

on green as Jason finally eased off. He wanted to beat the prison van and police cars to the four-way junction but didn't want to cross before they got there.

Forty miles an hour, thirty: still green. Where was a red light when it was needed?

To Jason's left, he had a view of the main road and the convoy trundling along, a row of cars in front slowing for the red light.

Twenty, still green.

In his mirror, a car flashed his headlights.

Fifteen, he couldn't go much slower.

BEEEEEEP!

The car swerved around, driving on the wrong side of the road and shooting across the junction just as the lights turned amber. Jason rolled the van to a halt, never more grateful to see a red light.

He was on the Prestwich border with shops on his right and Barnfield Park directly ahead. The motorway was a mile away at most.

Jason's heart was thumping: this was his only shot. The lights on the main road changed to green and the stream of traffic began slipping through. Over the top of the hedge, Jason could see the three police cars sandwiching the van. He was counting the seconds as the cars continued to move along. Eight, nine, ten: would the lights turn back to red before the convoy got through? If so, what would he do then? He couldn't wait at a green light through an entire cycle.

Above, the traffic lights burned red; on either side they remained green. It was going to work . . .

Jason put the van in gear, dropped the handbrake and rested his foot on the accelerator. All he had to do was time it – when the bumper of the first police car reached the junction, he'd stand on the accelerator and by the time he reached the junction, he should be able to clip the back of the prison van with enough speed to set it spinning. His van would continue moving across the junction where he could bail out and disappear into the shadows of the park and the golf course beyond. Meanwhile, the second team, wherever they were, would do their thing and rescue Samuel Yates. By the time the police had the helicopters up, he would have changed clothes and be sitting in a pub somewhere. Easy peasy.

Closer . . . closer . . .

Two vehicles to go . . . one . . . next up was the police car.

Jason revved the engine and then . . . hurtling across the junction directly in front of him, straight through the red light, were three more police cars, blue lights spinning. Jason gasped in surprise, stalling the engine as the three new cars joined the others, providing a protective escort on all four sides of the prison van. The convoy slipped across the junction, six sets of blue lights now spinning and disappearing into the night.

BEEEEEEP!

Jason realised he was waiting at a green light. He pulled steadily across the junction, heart thumping, hands shaking. He parked on the edge of the road, staring into the distance. Not only had more police cars turned up but there were no vehicles behind the convoy. If he *had* set the prison van spinning, then where was the supposed pick-up team for Yates?

He tried to run through the events of the night, hearing Harry's voice tell him not to intervene too close to the centre or too far away from the motorway. Jason had thought that intercepting the prison van at this spot was his idea but it had been Harry's all along: he'd just been led into it.

If that was the case, and the additional police cars had appeared at this *exact* spot, did that mean he had been set up?

32

Jason didn't know if he screamed as he woke up, or if it was just in his mind. His bedroom was freezing, the window wide open, not just on the catch. His head was throbbing, vision hazy. He went across and closed the window, wrapping his arms around himself and trying to keep the cold out. Could he really be sleepwalking and opening it every night? It sounded ridiculous but no more than either Chris or his mother coming into his room without waking him, opening it, and then leaving again. Why would they?

Outside was the usual scene: schoolchildren, buses, cars, people walking, talking, complaining. No one paying his flat a blind bit of attention.

Jason shivered again, not because of the cold, but remembering how close he had been to disaster the previous evening. Had Harry set him up or was it one big misunderstanding?

What was happening to him? He was riddled with paranoia: sleepwalking, seeing demons, second-guessing those he once trusted.

In the kitchen, Chris was fully dressed, looking almost like his old self apart from the purple and yellow bruises around his eyes. He plucked two pieces of bread from the toaster and began to smear marmalade across them.

'Mum's up then,' Jason said.

His brother smiled, licking the knife. 'How'd you guess? You look like shite by the way.'

'Can I ask you something?'

'That depends.'

'I don't care if the answer's yes or no, I just want you to tell me the truth.'

Chris dropped the knife into the sink. 'Shoot.'

'Have you been opening my window?'

'What window?'

'The one in my room.'

Chris frowned in confusion. 'Are you high or something? Why would I open your window?'

'I don't know, I just . . . forget it. How are you feeling?'

'Fine – I spoke to the probation guy, like you said. I told him I'd fallen down the stairs. He wanted a doctor's note but I said I'd go in and show him the bruises and he said it'd be okay. I'm going round Kat's in a bit. She says I need some "looking after" if you get what I mean.'

'I think a blind, deaf nun would get what you mean.'

Chris sniggered. 'Seriously – you look like you could do with some kip.'

Jason turned, ready to leave. 'I'll bear that in mind.'

On his way to the front door, he stared at the doormat, looking for the advertising card that wasn't there, which left the obvious question: if Harry didn't want to see him, was that a good or bad thing?

Jason's phone buzzed as he was sitting at the computer terminal in the library. Lucy presumably wasn't working, although he hadn't gone there to see her anyway.

With a whisper, Jason answered it.

'Oh, so you do answer your phone,' Natalie's voice said.

'I was busy.'

'Can we meet? It's urgent.'

'Where?'

'You pick – wherever you're comfortable. Send me the address. One hour.'

The line went dead, leaving Jason looking at an empty screen and then the scolding face of an old woman two seats down. She nodded at the 'no mobile phones' sign on the wall next to them and then turned back to her screen.

Jason knew just the right place to meet. He texted Natalie the address and then focused back on the screen: £330,420. He hadn't been paid for the last two jobs, not that he'd been successful in either. He checked the temperature in Crete – twenty-two degrees – and then logged off, getting a 'shush' from the old woman for good measure because he had the temerity to accidentally, and painfully, bang his knee on the desk.

Outside, he peered across the road towards the newsagent. He felt the pull to buy ten more scratch cards but hadn't been paid this time. He'd be breaking his ritual if he went ahead. Jason only realised he was staring when a woman with a pram wheeled her way around him, tutting despite not having bothered to ask him to move. With the casino a part of his everyday life, he thought it strange that the one aspect of gambling to which he'd succumbed involved a coin and a piece of cardboard.

*

'This is nice,' Natalie said sarcastically, sliding onto the chair opposite Jason and making it obvious she was trying not to touch anything.

For once, she hadn't dressed for the occasion. He'd chosen a typical cafe nearly in the shadow of Old Trafford football stadium, yet she was wearing a suit. The walls were almost as greasy as the food but the constant smell of bacon was as reassuring as it got. From the kitchen, there was a steady sizzle of meat on griddle.

Natalie flicked her hair back, straightening her top as she sat. Jason could barely remember what she'd looked like in the bar when they'd first met. Like so many other things, it was a memory that had become a dream. Most of the past week or so had a haze around it, as if he'd been drinking the entire time. Perhaps that was what life was like for his mother?

She plopped a ring binder on the seat next to her, followed by a box file. 'You don't even know what thin ice you're on, do you?' Natalie said.

Jason shrugged. He didn't really like coffee but he'd already drunk one and was starting on his second to try to keep himself awake.

'Didn't I tell you to stop that robbery?' she said.

'I did, didn't I?'

'I didn't tell you to burn an entire van out, stolen goods and all.'

'Who says that was me?'

Natalie raised a single eyebrow and picked up the lever file. 'A handful of people know what's going on. I've had to persuade them to stay off your back, telling them you're the right man. They're unhappy, though. They're saying what I have been – that it doesn't feel like a two-way thing. We can't turn blind eyes if we're not getting anything back. I've been pretty clear about what's expected from you. The fact you sabotaged that robbery does at least show some goodwill – even though you bodged it.'

She paused as the server came across with a steaming cup of tea, which he put on the table in front of her. Jason asked for a third coffee and stifled a yawn.

'You look tired,' Natalie said.

'So people keep saying.'

'Where were you last night?'

'At home.'

'Really?'

'Why?'

'You sure you weren't in Prestwich?'

Jason couldn't stop his mouth from flopping open, giving Natalie her answer. The waiter returned, swapping Jason's empty mug for a full one.

Still he didn't close his mouth. 'How . . . ?'

'You were set up – which you would have known if you'd bothered to answer your phone. I didn't know if you were involved but there was a tip to say someone was going to try to intercept a prison van. Some extra police cars were sent out, I believe.'

'I . . .'

'You should've called to say what was happening,' Natalie said firmly.

'I couldn't prove any of it – nothing happened anyway.' Jason was playing fast with the truth: nothing *had* occurred but it wasn't for the want of trying. Natalie didn't have to know that, though, and he hadn't expressly admitted he was there either.

'Do you have anything for me?' Natalie asked.

'The family that were burned in their home – the Guptas – that was ordered by Harry.'

Natalie took out a notepad. 'Really? Who carried it out?'

'I don't know.'

'What else?'

'There's a room under Casino 101. It's made from concrete, no windows, just a door. Harry's right-hand man, Carter, carries out beatings and the like there.'

'I need more.'

'How do I know you'll look after me?'

Natalie reached for the box file, unclipping the top and sliding a sheaf of papers across the table. Jason read the top page, words like 'immunity' and 'refuge' jumping from the paper, even though they were buried among a wealth of legal jargon.

'You can get a lawyer to look that over for you if you want,' Natalie said.

Jason scan-read the rest of the page but didn't bother flicking to the second. He shook his head – he had taken things too far to go back now.

Then he went back to the start. Harry had betrayed him and so he betrayed Harry. He told Natalie about the black car pulling up next to his thirteen-year-old self on the edge of the estate, about 'Uncle' Graham going missing, about the business names he'd seen and heard of at various points over the last few years – places that were most likely laundering money. He downplayed his own role in every-thing but talked about the beatings and robberies that had been ordered, about the garages where they swapped cars and the drop-off points for the things they stole. He gave the names he knew, which weren't many.

By the end, it felt as if a massive weight had been lifted. It was the first time he'd ever said most of it out loud.

Throughout, Natalie wrote, nodded and asked the odd question. Mainly, she just let him talk – like a therapist listening to an unloading patient.

'Is that what you were after?' Jason asked when he was finished.

She snapped the top of the pad closed. 'More or less.'

'What's going to happen now?'

'I'll have to come back to you later today. This is all very good but there are still channels I have to go through. I'm not going to ask about what nearly happened last night and I don't want to judge anything you've told me but I'll ask you something you should be asking yourself.'

She paused for dramatic effect.

'Given the events of last night and what happened with your brother, how well do you know Harry Irwell?'

33

Jason drove back from the cafe with a constant eye on his rear-view mirror. Every time someone pulled in behind him, he'd carefully examine their features, wondering if the person was watching him. He weaved in and out of the side streets, getting stuck behind a dustbin lorry but not worrying because it meant anyone who was following him would stand out.

He shouldn't have brought his own car – he should have taken the bus, or left his vehicle somewhere in Salford and walked. Jason was feeling a strange mix of relief and panic. Finally saying it all out loud made everything with Harry feel real but, at the same time, there was no going back now. Harry had tried to double-cross Jason with the prison van ambush – which meant that he had played his cards.

Now it was time for Jason to play his – even if he still hadn't figured out what had happened with Chris. Was his brother's abduction a punishment for the money he owed Richard Hyde, or payback for Jason kicking one of Harry's dealers down the concrete steps? Hyde had given a firm denial and Jason had not had the guts to ask Harry directly.

Back at the flat, Jason parked and took the stairs at the far end, walking around the dried pool of blood that was either Chris's or the dealer's.

Inside and there was no advertising card waiting for him on the doormat, which only left him more convinced by what Natalie had told him. If the prison van job was as important as Harry had made out – a friend of a friend, fifty thousand's worth – then he would surely want a word after it all went wrong?

His mother was lying on the sofa, half-full vodka bottle in her hand, cackling at the television. On the floor was a plate covered with toast crumbs from earlier on. Unsurprisingly, she'd almost certainly not moved for the entire morning.

The room was dimmer than usual, so Jason tried the light switch, although it made no difference.

'Bulb's gone,' his mum said.

Jason perched on the edge of the sofa. 'When did that happen?'

'Dunno. This morning? Yesterday?'

'Do we have any replacements in?'

She didn't look away from the television. 'How would I know?'

Jason went into the kitchen and hunted through the cupboards. Buried behind the plates, underneath an empty plastic pot was a damp cardboard box with nibble marks in the corner. His mother complained that he was blocking the television but Jason changed the bulb anyway, trying to balance on the coffee table as he strained. With a flicker and a blast of heat, the room came to light again.

His mother shifted positions to have a drink as Jason perched on the end of the sofa. 'Was there any mail, Mum?' he asked.

'Dunno.'

'Well, did you get up and pick anything off the door-mat?'

'Why would I do that?'

Jason didn't reply, though he would love to have said: 'Because you live here.'

'Was there anything at all for me – a card? A parcel? Did anyone knock on the door after Chris went out?'

'Stop bothering me – I'm trying to watch this.'

She took another swig from the vodka and then burst out laughing, pointing at the screen, even though Jason wasn't sure what she found amusing. From what he could make out, it was a history documentary. Under her arm was the cushion filled with painkillers that he'd switched. The zip of the cover was undone slightly and when she noticed him watching, she tucked it firmly against the back of the sofa.

Jason went to his room, feeling the chill as he entered. The window was open again – and this time he definitely hadn't done it, sleepwalking or not, because he hadn't been in. Chris could have come in here on the way out and done it specifically after Jason had asked him about it, but he thought they were past that pettiness. Regardless of how bad the abduction and beating had been, it had at least marked a turning point for them as brothers.

That only left his mother – who claimed she'd not left the sofa. Yet she had to get the alcohol from somewhere, either buying it herself or having someone bring it to her. He had no idea why she would keep coming into his room to open the window but then what did he know about alcoholism at all? What did he know about his mother for that matter? She was just the woman who lay on the sofa for days at a time and bellowed when she wanted toast. Could she have been lying about his sleepwalking the entire time? He didn't know what to think, his mind a mangled maze of deception and suspicion.

Jason closed the window and sat on his bed, screwing his eyes closed and flopping backwards. It wasn't just Harry who had betrayed him, it was his mother too. She had brought a string of uncles into his and Chris's lives and then abandoned them to be beaten. She must have money somewhere, because where else would the booze and tablets be coming from?

Another hoot of laughter breezed through from the living room. What exactly was it she found so funny? Was she laughing at him? Perhaps they all were? This was the game – put him in awkward situations and then swap notes.

Then Jason's memory flicked back to the morning. Perhaps he *hadn't* shut his window after all? It had definitely been cold and it was open wide but could he remember for absolute certain closing it?

He screwed his eyes shut, resting on his pillow and staring into the darkness. Everyone kept saying he looked tired and now he was feeling it. His head lolled to the side, thoughts of Lucy flitting through his mind. Through all of this, she was the normal one at the centre of his disjointed world.

Buzzzzzzzzzzzzzzz.

Jason's hand shot down to his pocket as his phone

started to vibrate. His eyes were lazy, wanting to rest, but the single letter on the front was something he couldn't ignore this time. In the instant that the 'N' had flashed, it disappeared once more and the missed call logo popped up.

Rubbing his eyes, Jason returned to the window, staring down at the street below. A teenager who almost certainly should have been at school was strolling past, chatting on his phone. Across the road, a hoody disappeared into the alley opposite. Jason waited, watching, as he emerged a minute later with his hands in his pockets.

Harry's influence had returned.

Jason watched the metallic-red estate car pull up and park on double-yellow lines next to the bus stop.

It was time to go.

34

Natalie sped away before Jason had a chance to fully close the passenger's door. Someone more interested in their phone than the road they were crossing jumped out of the way, bellowing a volley of swear words in their direction.

'Whoa . . .' Jason said.

'Double-yellows,' Natalie replied.

'Are you really worried about tickets?'

Natalie was wearing the exact same clothes as before but her car was far more cluttered, the back seat laden with files and cardboard folders. 'I've been talking to people ever since I left you,' she said.

'Doing what?'

'Talking them through everything you told me.'

'So, is everything okay? We need to talk about how everything will work and . . .' Jason tailed off, realising Natalie was shaking her head. 'What?' he added.

'Why didn't you call me about the attempt to break Samuel Yates from that prison van?'

'Who's saying I knew? You've just told me that name, I didn't know it before.'

Natalie glanced away from the road, letting him know she wasn't convinced. 'You could have proven your intentions by letting me know something was going on but you didn't. Instead someone else tipped us off.'

Jason couldn't reply because he had no answer – he'd been thinking of the fifty thousand and his other way out. When that had fallen through, it had left him with this.

'What else do you know about it?' Natalie snapped.

'Nothing – it wasn't me. I wasn't there. I just heard rumours that something important was happening last night. I would have called you but didn't know any details – plus I didn't have my papers anyway, remember. You only gave them to me this morning. You said it was a two-way thing and that was your half.'

'Does Harry know Samuel Yates?'

'I don't know.'

'Have you ever heard Harry or anyone else talking about Yates?'

'No.' That part was true at least.

Natalie indicated off the main road and pulled into a parking space outside a row of red-brick terraced houses. She checked her mirrors and then turned the engine off, turning to Jason.

'Do you remember when you asked me if we had people working within Harry's organisation?'

'Of course.'

'Things are complicated, Jason, but there's something I need to tell you. You must have wondered how I found you in that pub.'

Jason felt the creeping sensation along his back again that wasn't related to an open window or the cold. He knew that his world was in the process of coming down around him.

'I was given your name,' she added.

Jason scrolled through the list of people in his group: Kev, Gavin, Pete and the others. It could be any of them, or none of them. Carter knew everything – he could have been careless in who he spoke to, if he ever spoke to anyone. It could be the doorman in the casino. It could even be Chris – he was stupid enough to have blabbed to Clarkey, Kat or any of the rest of his mob.

'Who by?' Jason asked.

'You know I can't tell you that – but I've worked my way up to you. It's exactly as you said – Harry's organisation is a complicated web of names and faces who don't know each other exist. I was looking for someone close to Harry and it took me six months to get this far. I knew about Carter, of course, but there was never a chance of approaching him, so I started with people at the bottom, gradually getting the names of people closer to Harry until I stumbled across you. I found out what happened to your father when you were a child and then . . . the pieces began to fall into place.'

Jason hadn't thought about his actual father for a long time. Hearing a stranger mention him didn't sound right and there was suddenly a lump in his throat. He had to turn away, watching through the side window as a car squeezed past.

'Want to talk about it?' Natalie said.

'No.'

'I didn't realise you were so close to Harry – it must be awful for a father figure to betray someone like that.'

Jason spun around, suddenly furious. He jabbed a finger towards her. 'Who says he betrayed me?'

Natalie didn't flinch, meeting his eyes and waiting for him to put his finger down. 'This is what I'm trying to tell you. You're not the only person I've spoken to in Harry's organisation but your name is known for more than one reason.'

Jason turned away again, trying to keep control. 'I don't know what you mean.'

'It's over.'

'What is?'

'Everything. I've asked for you – *begged* for you – but you're no use to me or my people if you're not trusted.'

'Who says I'm not trustworthy?'

'That's not what I'm saying. I've heard from people that Harry knows about you.' She checked her mirror again. 'He set you up because he thinks you're a liability. He thinks you're talking – which I suppose is true.'

Jason sat in silence, staring directly ahead through the windscreen. At the end of the street, two children were chasing after a smaller kid. Perhaps it was playful or maybe they were bullying in the same way that Jason had been picked on all those years before.

He watched them run out of view and didn't say anything for a long time. Eventually, Natalie's upbeat ringtone broke the impasse. She checked the screen and didn't answer.

'Anything important?' Jason asked.

'No.'

'Who told you that Harry knows about me?'

'I can't tell you.'

'It means I'm in danger!'

'That's what I've been trying to tell you – but giving you the name of the person who told me isn't going to change that. I'm doing you a favour by being here.'

'How is this helping?'

Natalie spun and gripped Jason's arm hard. For the first time, he saw the fire in her. 'You don't get it, do you? If he doesn't trust you, he's not going to tell you anything. You've got no chance of making him incriminate himself, so any deal we might have been talking about is worthless. You've said there are no documents you can get hold of that might be useful, no computer systems you can access. If you don't have access to Harry, you don't have anything at all.'

'What about everything I told you this morning?'

'You say he owns certain companies and moves money around. You say he arranged for all sorts of things to occur – but it's your word against his and it wouldn't even get to court.'

Jason suddenly realised why she seemed so panicked – it wasn't just his world crashing down, it was hers too. She'd worked to get this close to Harry, found the person she was after in Jason, and then it was all over. She could have walked away without a word but she'd come to him with a warning.

'We had an agreement,' Jason said limply.

'We didn't because you've not kept your end of anything. I told you all of this the first time you were in the car with me. I wanted enough to get Harry Irwell off the streets. You've not provided anything like that.'

'I've told you all I know.'

She shook her head. 'I'm sorry.'

'What can I do? If he doesn't trust me, there's no way I can stay around.'

Jason thought of the money in his account, knowing the vague escape plan of getting on a ferry was only ever a fantasy. He'd never get his mother off the sofa and he doubted she had a passport anyway. If she did, she wouldn't know where it was. As for Chris, he was so unpredictable, he'd probably tell Kat where he was going, not knowing one of Harry's men would track her down and get the information. He could run away himself, of course, but could he really go without them, knowing he was potentially leaving them at Harry's mercy?

And what about Lucy? Was there something between them or was it all in his mind?

Natalie's voice was so soft, so solemn, that she sounded like a different person. 'Down among the dead men let him lie.'

'Sorry?'

'You heard.'

Jason took a deep breath, running the words back over, trying to pretend they meant something other than what he thought they did. 'Where does the saying come from?' he asked.

'It's an eighteenth-century folk song and then the chorus became a sort of socialist anthem at one point.'

'How do you know that?'

She shrugged. 'How do we know all the things we do? Some things stick in our minds, some don't.'

'You weren't talking about socialism or folk songs when you chose those lyrics though.'

Natalie laughed, glancing away out of the window on the other side. 'No, I wasn't.'

'You think I should kill him?'

She paused. 'No, I don't. I wanted you to bring me something I could use to get him off the streets.'

'You said you were my salvation.'

Natalie didn't reply for a long while, wiping the condensation from her side of the glass and resting her head against the window. She closed her eyes. 'Perhaps you're your own salvation, Jason.'

35

Jason stood in Lucy's kitchen as she fussed around, partly cooking but mainly distracting herself by chatting. Her flat felt hotter than usual and she was wearing a black pleated skirt shorter than the red one and a loose black top that had thin spaghetti-width bands that didn't cover the black straps of her bra. Jason tried not to stare at her, telling himself she was dressed like this because it was hot and not because she knew he was coming over.

She was utterly breathtaking.

Her hair was down, curling gently but naturally around her face and flicking dramatically every time she turned from what she was doing to face Jason – which happened a lot. Her eyes were bluer: a bright oasis of colour.

'. . . so have you ever baked a cake?' Lucy spun from the stove, still stirring whatever it was she was cooking.

'I've *eaten* a cake.'

She turned back, laughing, which felt wonderful, not just because of the sound but because Jason had caused it.

'That's not what I asked,' she said.

'I've never *made* a cake. I don't even know what goes in one – except for sugar.'

'Didn't your mum ever let you make a mess in the kitchen?' She twisted to face Jason again and must have caught his expression. 'Oh, sorry . . . I forget not everyone has parents like mine.'

He shrugged. 'It's okay – but, no, she didn't.'

'We should make a cake!'

'I thought you wanted to paint me?'

She batted a hand in his vague direction, absent-mindedly spattering boiling water across the floor without realising she'd done it. 'We've got all evening.'

'I do have to go later.'

She turned and half-squinted, half-winked in the way that left Jason with no idea what her intentions were. 'Why? Did you think I was asking you to stay the night?'

'No, I—'

'I'm joking, Jason.'

'Right . . .'

'So are we making a cake or aren't we?'

'Do you have the stuff we need?'

She twiddled one of the knobs on the cooker and the bubbling water slowed to a simmer. She dropped the spoon on the side and crossed to the cupboards next to Jason, edging him out of the way and crouching. As she spoke, she placed various bags on the counter. '*Stuff?* What type of cook are you? Anyway, I've got sugary stuff, floury stuff, eggy stuff, there's buttery stuff in the fridge – and I might even have some chocolaty stuff somewhere.'

With the spaghetti bolognaise officially turned down, Lucy taught Jason how to bake a cake. For the most part, it involved dumping a bunch of things into a bowl, stirring until their arms felt like they were going to drop off, pouring the mixture into a circular tin, and then putting it in the oven.

Jason wondered how this type of life had escaped him for so long. Lucy giggled, twirled her hair, smudged cake mixture on his nose and then they took turns to lick the bowl – although she insisted she wasn't sharing the spoon with anyone.

When everything was ready, they moved into the living room, dragging the furniture around and – for the first time Jason could remember in a long time – he had a meal in a house without the television on. The pasta might have been mushy because it had been on the stove for the best part of an hour but neither of them cared. It wasn't what he was eating that mattered anyway. She offered to open a bottle of wine from the fridge but Jason said he had to drive later.

In the time between talking to Natalie and coming to Lucy's, he'd been thinking about what he had to do. There was really only one answer – he'd backed himself into a corner with no easy way to get out. If this was to be his last supper, then it couldn't really have gone much better. If only for a few hours on an autumn evening, he was living the type of life that everyone else had.

They finished the spaghetti perfectly on cue, just as the oven began to beep. Sugary-scented wafts escaped as Lucy pulled the oven door down and took their cake out, placing it on the counter.

'Ta-da!'

'It's a bit flat, isn't it?' Jason said.

'I think you're supposed to use self-raising flour but I've

only got plain. Anyway, aren't you excited? An hour ago, this was all stuff in the cupboard and now it's an actual cake.'

Jason prodded the warm surface. 'It is kind of cool.'

'Isn't this fun? I've not made a cake in ages. We could try cookies, or brownies, or something else next week.'

'We should probably make sure this one is edible first.'

Lucy reached into a drawer and took out a large knife. 'Good idea.'

As she cut, she was listing more sugary creations they could make but Jason could see only the blade. For her, it was a kitchen instrument; for him, it was a reminder of the life with which he'd landed himself. Harry's letter-opener was hidden under the carpet in the back corner of his bedroom – a memento of his paranoia, which was apparently not misplaced.

'. . . so do you think we should ice it?' Lucy said.

'Oh, er . . .'

'I've got some icing sugar and jam. What do you reckon? We'll have to let it cool first.'

'Okay . . .'

'You look like I've just asked if you want to jump out of a plane without a parachute.'

'It's not that, it's just . . . I've never done anything like this before.'

Lucy smiled but not in the way she usually did. There was an understanding behind the blue of her eyes, like she knew who he was. *Really* knew. 'Well, there's a first time for everything and I have no intention of eating a cake without icing, so let's get on with it.'

A bit of butter, some icing sugar, a whole lot of mess, and they were there.

Sort of.

The horizontal slice through the centre of the cake wasn't quite straight, so the top half had started to slip, causing the icing to slide as well. Everything was slightly lop-sided: jam had dribbled onto the floor and the finished product looked as if it had been dropped.

It was still theirs though.

Lucy stepped back and held her arms out. 'Ta . . . duh . . .'

'It's a bit rubbish, isn't it?' Jason said.

'It's the taste that counts.'

Lucy cut two large wedges and put them onto plates. She led Jason back into the living room and they sat at the table again.

'You go first,' she said.

'What if it's, I don't know . . . *off*, or something?'

'How can a cake be off?'

'I don't know.' Jason prodded the lumpy, misshapen slice with a fork. 'When I said I'd eaten cakes, I meant ones that didn't look like they'd been used for a game of football first.'

Lucy scowled at him, jabbing a fork in his direction and trying not to smile. 'It's your fault – my cakes aren't usually so . . . fally-aparty.'

'You should definitely try it first,' he said.

'Fine – be like that.'

Lucy cut through the cake with her fork and lifted it to her mouth as Jason hummed the theme tune from *Jaws*.

She swallowed a small amount before bursting out laughing and spraying the rest across the table.

'Can you stop the humming?' she said.

'What did it taste like?'

'Surprisingly, it tasted like a cake.'

Jason risked a forkful and she was right. 'Definitely cakey,' he concluded.

'There's a massive stack of washing-up in there,' Lucy said, nodding towards the kitchen.

'It's your flat.'

'Yeah but you made at least half of the mess.'

And so, after finishing his slice of the ropey-looking cake they'd made, Jason joined Lucy in the kitchen and spent fifteen minutes of the best evening of his life drying up.

Eventually, with the kitchen as clean as it was going to get, Lucy led him back into the living room and they re-arranged it to the way it was when Jason had arrived. He took his seat in the centre of the room, put the hat on and gazed at the usual spot on the wall.

Lucy wriggled herself onto the stool behind the easel and picked up the paintbrush. She chewed on the wooden end, peering across the room towards Jason.

'What?' he asked.

'You've got an interesting face.'

'Er, thanks . . .'

'It's not a bad thing – you're sort of . . . weird. Good weird, though.'

'Right . . .'

She popped her head around the canvas and dabbed the

brush onto her palette. 'I think I'm just fascinated because what I've thought of as standard – mucking around in the kitchen, reading, travelling, and so on, are things that aren't normal for you. I'm sure there are loads of things you know that I wouldn't have a clue about.'

She didn't realise how right she was but there wasn't an awful lot Jason could reply with.

'Sorry . . .' Lucy added.

'It's okay – you're right.'

'What's wrong with your mum? You said she hadn't been well.'

'It's awkward – she's . . .'

Lucy's brush swiped across the canvas. 'You don't have to say – I'm just being nosey.'

Jason shuffled uncomfortably before shifting back into the position he was supposed to be in. With a sigh, he made his decision: 'She's been an alcoholic for almost as long as I can remember. I don't even know the last time she left the flat but she somehow manages to have money for the booze. I don't know if it's my brother who's getting it for her, or . . . I just don't know.'

There was a silence broken only by the delicate strokes of brush on canvas. 'I don't know what to say.'

'It's okay, nor do I really.'

'Do you look after her?'

'Sort of. She refuses to eat anything but toast most of the time, so either me or my brother has to go shopping. Usually me, because he never has any money.'

'What exactly is it you do . . . ?'

Jason knew this was the moment where he either had to

tell the truth and stand by whatever came with it, or lie and stick to it for as long as he was going to know Lucy.

There was only one option: 'It's mainly courier work – delivering packages and so on – like I said. Not particularly skilled, I suppose.'

'Everyone has to start somewhere. It's not where you begin that matters – it's where you end up.'

Jason wondered if that was true. Could everything up to one point in a person's life be discounted because he or she ended up in a better place at the end of it? It sounded too easy and yet that was what he'd spent the past few years building towards. He'd tried to save his money so he could run away to a better place.

'Are you nervous about something?'

Lucy hadn't stopped painting but her remark came out of the blue.

'Huh?'

'The other times you've posed for me, you've been really still but you're fidgeting.'

'Sorry.'

Lucy put the brush down and began using her fingers, dabbing small blobs of dark paint onto the canvas. Jason didn't know what to say to her; when they were talking about her life, he felt comfortable because she was everything he wasn't. After a few minutes, she dipped her fingers into a pot of water and then dried them on a tea towel.

She stood and looked at Jason over the top of the easel. 'It's finished.'

'Can I see it?'

Lucy made a 'hmm' sound and tilted her head, chewing on her bottom lip. 'I'm not sure if I want you to.'

'Why?'

'I don't want you to be offended.'

Jason took the hat off and stood. 'Why would I be?'

'It's not meant to be a perfect likeness. It's Expressionist—'

'So it's your impression *of* me, rather than what I actually look like.'

Lucy bobbed awkwardly on one foot and tugged her top up. 'I suppose.'

Jason shrugged. 'I'd like to see it.'

She smiled weakly but this was the most vulnerable Jason had seen her. The confidence and smartness she exuded was replaced by an insecurity that didn't befit her. She stepped across to the easel and turned it around.

At first, Jason wasn't quite sure what he was looking at. Swirls, smudges and swipes were combined with gentler, far more subtle, brushstrokes. He moved closer, wanting to touch it but stopping just short. The texture was as fascinating as the content itself: thick mounds of paint in some areas, barely there smears in others.

It was undoubtedly him and yet it wasn't.

There were deep, dark bags under his eyes: thick blobs of black and grey blended with the colour Lucy had used for the rest of his skin. The hat he'd been wearing at her request was hardly there, replaced by a halo that was grey and decaying, like crumbling, weathered stone. The rest of the image was relatively accurate – his ears, nose and mouth all in proportion, the only confusion being that he had one grey eye, one green.

When Jason turned, Lucy was biting her fingernails, glancing nervously from him to the painting and back again.

'I'm not sure I get it,' Jason said.

'Do you promise you won't be offended?'

'Yes.'

'Say it.'

'I promise.'

Lucy stepped forward and took his hand, interlocking their fingers as she had in the library. Her fingers were still slightly damp but they were wonderfully warm. Jason brushed his thumb across the shape of her fingers as she reached forward with her other hand, pointing towards the halo.

'It's like you're two people and I'm not sure who the real you is.'

Her fingers twitched but didn't release his. Jason continued staring at the painting. 'I really like it,' he said.

'Honestly?'

'Sometimes I feel like two people: as if I don't quite know what I want.'

He paused to lean in and have an even closer look at the textures. He could see individual thumb- and fingerprints in the halo, as if she had been massaging his thoughts as she'd created it.

'What are you going to do with it?' Jason asked.

'I've got to hand it in for my project.'

'Do you get it back?'

'I suppose – do you want it?'

'I don't know – it'd be a bit strange to have a painting of me on the wall.'

Lucy released his fingers and snaked an arm around Jason's back. Instinctively, he draped an arm around her shoulders as she wedged herself into the crook of his shoulder. 'I'm sure we can think of something to do with it. I thought you'd hate it.'

'I don't.'

'Do you remember when I said I liked you because you'd never asked me out?'

'Yes.'

'I'd quite like you to ask me out now.'

Jason took a breath. Thinking. 'Where are we going to go?' he said.

Lucy giggled and squeezed him. 'It's questions like that which are why I'd like you to ask me out now.'

Jason breathed again. In through the nose, out through the mouth, not knowing how to phrase things. 'I don't think I can today.'

'Why?'

'There's something I have to do later.'

Lucy wriggled her way away from him and locked eyes. 'If anyone else had said that, I'd have told them to get lost.' She didn't sound aggrieved.

'Can I ask you tomorrow?'

'If you ask me now, I'll say "yes". I don't know what I'll say tomorrow.'

'I'm sorry.'

'What do you have to do later?'

'I can't tell you. Will you trust me?'

Lucy turned back to face the canvas: her reply implicit through her painting.

36

Jason sat in his car, staring at the intimidatingly high gates of Harry's house. A chill autumn mist had enveloped the city, seeping into the very fabric with its whispering, freezing tendrils. Somewhere in the distance, a set of headlights zipped through the cloud but Jason hadn't seen anything moving close to the gates in almost half an hour. Not even dog-walkers were insane enough to go out in this weather.

For the third time in the past sixty seconds, Jason checked his watch: eleven minutes to midnight. He got out of his car and buttoned his jacket tight, heading to the gate and not worrying about the height this time. With a few quick heaves and a scrambling of feet, he was at the top and then dropped into the same bush as before. After the first occasion, he knew how to roll and where to aim for. A grunt of gentle pain still slipped out but nothing more.

As Jason headed along the driveway, the mist grew thicker, shielding the cars and most of the house. At the top, the security system switched on, sending fibres of white light threading through the ethereal night, but barely providing any clarity.

Jason rang the doorbell and waited, unbuttoning his jacket, as he realised he wasn't even cold. He turned in a full circle, feeling the haze around him, enjoying its embrace. As he was thinking about ringing a second time, a light flicked on inside and then there was the sound of a heavy bolt and chain.

Harry was suddenly in front of him: heavy brown dressing gown tied tightly around his waist with matching slippers. His legs were sticking out of the bottom, thin spider-like hairy knees barely seeming enough to hold him up, let alone provide any athleticism. His face was grey and pale, bristles of black and white stubble on his chin. He was an old man.

'I'm going to have to build my gate a little higher,' he said with the merest upturn of his lip, nodding his head sideways and holding the door open wider.

He led Jason through to the room that was similar to his office, flipping the lid on the globe and pouring himself a drink.

'Want one?' he asked.

'I'm driving.'

Harry pushed the crystal lid back into the decanter and crossed to the leather armchairs. Jason joined him, half-wishing he'd taken a drink after all.

'Did I ever tell you where that globe came from?'

'No.'

'It was a gift from many years ago – housewarming if I remember correctly.'

'Who from?'

Harry snorted a smile before taking a sip of his whisky. 'It was handmade in one of the souks of Marrakech and then imported especially for me. I was told it cost five hundred not including transport, so who knows what that would be nowadays.' He drummed his fingers on the side of the chair. 'I remember now – it wasn't housewarming at all. It was for our tenth wedding anniversary – not that Barbara's had much use from it, of course.'

Jason didn't know if he should interrupt – he didn't need many fingers to count the number of times Harry had been in a chatty, reminiscent mood like this.

Harry nodded towards the photograph of his wedding day on the wall that Jason had looked at previously. 'Thirty-eight years – that's how long it is since we got married. Her father hated me. He used to own a pub just down the road from here. It's long gone now, of course. He always said I wasn't good enough for his princess and didn't even bother coming to the wedding. Her mum came along and apologised, saying he was ill, but he was down the bookies the whole time.' Harry stopped to indicate the house. 'I wonder if the prick thinks I'm good enough for his daughter now?'

He peered across to Jason who was trying to do the maths in his head. 'We were married at seventeen,' Harry said.

'Wow.'

'It was a different age then, m'boy. Everyone was ex-pected to settle down and start popping wee bairns out. Course, with Barbara the way she is . . .'

Harry nodded towards the wedding photograph again. 'Have a look.'

Jason crossed to the wall and did as he was told. When he'd seen it the first time, it had just been a cursory glance. Harry was so young: the dark hair, the trim physique. It was still undoubtedly him though, the steely, intense gaze apparent, even though he was smiling. Barbara looked striking in the way people did in faded, grainy photographs. Her blonde hair was overexposed in the picture, the colour spilling into the sandy shade of the building behind and the whiteness of her teeth glinting distractingly. They were each toasting the camera with champagne flutes but Jason was drawn to the people around them, wondering why Harry had wanted him to take a second look. Behind Barbara was a woman Jason assumed was her mother. They shared the same wide cheekbones and round noses. Around them was a host of people, the men wearing a mix of suits with wide lapels and thick ties, the women in flowery bright dresses.

And then Jason saw him.

The man at Harry's side had thick dark hair greased back into a quiff. He had far fewer wrinkles and his glasses had thick black rims but his eyes were the same sharp, intense brown that Jason had seen in person.

'Richard Hyde was at your wedding?' Jason said, not believing it.

'He was my best man. That's where the globe came from ten years later.'

Jason couldn't take his eyes from the picture, trying to put things together in his mind. Richard Hyde had always been on the periphery of his own life at Harry's side. He was an almost mythical figure, a ghoul in the shadows who caused only trouble. Every now and then, Harry would mention him but never in positive terms, always pointing out how Hyde had invaded his territory and hurt his men. Then there were the odd occasions they were pictured together at functions: always smiling cordially, the truth of what was going on between them carefully disguised. Now it seemed the truth about their relationship had been hidden completely.

'How long have you known each other?' Jason asked.

Harry downed the rest of his drink in one. When he replied, there was a clear rasp in his voice. 'We used to knock around as kids. There was an estate perhaps a mile away from here where we both grew up. He lived on the street out the back of mine and we'd play cricket and football. Every now and then we'd skip out of class, which I've always regretted. Kids should really stay in school.'

'What happened between you?'

Harry reached for his glass again, forgetting it was empty. Jason stepped across the room and took it from him.

'Another?'

'There's a fifteen-year malt in there.'

Jason stood at the globe cabinet, his back to Harry, hand flashing in and out of his pocket as he poured a generous measure and swilled it before returning to the chairs. Harry held it to his nose, breathing the heavy fumes and peering into the cloudy bottom before taking a sip.

'We had a disagreement,' Harry said. 'There was an accident at my father-in-law's pub . . . a fire.' He paused, letting the sentence sink in as he gulped another drink, wincing as it went down. 'This was eleven or twelve years after the wedding. Cancer had taken Barbara's mother, God rest her soul, but that miserable bastard kept going and going until the flesh was dripping from his body as he slept. At least it finally gave him something to complain about.'

He paused for another drink, venom dripping from his lips. His voice was now hoarse. 'Afterwards, there was a big investigation into what started the fire but the place eventually went on the market. I thought I'd buy it for Barbs and the papers were all in place but then Richard arrived late in the day and the administrators sold it without allowing me to make a counter offer.'

Jason didn't know how to reply, other than a pitiful-sounding 'Oh . . .'

'I made it my sole aim that day to do everything I could to run him out of business – out of town, I suppose. It's not quite happened of course – for various reasons. I guess you could say we know each other too well.'

Jason let it sink in, thinking about how such carnage had spread from a simple act of buying a pub. 'Can I ask something?'

Harry raised his glass. 'That's why you're here, isn't it?'

'When I was in Oldham, Mr Hyde told me something strange. He said his children had been sent away when they were young because he didn't want them being drawn into anything. I don't really understand why he said that. Then he said that he doesn't get involved when it comes to other people's families.'

Harry paused for a moment, lips pursed. 'Did he now? Richard always was the edgy type – worrying about things he needn't have.'

'He sort of implied that maybe you . . .'

'What? Targeted his family?'

'I suppose.'

Harry shuffled until he was facing the other seat. His gaze was slightly unfocused, more looking through Jason than at him. 'So things didn't go as planned last night . . .'

'More police cars arrived just as I was in place.'

One of Harry's eyelids flickered involuntarily. 'Sometimes things don't work out as you plan.'

Before he knew it, Jason felt the now-familiar tingle tiptoeing along his spine. He shivered, goosebumps rising on his arms.

'I didn't see any other people there last night,' Jason said.

'That was kind of the point, wasn't it?'

Jason shrugged, unable to argue. 'Why didn't you want to see me today?'

'I thought you probably had a rough night.' Harry sighed, glancing up to a grandfather clock in the corner and finishing his second drink. The ornate dark wood had a beautiful spiralled pattern around the edge. It was nearly twenty past midnight. 'What's troubling you, Jason?'

'I suppose it's just how close everything was last night. If I'd moved a few seconds earlier, I wouldn't have seen the extra police cars and, well . . . I wouldn't be here now.'

'That's the game, m'boy. More money means bigger risks.'

Jason pointed at Harry's empty glass. 'Another? I think I might have a little if you don't mind.'

Harry passed it to him. 'Try the malt.'

Jason kept his back to the room as he stood by the cabinet, pouring a small amount into an empty glass and refilling Harry's most of the way to the top, before rotating the glass to mix the drink.

'You don't need to shake it,' Harry called from behind.

Jason turned: 'Sorry, it's not usually my drink.'

Back in the warmth of the comfortable leather chair, Jason breathed in the liquid but couldn't stop himself from gagging at the sulphuric peat aroma. He tried a small taste anyway, swallowing it quickly.

'You need a proper mouthful to appreciate it,' Harry said, watching Jason carefully.

'I'm not sure it's my thing.'

He nodded acceptingly. 'You've still not really told me why you're here.'

'What would you say if I wanted out?'

Harry paused, glass pressed to his lip, contemplating the wall of photographs. 'Of what?'

'Of everything.'

A hint of a smile. 'Sometimes we're defined by the ruthlessness of our decisions.' He raised his glass, angling it towards Jason. 'To the future?'

Jason clinked his glass into Harry's. 'To the future.'

He downed the toxic-tasting liquid in one and stood, nodding towards Harry's glass. 'Another?'

37

EIGHTEEN YEARS AGO

Jason wriggled his way about in the seat that was so big, his feet didn't touch the floor. He hugged the soft toy dog onto his lap and began stroking the feathery material under his large, drooped ears.

'I told you Flopsy wouldn't need a passport, Mum,' Jason said.

His mother smiled down at him from the adjacent seat. 'I was only joking, sweetie. You don't have to believe every-thing everyone tells you.'

She clipped her seatbelt into place as the air stewardess walked along the aisle, making sure everyone was belted in – as if that would make a difference if the aeroplane actually came down mid-flight.

The stewardess stopped next to Jason, beaming. 'What's your name, young man?'

'Jason.'

'I love your doggy – what's his name?'

'Flopsy.'

She leant forward and patted the toy on the head. 'Have you ever flown before, Jason?'

Jason looked at his mother, taking in her long brown hair and gently tanned skin, then turning back again. 'No but Mummy says that when Daddy gets home, we'll go to all sorts of places.'

The stewardess stood back up, smiling again. 'That sounds wonderful. My name's Katie – if you or Flopsy have any problems on the flight, you make sure you call me over, okay?'

'Okay.'

As the stewardess continued along the aisle, Jason turned to his mother. 'Do you think Flopsy will enjoy Cuh . . . right?'

'You pronounce it "Crete", honey. Does Flopsy like the sun?'

'Yes.'

'He'll love it then.'

Flopsy's tongue lolled out of his mouth, as soft as the rest of him. Despite the fact Jason had slept with him for as long as he remembered, the toy never seemed to lose its spongy, cosy feel. Jason loved him as much as anything.

'Mum . . .'

'What?'

'How long until Dad gets home?'

'We've talked about this.'

'I know but I like hearing it.'

Across the address system, the pilot said something incomprehensible because of the echo. Somewhere underneath, there was a buzz of activity and the plane began its taxi towards the runway. Jason pressed himself deeper into the seat, clutching Flopsy more tightly as he felt the power of the plane humming through him.

'Your father's a very brave man. He's away with the

army at the moment but he'll be back in six weeks' time.'

Jason began counting on his fingers as the plane gained a little speed. Across the aisle, a woman strapped a pillow around her neck and leant back in her chair, muttering a swear word to the man sitting next to her.

'Forty-two days?' Jason said.

'Good boy.'

'When he gets home, can I get a real doggy?'

Jason's mother breathed out a laugh, knowing it had been coming. 'We'll see, sweetie. We'll have to ask your father. Our flat isn't really a place for doggies – they need space, gardens and people that walk them.'

'I'll walk him.'

'It's still not really a place for pets. Let's wait until your father is home and we'll see what he thinks.'

Jason hugged Flopsy even tighter, sitting in silence for a minute or so and feeling edgy as the plane came to a gradual halt, waiting for its take-off spot. Katie hurried back along the aisle and took a seat at the front, offering Jason a grin.

'Mummy . . .'

'What?'

'How do planes work?'

Jason's mother took her son's hand, gripping him firmly. 'You really don't need to worry about that – they just do.'

'I'd like to fly planes when I'm older.'

'Last week you said you wanted to be a bin man.'

'Can I be both?'

His mother laughed, tucking a strand of hair behind her ear. 'I don't think so, sweetie. You'll have to choose.'

The plane juddered forward again, moving closer to the runway.

'What do plane-men do?'

'They're called pilots and they fly people all around the world. They see a lot of countries but they don't spend a lot of time at home.'

'Like Dad?'

'A bit.'

'What does a bin man do?'

'He empties everyone's bins.'

'Hmm . . .'

With another shuddery vibration, the plane edged forward again. Jason's mother peered through the window, craning her neck around the impossible angle. 'We're up next, sweetie.'

'How hard is it to drive a plane?'

'You *fly* a plane and I'm not sure. I think your dad will be able to tell you – he knows people in the air force. Perhaps Katie will know a little too?'

'I'm not sure I want to be a bin man or a pilot.'

'What would you like to be?'

Jason scratched his chin with one hand, hugging Flopsy a little harder with the other. 'Maybe a footballer? Or a singer? P'raps I'll be like Daddy?'

She squeezed his forearm. 'You want to be in the army? That means you'll have to be big and strong, plus you'll be away from home all the time.'

'I wouldn't want to be away from you and Daddy.'

'I'm sure you'll have someone else by then – a girl.'

'Ugh.'

'You won't be saying that when you're older.'

'I will.'

Jason's mother squeezed his nose between her fingers, smiling as he squirmed away. 'I'll remind you of this when you bring your first girlfriend home.'

There was a pause as the engines blared loudly.

'Mummy . . .'

'What, sweetie?'

'I'm scared.'

'It's okay, honey, Flopsy will look after you and I'm not going anywhere.' She took his hand, wrapping her warm fingers around his. 'We'll be going on lots of planes in the future with Daddy: seeing the world and enjoying the sun. There's a lot more to life than Manchester.'

Jason relaxed back into his seat, clasping his mother and Flopsy tightly as the plane surged forward with an excited roar. The back of his head was pressed into the material of the seat as the speed increased. He gazed out of the window at the grey of the runway and the green hedges in the distance. With a final rush of air, Jason suddenly realised he was looking down upon the hedges – then houses, roads, trees: everything. He released his hand from his mother's and began tickling Flopsy's ears, enjoying the whooshing and popping in his ears and knowing that what his mother said was true: there was an entire world out there that he was going to go and enjoy.

38

Jason opened the door to the flat just as his watch reached 03.42. He clicked the door closed and tiptoed towards the living room, peering through the open doorway towards his mother. She was curled up on the sofa, half-covered by the blanket and bathed in the blue-white glow of the television. For a few moments, he stood watching, arms crossed, wondering if she would ever be better again. She let out a soft moan and rolled over until she was facing the back of the sofa, her face nestled in the crease. Jason padded slowly across the floor and lifted the blanket over her properly, tucking it under her chin and whispering 'good night', before switching the television off.

His bedroom was snug and warm, the window closed and untouched. Jason tried the handle just in case but it was locked firmly in place. He tried calling Natalie one final time but it gave five rings before plipping and going dead. It was late but he thought she might have picked up one of the six calls he had made to her. Then he reminded himself she might turn her phone off, or put it on silent, before going to sleep. At least she'd see the missed calls in the morning and contact him.

After setting his phone to charge, Jason undressed and

climbed under the covers. For the first time in a long while, he felt . . . okay. He didn't really know the words for it. He wasn't happy as such but there wasn't that nagging voice in his mind, either, telling him that things were going to go wrong and Chris and his mother would be left to fend for themselves. He pulled the duvet up and wedged it underneath his chin, twisting his feet into the lower half and winding it around himself until he was almost cocooned. He rolled over so that he was facing the wall and closed his eyes, knowing that sleep would not be an enemy tonight.

'Jase, you awake?'

Jason's arm was being rocked, which would usually make him panic and thrash wildly to grab whoever was touching him. Instead, he was calm, knowing it was Chris and feeling refreshed. He couldn't remember sleeping this well since the days when he would bury himself under the covers with Flopsy, shut his eyes, and wake up eight, nine or ten hours later.

Slowly, Jason opened his eyes, stretching at the same time. 'I'm awake now.'

Chris reached across to the bedroom door, one hand on the frame. 'Come on – hurry up. It's massive.' He hurried out of the room, banging the door closed behind him.

Jason didn't hurry.

He sat up, taking in the familiarity of his room: the folded clothes, his phone charging on the floor, the closed window. The warmth was wonderfully energising. He doubted he'd moved since going to sleep the night before.

Jason stretched out towards the radiator, holding his palms a few centimetres away and allowing the haze to blanket him before sitting on the floor next to it. He picked up his phone, pulling the cable out and yawning as he tapped in the unlock code. There was a tingle of uncertainty as he registered the lack of activity: no text messages, no missed calls, no voicemails. He tried calling Natalie once more but after five rings it went silent again. He stared at the blank screen, wondering why she hadn't been in contact.

She was probably busy, he told himself.

Out of the window, the road was almost clear, the school run over and everyone who was going to work already there. The sun was even out and the trees were still.

Another yawn.

Jason made himself a cup of tea before heading into the living room, where his mother was jealously guarding her blanket in one corner of the sofa. At the other end, Chris was sitting, hunched forward, eyes fixed on the television.

'I want my programmes,' their mother protested.

'No,' Chris replied, holding the remote control in the hand furthest away from her.

He glanced up as Jason entered, nodding towards the screen, his face pale with anxiety. Jason perched on the arm of the sofa, shaking his head as Chris offered him the remote. The newsreader was talking about the previous evening's football results.

'Wait,' Chris whispered.

Their mother continued to complain, in between nibbling her way through marmalade on toast. Her lap was covered with crumbs, an almost-empty vodka bottle nestling between the sofa and the wall. As Chris fidgeted slightly, she pulled the blanket again, tutting in annoyance and tucking it under her legs.

Jason turned back to the screen as his brother took a sharp intake of breath.

'. . . and our top story this morning: local businessman Harry Irwell was found dead at his home this morning. Mr Irwell, the owner of Manchester's Casino 101 and the patron of numerous charities, died from what is being called "a lethal cocktail of alcohol and prescription drugs" . . .'

Chris turned, open-mouthed. 'Jase . . .'

His eyes were still rimmed by the multi-coloured remnants of bruises and he was holding his shoulder at an angle. Jason stood and smoothed his top down. 'I'll see you later.'

Jason sat on the cold concrete of the stairwell at the end of his rank of flats, staring at his phone screen, a gradual sense of dread crawling through him. He pressed the name 'N' again but this time it didn't even ring: instead there was one long dial tone. A stab of the speakerphone button allowed the tinny sound to reverberate around the hard enclosed area.

'. . . The number you have dialled has not been recognised . . . The number you have dialled has not been recognised . . .'

He tried again.

'. . . The number you have dialled has not been recognised . . .'

Jason stared at the screen, willing it to ring, or for a message to arrive. Other than the hooting of a car horn somewhere in the distance, there was only silence. He felt the icy spider feathering its way along his back again.

Bringing his knees up to his chest, Jason pressed himself more rigidly against the hard surface and dialled Lucy's number. This time it did ring: once . . . twice . . . three times . . . four . . . 'Hi, this is Lucy – I'm probably busy. Leave a message.'

Her voice was breezy: so refreshingly different to Jason's mood. He closed his eyes, picturing the way she looked the night before when she was standing inches away from him: her golden hair, the relief in her face that he liked the painting, the softness of her skin as she held his hand.

He coughed slightly as the beep ended and he suddenly realised he had no idea what he was going to say. He stammered his way through the message: 'Hi, er, it's me . . . I mean it's Jason. I was just hoping that perhaps we could do something sometime. I'm sorry about last night – things were complicated and I think I was a little confused. I just wanted to say that it'd be nice to see you again . . . oh – and I love my painting. Hope to hear from you soon . . . er, bye.'

39

The wind bristled across the patch of grass as the small crowd of people huddled together, pulling coats tighter, readjusting scarves and breathing into cold hands. There was a low chatter: anticipation combined with something Jason couldn't quite place. It wasn't excitement or relief, perhaps a sense that it was always going to end this way.

The green patch had a low stone wall behind and a pavement in front next to the road. Through a rickety wooden gate, a cobbled path led to the small Edwardian church. Standing halfway along, Barbara Irwell was being comforted by an ageing priest. Jason felt bad for thinking it but she looked almost ghoulish dressed entirely in black: a broken woman whose slumped frame and crooked back screamed that she had given up.

Jason turned in a circle, taking in the crowd of mourners who were waiting next to the road, recognising almost none of them. The ages were a complete mix – people of Harry's generation and older, all the way down to street kids a little younger than Jason. He wondered how far Harry's influence stretched, how many 'sons' he had.

As Jason took a step towards the path, he felt a tug on his sleeve. Carter was wearing the smartest suit Jason had ever seen him in: cut perfectly around his wedge-shaped frame with a smart black tie. He shook his head slightly and mouthed a 'not yet'.

Jason felt uncomfortable in his own itchy black suit. It had been in his wardrobe for years but he couldn't remember where it had come from. He must have bought it at some point because his mother never would have done, perhaps for an interview he couldn't remember. He really needed a clear-out of everything he owned.

Carter patted Jason on the arm again, nodding along the road to where a familiar black car with blacked-out windows was cruising. Jason had to squint closely at the number plate to remind himself it wasn't *the* car. The similarity was striking, though: a symbol of memories past.

As it pulled up to the kerbside, the crowd parted slightly, allowing the door to open. The man who stepped out was wearing a long woollen coat over the top of a smart suit and shoes so shiny that the black was almost transparent. He peered across the crowd and then honed in on Carter, stepping across to the grass and offering his hand.

'Good morning, Mr Carter.'

'Morning, Mr Hyde.'

The two men shook, though there was a clear frostiness, illustrated as they quickly withdrew their hands.

Hyde turned, stretching his arm out towards a second, younger, man who had climbed out of the car behind him.

'This is my son, Richie,' he said.

Richie didn't look much like his father but then it didn't particularly matter. Carter shook Richie's hand, not bothering to look at him as Hyde turned to Jason. 'Mr Green, I believe.'

Hyde's handshake was firm but not overly so and he offered a thin smile. 'Richie returned from Spain yesterday for this occasion. He's been living there for the past few years.'

Richie held out his hand, so Jason shook it. Hyde's son had a curious half-grin on his face that Jason couldn't quite figure out: as if he knew something that no one else did. When his father caught his eye, Richie's smile disappeared and he moved away to the side.

'Curious one, isn't it?' Hyde said, addressing Jason and Carter but speaking quietly so that no one else could overhear. 'Who could have realised my old friend was into so many things. I can't even pronounce them: oxy-something-or-another, hydro-me-bob, something with pam in it. That's quite the list.'

Carter held his gaze, growling a firm reply. 'Steady . . .'

'It's not just Richie who's back in the country, of course,' Hyde continued. 'My daughter's here too. If there's one thing that funerals do, it's bring other people together.' He nodded towards Barbara and the priest on the pathway beyond. 'It's a devastating loss, of course – awful – but it's been nice to see my family again.'

At the far end of the road, a familiar car was approaching slowly.

'She's only been back for a short while but she's been so helpful. She's so sharp and incredibly persuasive.' Hyde laughed gently to himself, now staring at Jason and ignoring Carter. 'I suppose you could say that she got the brains in the family. I was never a school person but she's got degrees in English language and history.' Richie was just out of earshot, peering towards the car as it glided to a halt at the roadside. His father nodded towards him. 'Sons are wonderful things but there's always that male urge to destroy and defy – to go against their fathers.'

As Richie opened the metallic-red door, and a heeled foot stepped out, Jason felt as if he was falling. His knees crumpled into one another as he grabbed Carter's sleeve for support.

'If it's any consolation – and I can't say any more than this – we do have a plan . . .'

Suddenly everything was clear. She'd never said she was police, speaking only of 'senior people', 'those above me' and 'my people'. Everything she'd told Jason about other people's misery had been reported well enough for it to be common knowledge. *She* was the one who'd instilled Jason's paranoia: making him question Harry and the motives around Chris's abduction. The paper she'd given him that he thought was some sort of legal immunity was simply a smattering of official-sounding words. She'd known Jason wouldn't take it to a lawyer because he wasn't the type.

She was a history graduate and she'd even used an eighteenth-century song lyric to plant the seed . . . telling him he was in danger.

'Down among the dead men let him lie . . .'

The woman finished climbing out of the car and thanked her brother for his help. Richard Hyde turned around, offering a welcoming arm towards her, beaming with pride.

'Mr Carter, Mr Green, allow me the pleasure of introducing you to my beautiful daughter, Natalie.'